HOPE, 120 AD

Gates McKibbin

For further information go to:

www.lovehopegive.com

Cover and text design by Kenneth Gregg

Cover artwork by Serena Barton

www.serenabarton.com

Copyediting by Sally Hudson

ISBN 9798525270923

Printed in the United States of America

First Edition

CONTENTS

Dedication

Foreword

Part One: Graci and Lucan   3

Part Two: Euphemia and Augustalis   121

Part Three: Yeshua and Alexios   229

Acknowledgements

DEDICATION

My mother was an avid reader of romance novels. She delayed applying for a library card until my youngest brother was in school, since she knew that once she dipped into a paperback she would never accomplish everything a family of seven needed her to do. Two of her preferred authors were my favorites as well. We spent hours on the phone recounting what we enjoyed most about their latest releases (gloriously male protagonists included).

Mother isn't here to read the stories in the *Love Hope Give* series, but I dedicate them to her nonetheless. They aren't what she typically checked out of the library, but she might still have enjoyed the adventures of Grace and Luke.

FOREWORD

The four novels in the *Love Hope Give* series arrived over a two-year period when I was living among ancient redwoods in Marin County, California. Whenever I had a free day on a weekend I would park myself on the sofa with a blank journal and a pen, ready to write whatever came through me. By the end of the day the pages would be spilling over with words, most of which I couldn't recall.

I never learned to type without looking at the keyboard – a particularly fraught process when handwritten material must be entered into the computer. So I used voice recognition software to transfer the narratives from my journals onto the hard drive. Reading each novel aloud was a fascinating process, since I had no idea what would happen next. I discovered the story arcs not as I was writing them, but as I was reading them afterward.

I shared early drafts with a few friends. One of them who lives in Portland told me a portrait caught her eye when she was visiting the art studio of her friend Serena Barton. It had an uncanny resemblance to how she envisioned Grace in the first novel *One, Beyond Time*. When we visited the studio a few weeks later, Grace was indeed waiting for us.

Serena gave me permission to use the portrait on my book cover. She also agreed to create artwork for the other three novels. As I was describing the storyline in *Love, 24 AD* she stopped me saying, "I may have a few pieces that would work." She hopped on a stool and retrieved three canvases from an upper shelf. "How about these?"

Incredibly, Serena had captured Grace in her three subsequent incarnations even though she knew nothing about the stories. Clearly she and I had connected in the realms beyond time and space. I purchased all four portraits on the spot.

May the *Love Hope Give* series fill your heart with your own deep inner knowing that anything is possible when love is your guiding light.

PART ONE
GRACI AND LUCAN

My first memory is of sea breezes gently rustling the folds of my mother's ankle-length tunic. The pungent smell of fish being eviscerated and deboned filled my nostrils.

My mother was a slave, cleaning a fresh catch piled on a long wooden table, standing as she worked. I was standing under the table, close but inconspicuous, watching my mother's legs. I was no more than two years of age, but I was already aware that good behavior made my life less troublesome.

We were living in Greece not far from Olympus. The year was less than a century after the death of the prophet Yeshua, during the Roman period.

I cannot with absolute veracity describe what occurred in my mother's life before I knew her. Nonetheless, I am commencing this narrative at a time that predates my birth. To that end I am recounting my mother's story as if I were witness to it based on what I knew of her. My purpose is to provide essential context for our relationship, how her first sixteen years affected my first sixteen.

My mother was strikingly beautiful and more alluring than most, even those of the upper classes. Men visited her often for their mutual pleasure. Some left a coin or two when they departed, although that was not the arrangement. Slaves were not at liberty to sell their services.

These encounters offered my mother temporary relief from a life of labor. Little gave her joy besides her beauty and a bangle or two when she could afford a trinket for herself. Despite her cascading dark hair,

3

sculpted bone structure, voluptuous body and seductive almond shaped eyes, my mother had the unmistakable air of someone who was perpetually dejected, unfulfilled, frustrated.

In her youth she believed she was intended for greatness and if not that then certainly some degree of comfort. She had designs on a young man, the son of a local vintner and tavern keeper, who was enchanted by her already abundant charms and enticing inexperience. Her gossamer garments enhanced her many ripe endowments. She was confident a commitment of marriage would be negotiated, and she would become a wife with a household complete with servants and slaves. It was her destiny.

But something went terribly awry. Her father, a shopkeeper who lived beyond his means, became overextended one too many times. The deeper in debt he became, the more he encouraged his family to enjoy unprecedented extravagances. He led them to believe he was more successful than ever. Why not allow them a few excessive pleasures? It would neither hasten nor delay the family's destruction.

Her father assumed the worst he would face would be the loss of his business and perhaps the family's personal property. But the obligations became so egregious, his creditors demanded retribution enough to satisfy their dark need for revenge. They confiscated his store and its contents and meted out a far worse punishment to his family. They were wrenched away from each other and their prior freedoms.

He and his wife, two sons and three daughters were locked in chains and sold into slavery. The money from the sale of those seven human beings did little to alleviate the debt, but the creditors felt vindicated. An entire family paid with their lives. That would have to be enough. Besides, it made for impressive storytelling among their friends and debtors.

My mother was thirteen at the time.

In one stunning blow my mother's life transformed from one of sparkling hope to murky despair. Losing her family was not half as difficult as the sacrifice of her future. She had barely reached puberty, that spirited time when everything is possible. Now nothing was possible, at least nothing she could contemplate.

My mother became a slave in the household of a prosperous Greek merchant with a considerable fleet of ships. His home was a testament to the architectural glory of marble, carved by dozens of craftsmen who devoted themselves to creating and maintaining a temple to the god of commerce. It was built on a ridge overlooking the sea, with panoramic views from every room and soft breezes blowing through the colonnades.

The merchant was not particularly handsome, but he carried himself with the unmistakable air of authority that usually accompanies great wealth. Such power goes a long way to compensate for relative unattractiveness.

The slave master assigned to get my mother situated after she arrived heard this new girl was quite imperious. No matter, she could be quickly brought down a notch or two. He learned over the years to be prepared for acquisitions of her sort, since the household often selected more civilized individuals who had fallen on exceptionally hard times and been sold into slavery. The relative refinement of these slaves was a mixed blessing. He found people who had known nothing but slavery to be far better servants, and not just because they were more malleable.

The slaves lived in reasonably maintained accommodations. All had their own private room, an unprecedented display of generosity on the part of their owner. Six buildings arranged in a cluster at the far eastern end of the property comprised the slave quarters. The cleanest, most solidly constructed building was reserved for the tenured, favored slaves. It occupied the best location, next to a garden spilling over with fig trees, grapevines and rambling bushes bursting with blossoms. The slave master determined that this new girl's accommodations would be quite the opposite.

My mother was assigned a room of her own at the gloomy end of a ramshackle building for female slaves situated near the outhouse and garbage mound. This despicable shack in a noxious location offended her sensibilities. She was from a good family and had done nothing wrong. Surely she deserved better than the others, most of whom were no doubt born into slavery. Instead she was being given the worst accommodations.

The slave master opened the door to her quarters. It creaked on rusty hinges, resisting my mother's entrance just as she resisted slavery. She stuck her head into the room. The stagnant air was thick with piss and shit and mildew. The stench burned her nostrils and brought on a surge of nausea so overpowering, she had to swallow hard to keep from vomiting. But her strength of will was stronger than her queasy stomach. She withdrew her head from the room, took a deep breath of fresh air and protested, "I can't live here. Find me another place to stay."

"Unfortunately, it is the only private room we have available," he declared. "If you want to share one, there is an extra bed next door. The slave quartered there is so sick with fevers, she will not last the month. It wouldn't bother her to have you stay there. Perhaps you could even help care for her."

This strategy was as successful with my mother as it had been with other willful slaves who preceded her. She acquiesced without further objection. "Is there a bucket of water and a scrub brush that I could use?" she asked. "If so, I can clean out the room assigned to me. It should be fine."

"I'll fetch them for you," the slave master replied, smiling to himself after he turned his back to take his leave.

Standing outside the room, my mother breathed the air that insinuated itself from the other side of the door. It was so vile she didn't know how she could even step inside that horrible place, let alone spend the night there. But step inside she did.

The rank odor was coming from a nearly full terra cotta piss pot standing nonchalantly in the middle of the floor. She grabbed it furiously by the handles and dragged it across the room and over the threshold. It bumped as it hit the dirt, sloshing its repulsive contents onto her shift.

"I can't do this!" she cried to herself in despair, tempted to topple the pot in protest. Then realizing she would be punishing no one but herself if she sullied her space even further, she dragged the pot across the grass to the outhouse, leaving a wake of uprooted green blades along the way. It took all her strength to lift the pot and pour the contents into one of the open holes. This small victory mattered a great deal to her. She would not succumb to the first challenge she faced as a slave. As an additional statement of dissent, she tossed the pot into the garbage heap in back.

A bucket and brush were waiting outside the door when she returned to her room. She made good use of both, scouring and rinsing every square inch. Sticky cobwebs and disgusting mold splattered her face along with drops of mucky water as she scrubbed the ceiling, perched precariously on a rickety three-legged stool. Still she persisted. If she was to survive in this miserable living space, she would exorcize every last remnant of misery suffered by its former occupant. It took all afternoon and eight more buckets of water before the space was cleaned to her satisfaction. Truth be told it would never be to her satisfaction, but it was bearable.

She discarded the rancid straw that served the prior tenant as a mattress and vowed to sleep on the bare floor if necessary. Once it dried, it would be good enough. She hauled one more bucket of fresh water to her room, undressed and bathed. She rubbed her skin and hair as thoroughly as she scoured the walls, then donned a clean shift.

Leaving the door open to allow the room to dry, she set the bucket outside the door and explored the grounds. A stalk of bougainvillea caught her eye, and she plucked it surreptitiously. This melancholy adornment for her room may not be as striking as a vibrant silk scarf, but it would provide a conspicuous counterpoint to the terra cotta piss pot.

Nearly everyone has the will to survive, no matter how wretched their circumstances. My mother was no different except that she was determined to survive on her own terms. She would use every situation to her advantage just as she did before. If she refused to accept the permanence of her slavery, she believed she could find a way out of it.

Her first order of business was to assess the household she was bound to serve. There was reason to be optimistic. The merchant had three sons, and she appraised them all. Perhaps her unexpected detour into slavery might prove to be a gift from the goddesses. Why not marry into a supremely wealthy family instead of only a modestly comfortable one?

Certainly the stars aligned in her favor. Her enslavement was nothing more than a temporary impediment on the road to lasting security and relative peace.

My mother managed to spend the first few months working in the merchant's household. She insinuated herself subtly into social events under the pretext of serving the food and made convincing arguments that she should have access to the family's private quarters to deliver packages or keep the potted plants watered. The family saw my mother's many overtures as evidence of her dedication. Her ploy worked.

The merchant and his sons prided themselves on their egalitarianism. Yes, they bought and sold slaves, who admittedly were human beings. But unlike most moneyed families in Greece, they allowed a measure of their slaves' dignity to remain intact. My mother, in turn, took advantage of the family's liberal ways. Since she had never known slavery, she found it impossible, and not incidentally distasteful, to think of herself in such terms.

Mother soon identified which son was the best prospect for her pursuits. He was more tentative and less self-assured than his brothers. Just as important, he was unfailingly kind to her. She found excuses to approach him with a question or ask for help carrying a heavy parcel. He seemed grateful to be of assistance, and she lavished him with praise after receiving even the slightest attention from him.

Below the estate was a tranquil private beach the slaves were allowed to visit on occasion, escorted to assure their return. One evening my mother saw her chosen one strolling on the beach ahead of her as the sun was setting.

"May I join you?" she asked sweetly. "I have been so busy lately, it's a pleasure to enjoy a few moments of leisure with you especially."

"By all means," he replied. "I too have been preoccupied, with my studies mostly. I am preparing to leave for Athens soon to learn from one of Greece's foremost history and literature scholars. I will be living with him, no doubt reading and discussing esoteric texts at all hours. I am getting a head start, on the reading at least."

In his excitement and anticipation, the young man strung together more words than my mother had heard in all of their prior encounters. She misread his talkativeness as evidence of his deepening feelings for her. Since he was leaving soon, she decided she must act quickly. She couldn't risk that a compliant, learned, virginal daughter of a rich Athenian nobleman – no doubt the scholar had numerous friends of noble birth – would erase her otherwise compelling charms from the memory of her intended.

My mother prayed quickly to Hera, the Protector of Marriage. Then she turned to her savior and revealed breathlessly, "I love you, and if you feel the same way about me, we can approach your parents about being married. Perhaps it would be best if we made the necessary arrangements before your departure."

The young man was so shocked by this pronouncement, he became lightheaded. How could she propose anything of the sort? Was she unaware of her pathetic circumstances? Beyond that, whatever gave her the idea he was interested in her?

She saw these questions in his eyes and the thunderstruck look on his face. His answer was clear, though not a word was spoken. Rather than realizing an apology was in order, my mother became furious.

"How could you do this to me?" she screamed at him. "I thought you loved me, but you never cared about me. I hate you!"

One of the household guards appeared within moments and pulled her away from the distraught young man.

"What happened here?" asked the guard, manhandling her into submission.

"He took advantage of me!" screamed my mother. "He should be punished, perhaps even banished! And he certainly shouldn't be allowed to go to Athens."

The guard, who knew the son's character, deduced his innocence and recognized his genuine distress. No matter, it was his job to protect the son without question.

"Please take her to the slave quarters," the son requested. "I will consult with my parents regarding what should be done."

My mother was hauled away and locked up in a miniscule stall. She was utterly alone and without even the most rudimentary freedoms. For the first time since she was bound in shackles and removed from her family home, she admitted to herself that slavery was her lot in life. She wept into the night, angry over the obliteration of her ambitions.

The next day she was taken to the family's private quarters, where the son and his parents were waiting.

"We understand that you approached our son last night and proposed marriage to him," the merchant stated. "Is that true?"

My mother nodded in agreement, hoping her apparent submissiveness was convincing.

"Then when your proposal was met with silence by our son, you turned on him and falsely accused him of leading you on," continued the boy's father.

"He was kind to me," replied my mother meekly, acting the part of innocent waif. "I thought he loved me, so I let myself fall in love with him in spite of my circumstances."

"I see," said the father. "You mistook his kindness for something more. Our son is compassionate and sensitive, but that is no indication of love. He told us he neither loves you nor feels any special emotion toward you. He was being thoughtful and respectful, nothing else."

"I am sorry for the misunderstanding," my mother replied contritely.

"You were not raised in slavery, so perhaps you don't realize your circumstances," the father observed. "Let me explain. You have no rights, you have no independence, you have no choices. You are not at liberty to marry anyone, even another slave. Your life will be more agreeable if you accept this. You would be well advised neither to resist your condition of subjugation nor to create a fantasy that can never be realized."

My mother bowed ever so slightly to express her subservience.

"You are fortunate to have been brought into this household," the father declared. "We treat our slaves with respect. Others do not. Slaves are often beaten and abused, sexually and otherwise. They live in circumstances unbefitting a dog and die young of starvation, disease or overwork. It would behoove you to recognize your good luck and modify your behavior accordingly. If we grow weary of your misdeeds and decide to sell you to someone else, the conditions of your life would surely deteriorate."

My mother's survival instincts served her well that day. She heeded the merchant's message and appeared to acknowledge her current condition. "Thank you," she replied. "I was unaware of the nature of my position. Now that you have explained it to me, I see the error of my ways. I promise there will be no more confusion in the future."

She might also have promised to behave herself, but she had no intention of doing that. She would let the issue subside then take back her freedoms, slowly and unobtrusively. For now, however, her behavior would assure her owners that nothing more than inexperience caused the problem.

"Very well," concluded the boy's father. "I will give you a second chance. But remember, you must always do what you are told. You are banned from entering this house ever again. There is to be no more trouble from you."

"I assure you of that," my mother stated, nodding submissively. Then she turned slowly and exited with the bearing of an equal instead of a slave with no rights whatsoever. She knew better, but she couldn't help herself.

The ensuing months were harsh. My mother's resolve to see herself as better than others vanished as she slipped into the apathy of her servitude. Her days were all the same: hard work, drudgery and exhaustion. Despite the brilliant sunshine, crystalline blue sky and azure sea, she saw only uninterrupted darkness.

"My life is over," she told herself. "I have nothing to look forward to. There will be no pleasures, no happiness, no luxuries, no joys, no frills, no love in my life. I deserve every last one of them, but they are withheld from me forever."

My mother wore her self-imposed victimization like a badge of honor confirming her slavery was unjustified. She was worthy of a gracious life, not her miserable existence. She would perish if she ever stopped reminding herself of everything that was her due before her father's devastation.

Inevitably, imperceptibly, she climbed out of her chasm of despair, having never lost her sense of entitlement. She took better care of herself and tended her hair so it sparkled in the sun. She even smiled every now and then. She accepted the fact that she was a slave. But that didn't stop her from imagining how she might introduce pleasure into her life, secretly and without punishment.

∞　∞　∞

Just after her sixteenth birthday, my mother declared to herself that she was going to exercise a measure of freedom. Having learned the habitual ways of the household, she could ingratiate herself with men who did business on the estate.

Most particularly she had her eye on the captain of a ship in the merchant's fleet. When he returned to port once or twice a year, he stayed on the estate in a separate building reserved for those of his rank and importance. She was also attracted to a man who brought exquisite fabrics gathered far and wide. He spent weeks at a time in a guesthouse while the merchant's wife and their two daughters selected and designed their finery. The first man was rugged, the second one refined. One of each would be perfect.

My mother had no experience with men other than her early flirtations. Some of the slave women told her of their sexual encounters, welcomed and otherwise. That gave her a working knowledge of the mechanics involved in coming together with a man. Despite her inexperience, my mother was confident her powers of seduction exceeded those of the whores in town. She simply had to find the right opportunity to prove that was true.

She found excuses to say a word or two to the sea captain during his previous respites between voyages, but he had been unfazed. Watching his ship come to port, mother decided she would seduce him this time.

The sea captain didn't acknowledge her advances, though the look in her eyes and the swaying of her hips were unmistakable. The merchant forbade the crews of his ships from fraternizing with his family, friends, servants and slaves. Whatever enjoyment the captain might derive from a tryst with this temptress wouldn't be worth the retribution if it were discovered. He took his pleasure in town, with the women who had a price.

On the last day before his ship set sail again, the captain was preparing to go into the village for one more night of entertainment. It would be a long journey before they arrived at the distant port with their cargo. He would spend the evening in decadent revelry, for memory's sake if nothing else.

An almost inaudible knock on his door was so soft, it seemed to have occurred at some distance. As he approached the door, he heard it again. This time it was more insistent, and definitely coming from the entrance to his quarters. Perhaps it was a servant bringing him a bite to eat. Opening the door, he saw the slave girl, the light of the full moon bathing her in luminescence.

"I heard you are leaving tomorrow," she said, "and I want to give you something to remember on your long journey. May I come in?"

"You aren't supposed to be here," he replied, surprising himself with his reservoir of willpower. She was gorgeous.

"That's true," she replied. "But everyone expects you to be gone all night. If we keep the room dark, they will assume you haven't yet returned. I will leave before dawn."

"Why me?" he asked. "Why now?"

"The answer to the first question is that you are a man of strong appetites and extensive experience," my mother explained. "I have equally strong appetites but no experience."

"No experience?" he asked, incredulous. "You are a virgin and yet you offer yourself to me in such a forthright way?"

"I have no life," my mother replied, asking for neither sympathy nor reassurance. "I can never do what I want. Pleasures are withheld from me. I can't survive under these conditions. I am asking you to help me experience pleasure if only for one brief night, that it might sustain me."

The sea captain looked at my mother thoughtfully. Then having made his decision, he pulled her gently into his room, closed and locked the door, extinguished the oil lamp and walked over to her. Standing before her he said, "You appeal to the modicum of compassion that resides within me. I can't fathom what a life of slavery would be like. I spend my days on the open seas, unfettered and free.

"I will give you this gift tonight, not for my pleasure but for your own. I will treat you gently and with the greatest respect. I will also take you to heights of ecstasy that you will remember until the day you die. I will hold you as you sleep, and when you awake I will love you again. You will leave here full of my seed and satiated with my lovemaking.

"I will do this on one condition, and you must agree to it. What we experience together on this night will be neither an affirmation nor a commitment of love. Don't decide you love me because I treated you well. Don't ask anything more of me, for I can't give it to you. And if we create a child, I will deny I am the father. Do you understand and accept these terms?"

"I do," my mother affirmed.

"And you promise not to love me because I am the first man you will have known?" he persisted.

"I promise," my mother replied.

"Then come my sweet young one," he whispered, taking my mother's hand and leading her to his bed. "Spend the night in my arms, in my bed, that you may discover freedom like you never imagined."

She stood still as he undressed her. The rough cloth and simple cut of her tunic had hidden her curves. Unclothed she was a breathtaking creature. He thought, "How is it possible that I am to spend the night with this woman as her first lover?" Then on the heels of that question he admonished himself, "And by the gods, don't fall for her!"

Something about her candid innocence brought out the best in him. He caressed her lovingly, kissing every curved surface of her body. He told her she was beautiful, captivating, unforgettable. He described how his rod throbbed for her and his chest was tight with passion. Then, when he could wait no longer, he touched her opening with his fingers. It was wet and velvety, even more enticing than her breasts and curved hips.

"I must have you now," he groaned, barely holding back his urgency.

As he was emerging from an orgasmic fog, kissing her passionately all the while, he said to himself, "It is amazing what taking pity on someone will do to a man's desires."

She opened her eyes and smiled languidly at him. "That was extraordinary," she purred. "I had no idea anything could make me feel so wonderful."

"Actually, that was quite extraordinary," he agreed. "Or better put, you are quite extraordinary."

They chatted about nothing in particular, making small talk in order to find their way toward whatever was to happen next. It took almost no time for him to grow hard again, still inside her.

"So now we can enjoy this again!" she effused.

"Yes, we certainly can," he replied spiritedly.

Afterward he rolled off her, swept her in his arms, threw his leg over her thighs and breathed deeply of the sublime aroma of their lovemaking. "I have never, ever, met a woman like you," he sighed. "How can you be such a phenomenal lover, and have no experience?"

"I longed for this pleasure until I thought the aching within me would tear me apart," she revealed. "You fed my soul, and I partook of you like a lost desert nomad who found an oasis."

"You have drunk deeply of me," he murmured. "I spilled more seed into you than I thought I had to give. My only hope is that there is still more in me for you."

And there was. They napped and loved all night. As the first light was appearing and my mother was preparing to go, the seaman held her to him one last time and whispered, "I will remember you every day that I am away, and especially every night. I will count the days until my return."

She kissed him gently and said, simply, "Thank you." Then she was gone.

The captain's head was reeling with thoughts of this woman. His heart pounded out messages of love, but he fought them off. "I cannot love her. This is impossible. We can never be together," he reminded himself. "Forget her the moment you set sail and, if she is interested, spend one more night with her when you return. Don't give your heart to her. Let her go, let her go, let her go."

But he couldn't. He thought about her night and day, even though he despised himself for doing so.

She, on the other hand, took him at his word. She committed not to love him, and love him she would not. With no other knowledge of lovemaking, she believed her night with the sea captain was typical of such encounters with men. She required the pleasure of a man's body and was determined to enjoy it frequently.

My mother had urgent sex with others soon after the captain's ship had sailed. These experiences were singularly unfulfilling, like two dogs rutting behind a fence. She decided to use better selection criteria. After all, she was doing this for her own satisfaction. If no enjoyment was forthcoming, whatever was amiss could be remedied.

The captain's ship was gone longer than anticipated. My mother heard rumors that it was lost at sea due to storms or pirates. Or perhaps because of an insurrection while they were anchored at a distant port, the captain and crew were imprisoned and the ship burned.

My mother realized that her anguish over the fate of the ship and its captain were less a function of the sexual disappointments she experienced while he was gone and more a reflection of how close she felt to her first lover. Yes, the lovemaking was incredible. But the tenderness with which he treated her won her heart. Nonetheless, she convinced herself that if he did return and she again shared his bed, it wouldn't be for love.

Much more time went by until finally everyone presumed the ship was indeed lost and the crew gone from the Earth. My mother accepted this with a sense of inevitability. It was her fate as a slave to have no love and no real gratification from sex.

This deeper, more destructive disillusionment precipitated an abrupt fall from grace. She became overtly promiscuous, seducing every male who would put his member into her even anonymously.

My mother was fully aware she was tempting fate. If the master of the house found out about it, she would be sent to the nearest slave market. But she didn't care. Better to have plenty of men while she could. The course of her life would be dictated either by her current owner or a new one. It mattered not.

She learned how to prevent pregnancy with herbs such as asafetida, which she grew surreptitiously in a small corner of the slave garden, and the liberal use of cotton to obstruct a man's seed. So far these methods were effective. She desperately wanted to avoid having a child. It would disfigure her body so wretchedly, no man would want her. Even worse, afterwards a needy infant would be suckling at breasts meant instead for male enjoyment. Becoming pregnant was as terrible a curse as being sold to an abusive slave owner.

Somehow her sexual encounters were kept from the family. The men who took advantage of her ready availability said nothing, preferring instead to return for more whenever they wanted. Beyond that, the slaves shared an understanding that forbade voluntarily offering information that harmed one of their kind.

Without much risk of being found out, my mother became a receptacle for the satisfaction of many men, although enjoyment eluded her. Blessedly her monthly flow always arrived. Relieved each time, she thanked the goddess for sparing her from pregnancy for one more moon cycle.

"The lost ship! It's back!" Hearing those exultant cries, my mother allowed herself to hope as she had never done before. Perhaps through some miracle the sea captain had indeed returned. She ran to a spot with the clearest view of the sea. Sailing into port was a ship outfitted just like his. Was he on board?

The merchant ran to the harbor along with many others involved with his business. My mother couldn't see what occurred, but based on the cheering and commotion she assumed that the ship with its captain had returned safely.

In spite of her exhilaration, she told herself to be patient. The captain would be unavailable for a while. No doubt many important people would want to find out what caused the long delay. There would be banquets and parties, none of which she could attend. He might have forgotten her completely and would be spending his nights in town to get his fill of the women there. She would expect nothing, though she wanted a great deal.

The celebration that night was unusually raucous. The ship's crew were treated as conquering heroes, back after an interminable struggle under unimaginably adverse conditions. My mother went to her room and tried to sleep.

In the middle of the night she felt a tap on her shoulder. "Wake up," whispered an unfamiliar voice. "The captain asked to see you."

My mother opened her eyes with a start and recognized a female servant from the house. She didn't know her name. "He gave me a coin," the woman whispered. "I promised to tell you and no one else about it."

"Thank you for your kindness," my mother replied, rubbing the sleep from her eyes. "I will be on my way shortly."

My mother freshened herself with water from a bucket and donned her cleanest tunic. She wore nothing underneath. Overcome with anticipation, she never thought to prevent pregnancy. When silence assured her no one was about, she stole to the captain's room.

The door opened before she could knock. He swept her into his arms, closed the door with his foot and carried her to bed. They kissed deeply, devouring each other, and came together with breathtaking urgency. She was gone from the world, away from her body yet with him completely.

They lay still for a long time, sweating and panting and descending slowly from their shared ecstasy. He lifted himself slightly and looked at her, smiling broadly.

"Hello," he whispered.

"Welcome back," she replied.

"I missed you," he murmured. "Every day I missed you. Every night I missed you more. I willed myself not to do so, but that only made it worse. Then we were detained along the coast of Africa – another civil war – and it took us an eternity to buy our freedom when the new regime took over. I thought I would die from missing you."

"And not from the civil war?" my mother teased.

"Enduring a war is nothing compared to the longing I felt for you," he declared.

She refused to say how much she missed him or to reveal how she had used other men to obliterate the memory of him. She also resisted the tempting idea that he might love her. Missing and longing didn't constitute loving.

"But you seem perfectly healthy and unharmed," she announced, "or at least, the part of you I find so delectable is perfectly healthy and unharmed."

"If it is harmed, it would be from desire," he laughed. "I am relieved to find everything is still in good working order."

"Do you mean that," my mother blurted out, then stopped, disbelieving.

"That I knew no women during my absence?" The captain finished her sentence. "I have been with no one since you."

Shame stabbed my mother's heart at that unexpected revelation. Just the night before she let a man have her, a rough itinerant wood carver brought in to repair the front gate. He couldn't be all that much of a craftsman, she thought, given the dreadful way he treated her.

She decided to preserve a scrap of integrity by not lying to her lover. So she said nothing and instead rekindled their passion. They made love again, more thoroughly and completely this time.

They found a rhythm that enabled them to ebb and flow like waves on a beach, almost achieving peaks of ecstasy, then receding only to be overtaken by another wave, another perfect coming together. There was more lovemaking and less napping than they experienced on their first night together.

Dawn insinuated itself, and it was time for my mother to leave. When she kissed the captain and pulled away, he drew her to him.

"I am leaving in a few hours," he told my mother matter-of-factly even though his heart was breaking. "A new ship is about to set sail, and I was asked to captain it. I'll be back before you know it. Please wait for me."

My mother couldn't believe what she was hearing. "Very well," she replied. "Come back safely. Promise me that."

"I promise," he replied, embracing her one last time.

She slipped out the door and tiptoed to her room. If anyone observed her, no one acknowledged it.

She never saw him again. The ship was caught in a storm and no one survived. It was returning to homeport when the tempest hit.

My mother was pregnant. I was born almost nine months after her night with the sea captain. That same day news of the lost ship arrived.

My mother told me she didn't know who my father was. But a girl knows these things. The sea captain was my father. He was on his way back to my mother, perhaps to convince the merchant to free her so she could become his bride. But their togetherness, married or otherwise, was not to be.

∞ ∞ ∞

My mother was desperate to exorcise the sea captain from her memory, and the best way to do so was with countless other men. But she had me to contend with. I cried and needed to be fed. Worse, her previously perfect body was misshapen from pregnancy, if only temporarily. That was my fault.

My mother's deepest desire from the day I was born until I was taken away at age sixteen was to rid herself of me. I would go unfed for days because she couldn't tolerate having me suckle at her breasts. When they became too swollen for her to bear, she would expel her milk on the ground rather than allow my mouth to touch her nipples. I wouldn't have survived had another slave not given birth shortly before my entrance into the world. Despite my mother's protestations, she put me on one breast and her son on the other. I drank of her sweet milk and her caring. Instead of faltering as my mother hoped, I thrived.

When I was old enough to understand that the woman who gave me suckle wasn't my mother, I faced a cruel reality. My own mother resented me. She bellowed that I must do exactly as she said, threatening to lock me in the shed without food or water if I didn't follow her every rule. I learned early how to behave perfectly and give her no excuse to punish me. Even when I was barely walking, I knew I must be quiet, request nothing and remain invisible.

One would think that after such obvious rejection I would learn early how to make my life without her. But the opposite occurred. I was consumed by fear that my mother would abandon me. I keep her within my sight at all times.

I learned how to be a good girl in the extreme, and she begrudgingly allowed me to remain physically near her as long as I was hidden from view. I spent endless days standing mutely under a table, staring at my mother's legs, watching fish bones, heads and entrails fall to the ground.

∞ ∞ ∞

The only existence I knew was that of a slave. The only people I saw were slaves. I was vaguely aware of other ways of life, but I knew they weren't available to me. So I didn't think about them.

By the time I was five years old I gained enough self-assurance to leave the close proximity of my mother and venture nearby to play. I was still too young to work, and my ability to remain unobtrusive garnered me more latitude than a misbehaving child might have had.

One day while I was playing by myself, chasing butterflies and reaching into the sky for them when they flew away, a slightly older boy approached me. I had seen him before, but we never talked.

"Don't you know you can never catch a butterfly?" he asked with uncommon certainty.

"Why can't I?" I retorted.

"Because they fly higher than you can reach, higher than you can jump, even," he explained.

"Do they fly higher than you can jump?" I wondered, noting he was a good head taller.

"Sometimes," he replied. "But I have caught one or two."

"What did you do with them?" I continued.

"I studied them all over then let them go," he revealed.

"What is the point of catching them if you let them fly away again?" I challenged.

"I just want to know I can do it," he explained.

"Will I be able to catch butterflies when I am as tall as you?" I persisted.

"I suppose, if you are fast enough," he conjectured. "If you do catch one, will you release it?"

"Oh, yes," I said, surprising myself with my answer. "I couldn't keep such a beautiful creature all to myself. Butterflies deserve to be free."

The irony that I would never be free myself was lost on me.

Every afternoon we met at the same time. I began to look forward to his arrival. He was kind to me, and kindness was something I experienced only rarely. One day I summoned the courage to ask him, "Why do you come here every afternoon when the sun is almost the same place in the sky?"

"I have a tutor who teaches me all day," he explained, "and by this time in the afternoon I start to get bored. So he sends me outside to get rid of the jitters."

"What are you learning?" I asked, though I had no concept of what one could learn. Such endeavors were never discussed with me.

"I am learning how to read and do mathematical calculations," he replied casually.

"What is reading?" I wondered.

The boy looked at me with such a quizzical expression, I didn't know whether to laugh or run away in embarrassment.

"Have you never seen a word written down?" he asked, incredulous.

"I have seen squiggles," I told him, "but I don't know if they are supposed to be words."

"You probably also know nothing about math – numbers," he conjectured.

"No, I don't," I affirmed, looking in shame at my bare feet and tattered tunic. For the first time I knew the difference between being a child of privilege and one of servitude.

"In that case, I will teach you," he announced decisively. "Tomorrow I will bring my stylus so you can learn your letters."

"What for?" I wondered, mystifying him even further.

"So you can read, dummy!" he exclaimed in response to my ignorance. "If I am going to be your teacher, you need to know my name. It is Alexios."

"I am Graci," I replied.

Alexios was a clever teacher. I was unaware there even was such a thing as the Greek alphabet, not to mention being able to differentiate one letter from another. He remembered how his tutor taught him and applied the same process with me. I was such a facile student, he soon began to show me how letters and syllables could be combined to form words. It was magical to me.

Within six months I was reading whatever he put in front of me and working with numbers as well. Alexios declared proudly, "You have caught up with me."

My heart sank. Our lesson time was the highlight of my day. Now that gift would be taken away because Alexios had no more to teach me. I felt bereft, but I tried not to let it show.

"So I talked with my tutor," he continued. "I explained to him that you learn fast and now know as much as I do. Then I asked if he could teach you, too."

"What did he say?" I asked, experiencing unfamiliar excitement.

"First he wants you to show him how much you know already, then depending on what he finds out he may go to my mother and father to see if they will allow you to participate in a brief lesson each day," Alexios explained. "He also said it would be unusual for a slave child, especially a girl, to have such an opportunity. He wants to meet you tomorrow in my classroom. I will wait for you here at the usual time."

I was practically paralyzed at the thought that what I learned as a form of play would be observed and evaluated by an adult. What if my mind went blank and I ended up embarrassing my friend? But Alexios reassured me saying, "Don't worry. I'll be there to help you, but you won't need it."

I revealed nothing to my mother about this prospect. She would have berated me for wanting to learn to read in the first place, asserting that I was a slave with no need for lessons. Besides, I had no hope that I would be given a chance to learn more than I already knew. Nonetheless, the next day I took extra care washing my face, hands and even my feet in an effort to make myself presentable.

I followed Alexios through a gate I dared not enter before. Sensing my hesitation to enter a prohibited area, Alexios took my hand and pulled me forward. We walked along spacious breezeways of cool marble that opened onto gloriously furnished rooms. I never dreamed anything so beautiful could exist, especially as someone's home. Once again I felt shame, this time for the seedy, smelly room my mother and I shared.

We entered a simpler room, where sea breezes wafted in and sunshine burst forth from open spaces in the walls. "What happens when it rains?" I asked, unaware that I should wait to be introduced.

"Where?" asked the tutor.

"There," I replied, pointing to the floor-to-ceiling gaps.

"Hidden doors can be closed," he stated. "Here, let me show you." The tutor pulled on a brass ring, revealing an enormous door inside the wall that glided into place.

"I have never seen such a thing," I said in amazement.

"Nor had I until I arrived here," he assured me, bending down to meet me at eye level. "Alexios tells me you have a keen mind for learning, so I invited you here to see if that is true. Here are some simple words I would like you to read." He handed me a wax tablet with writing on it. "What are they?"

I read the words easily, my confidence growing each time he said, "Correct."

"Now let's see if you can read this," he encouraged, handing me a small papyrus roll with words written from top to bottom in lines that formed columns.

I began to read haltingly, but after I got a sense of the story being told, I relaxed and kept going. I wanted to find out what happened to the central characters, a mouse and a bird.

"Remarkable!" the tutor exclaimed with genuine enthusiasm. "Can you work with numbers?"

"I think so," I replied.

"Good, then take this tablet to the table over there and figure out the answers," he suggested. "You can write with this stylus."

Alexios and his tutor talked quietly on the other side of the room while I solved the mathematical problems. The ones at the bottom were more difficult, but I thought through them and counted with my fingers to check my answers. When I was done, I put down the stylus and sat quietly.

"Finished?" asked the tutor.

"Yes," I assured him. "But I'm sorry. I don't think I got every one right."

"Never mind that," he replied. "I included some problems that even Alexios hasn't been taught, just to see how far you could go."

He glanced over my answers, then reviewed them again more carefully. "My child," he began, "you are an intelligent young girl and a natural student. I have been teaching for over thirty years, and never have I seen anyone so young show such capability. I will use all my powers of persuasion to gain permission for you to be tutored by me every day, even if it is only briefly."

"Thank you, sir" I answered politely. "But I am not allowed in here. I don't want you or Alexios to get into trouble. Maybe you shouldn't ask."

Patting me tenderly on the top of my head, he said softly, "Please call me Errikos. And don't worry. I will ask respectfully. I won't anger anyone with my request."

"All right," I agreed. "I enjoyed being here today. I will always remember how pretty and clean everything is, and what a nice man you are, even if I can't come back."

"Thank you for visiting me," Errikos said, his tone softening.

"Thank you for letting me come," I told him, trying to be more than the lowly little girl I knew I was.

Alexios means "defender" in Greek, and my friend proved to be just that. At first his parents disapproved of having a slave participate in even a minor aspect of his tutoring. They were concerned he would become distracted or the usual decorum would be compromised by the unruly behavior of a slave girl. The tutor's initial request was met with a flat refusal.

Alexios appealed to his parents to change their mind. I was playing near an open window and overheard the conversation he had with his father. I barely breathed while it was occurring.

"Why can't Graci be tutored when I am on break playing outside?" Alexios suggested. "Then I would miss none of my normal instruction."

His father challenged, "Wouldn't you rather play with her than be by yourself?"

"Yes, I truly would," Alexios answered.

"Then why are you suggesting she spend time inside when you are outside?" his father asked pointedly.

"Because she is smarter than I am and deserves the chance to learn," Alexios replied.

"How do you know she is smarter than you?" his father queried.

"I taught her everything I know, to read and do her numbers, even though she is younger than me," explained Alexios. "She even solved difficult mathematics problems on her own that I haven't learned myself."

"But you have been her teacher," persisted his father. "Doesn't that make you at least as smart as she is?"

"Maybe," replied Alexios noncommittally. "But think of how much faster she could learn if Errikos could teach her instead."

"You have a point there," his father admitted, yielding ground to his young son. "Let me see what I can do."

The next day Alexios informed me I would be tutored during his afternoon break while he remained outside. As I was receiving my first lesson from Errikos, Alexios stood by the gate. He waited for me to emerge so I could tell him quickly what happened before he went back in. I was so thrilled I could barely contain myself. I babbled on and on about what I was learning before I remembered to thank him. Every day he was there waiting, and every day I poured out my enthusiastic update to him.

After a few weeks he met me at the entrance when it was time for my lesson, escorted me inside and remained there. That change concerned me. If he was present in the room, I would surely be sent outside. Those were the rules.

"You may be wondering what is happening," commented Errikos. "I noticed that without you to romp around with, Alexios was still jumpy when he returned to the classroom. Apparently he has no interest in playing by himself, not even in chasing butterflies.

"I discussed this with his parents, and they agreed that he may continue his lessons while you are here. Then if you both do well, I can release him to play outdoors with you. Now you must each work hard and do your best."

And so we did.

My life was transformed as a result of Alexios' generous heart and Errikos' kindness. The learning I experienced each day, coupled with the time I spent with Alexios in the open air afterward, were a wonder to me.

Nonetheless, I continued to be a mute, prosaic little girl when I was with my mother. She couldn't stand to see me smiling or joyful. It reminded her of the loss of her own childhood innocence at the hands of her charlatan of a father. Whenever she spotted a hint of happiness on my face she railed against it, insisting I would fall ever more deeply into a chasm of misery for having known fleeting delight.

I kept my learning to myself and remained unexceptional in her eyes.

Years passed, and I continued to attend brief tutoring sessions each day. Errikos chuckled on occasion and commented that because of me he was delaying retirement. "I will be an old man with no teeth and my mind half gone, and if you are still around I will be tutoring," he declared.

He and Alexios became my surrogate family, the uncle and brother I would never have. I enjoyed more affection and respect from them than I could ever hope to receive from my mother. The miracle of their caring healed my wounded heart.

Around my tenth birthday I was informed that it was time for me to start working. Although my tutoring sessions were common knowledge by then, they were irrelevant compared to the labor I was required to perform as a slave. Blessedly I was assigned to the kitchen, away from my mother.

"What about my lessons?" I asked in desperation when I heard about the many hours I would be required to work each day.

"What about them?" the head cook replied. "You were treated like anything but your kind for so long, you forgot who you are. You are a slave. You may believe you deserve the life of a rich girl, but you are entitled to nothing. You have nothing and never will. Get used to it."

Alexios and Errikos were stunned at the news that I could no longer continue my lessons. They were told of the decision as abruptly as I was. The pronouncement seemed more arbitrary to them than it did to me, for they were unaccustomed to a life that starts with deprivation and declines into desolation.

I was attending my last class when Alexios spoke up. "I won't allow your lessons to cease," he decreed, every bit the authoritative young man he was groomed to become.

"But it has already been decided," I reminded him. "What can you do?"

"First, the determination was made by a man who places no value on education," he explained. "My parents were informed of the decision after it was announced by the slave master, and they chose not to contradict it.

"Second, there is no reason you can't do both. You spend only a small part of the day being tutored. Certainly you can be spared from your duties for that brief period. Perhaps you can work later, or start earlier, to make up the time."

"You have thought through this quite nicely," commented Errikos. "I am impressed. Your use of logical arguments is most convincing."

"We'll see how convincing I am tonight with my parents," Alexios replied, revealing an uncharacteristic sliver of self-doubt.

Once again Alexios persuaded his parents to change course where I was concerned. They sent word to the kitchen that although I was expected to do the same amount of work, I should be released for my daily lessons at the appropriate time.

"Retirement evades me still," chuckled Errikos when I returned to the classroom the next day. Alexios was beaming.

My work in the kitchen was menial. I was given the chores no one else wanted. Rather than resenting my mindless tasks, I focused on my lessons while I worked. I swept the floor and recited poems to myself in Latin. I scrubbed the countertops and relived Greek epics. I scoured pots and imagined sarcophagi in Egyptian tombs. I filled water jugs and conversed with imaginary gods and goddesses.

The same wasn't true for mathematics, however. Although I excelled in that subject, rarely did complex problems occupy my mind as I worked. They represented the opposite of a happy diversion.

One day I was assigned to clean the spice cupboard. I had done so before, but I never opened any of the decanters. Not much was left for me to do that afternoon, so I lifted the lid off one of jars, stuck my nose inside, breathed the sublime fragrance of the spice it contained then replaced the lid. I closed my eyes and felt myself being transported somewhere unknown yet strangely familiar. The scent of the spice had taken me there. It was a surprisingly comforting sensation.

When I opened another jar, I had a similar experience. The aroma was unmistakable to me although I had never before inhaled it.

I had worked in the kitchen a couple of years by that time and was assisting with food preparation – mincing vegetables and herbs, peeling fruit, stirring sauces. It was a welcome relief from the constant cleaning I did initially.

A few days after my tour of the spices, I was tending a sauce when I mentioned to the cook without thinking, "A spice in the pantry might enhance this sauce. Isn't it to be poured over roasted boar?"

Once those words left my lips, I regretted my effrontery. If anyone sensed I felt superior, they would take steps to halt my lessons. I could continue to learn only as long as I remained an ignorant slave to the rest of the world.

"I'm sorry," I said immediately. "I don't know what I was thinking."

Unperturbed, the cook queried, "Which one is it?"

"You want me to get the spice?" I asked, afraid I had misunderstood her.

"What else could I be referring to?" she replied.

I wasn't sure where it was, but I knew I would recognize its aroma. "May I take a moment to find it?" I requested.

"Yes, but just a moment," she warned as I handed her the spoon to stir the sauce.

I walked over to the shelves of spices, closed my eyes and willed my nose to locate the one I was looking for. At first the assortment overwhelmed my senses, even with the lids on. But then I picked out its piquant fragrance. I opened my eyes and my hand reached for the jar I was looking at. I removed the lid and sniffed. That was it!

I gave the decanter to the cook, prepared to offer another apology.

"That is remarkable," she said. "I forgot to flavor the sauce, and you recognized something was missing. You also knew which seasoning would go well with the strong taste of the boar. This spice is called turmeric."

I flushed, unable to receive the compliment. "It was just an accident," I replied.

"I don't believe so," she countered. "You have a talent for selecting appropriate spices and herbs. I watch you add herbs to the fresh ones you are chopping to balance the flavor, and you are correct every time."

"I wasn't really thinking about it," I declared honestly. "Something just happens, and I find myself including a few additional ingredients."

"There's no way you learned this anywhere," replied the cook. "You have a natural ability that can be put to good use. Let's start with this sauce."

We added the spice and I stirred the mixture until it had a thick, aromatic consistency. Then I did something even more uncharacteristic. I suggested we add a second spice. The cook gave me permission to retrieve it.

"This is cumin," she commented. "I have never mixed it with turmeric before, but it just might work. Let's see."

When it was time for the main course, we poured the unusual sauce over the roasted meat and sent the platter to the dining room. It came back empty, accompanied by high praise.

Thus began my ongoing collaboration with the cook, for which I took increasing responsibility. I created ever more innovative spice and herb combinations, all of which were well received by the merchant and his guests. Sauces seasoned with saffron, sweet pepper and garlic were delicious with seafood. Rosemary, caraway and allspice enhanced root vegetables perfectly. Cardamom infused cream served with fresh fruit made even the ending of a meal memorable. The compliments continued.

The cook requested that the merchant's ships return with every variety of spice available from caravans and distant ports. She also asked that seeds and cuttings be brought back so we could grow an assortment of herbs in our garden, the more exotic the better.

Our inventiveness expanded along with the variety of ingredients and seasonings we had at our disposal. Many of the spices we acquired had no recognizable name, so we took to storing them in numbered containers. Number 59 turned out to be fenugreek, number 43 tamarind, number 22 capsicum.

The merchant became known for his dinner parties in the men's dining room, where dishes unavailable anywhere else were served, one course after another. We combined figs and pheasant, curry and lentils, arugula and fennel, coriander and sea bass, artichokes and sprats. I stopped cleaning the kitchen altogether and spent my time creating ever more interesting meals.

Alexios and I were chatting one day in the classroom while Errikos napped. Since he had grown too old to teach all day, we often found ourselves together for a tutoring session without the tutor. It didn't matter. By now we were both so proficient at most of what Errikos knew, there was little else for him to teach us.

"You have become a phenomenal cook," Alexios declared, smiling happily. "Every night I look forward to the men's meal, which is inevitably more delicious than the one we had the day before. I enjoy it all the more because I know it is your creation. It's like getting a daily gift from you. The fish you made last night was sublime."

"You give me too much credit," I replied. "I am not in charge of the kitchen. I only help out."

"That may be true," he said, "but I know for a fact that you are the magician in charge of the herbs and spices. Tell me how you do it."

I spent the next half hour recalling my experiments with unexpected combinations of ingredients. He listened intently, saying little in response. I got so caught up in my stories, I almost forgot it was time to return to the kitchen. In fact, I was late.

"I never thought it would be possible," Alexios commented as I was putting away a papyrus roll.

"What?" I asked.

"That anything would stimulate you as much as learning something new during your lessons," he replied.

"I love learning and creating," I admitted, "even though they are so different, perhaps because they are so different. One involves my intellect, the other my senses."

"There is no one else like you anywhere," Alexios said to me as I ran out the door.

"You haven't traveled very far," I called back to him. "When you do, you'll find that I am as ordinary as an old pair of sandals."

As I became a young woman, other aspects of me developed besides my mind and my senses. I grew breasts. My waist narrowed, my legs grew long and shapely, my hips became more curved, and my hair shone copper in the sunlight. I noticed these changes, but given that I had neither a reason nor a means to flaunt them, I kept them well concealed. Or so I thought.

My mother continued her activities with men and managed to avoid any subsequent pregnancies. She loved her "pleasures" as she called these encounters. I was grateful they were available to her, since usually afterwards she was in a better mood even if it was just for the night.

I was walking back to our room from the kitchen one evening when I heard her angry voice. I ventured closer to hear what she was saying.

"How dare you even consider doing it with my daughter!" she hissed. "She is untried. And besides, she doesn't have any charms."

"She has charms aplenty," growled the man. "If I had my way I would take her by force right now."

"You bastard!" screeched my mother. "You say this after you just enjoyed plowing me with your puny little stick. If you took her by force, she wouldn't realize anything had happened."

I heard a slap, and my mother cried out in pain. I was about to help her, but I didn't want to take a chance that the man would do to me what he threatened. I also didn't want my mother to be faced with me after hearing I was desirable, even to such a despicable character.

I tiptoed away and returned to our room, where I pretended to be asleep when she arrived.

My plan worked for the night, but the next morning my mother was furious with me. The left side of her face was bruised, and her eye was swollen shut. Her lip had been bleeding. She paid the price for her belittling words.

"It is your fault," she spat out to me as I was getting dressed. "I never should have let you live. You have been a problem for me since the day you were conceived. And now look at me. This is your doing, and you won't get away with it."

Her words were so irrational, there was no use responding to them. I finished dressing and walked out the door. Even more offended by my silence, she began yelling obscenities at me. If the slaves were not already awake, they would be.

My mother was twice my age. She had lived a hard life, some of which was self-imposed. It showed on her face and in her sagging breasts. I say this not to assert that I was better or more attractive than she. Rather, I was simply younger. I had the body she once enjoyed, the one that captivated the sea captain. She wanted it back. She also wanted to deny it to me. Neither was possible.

That afternoon as Errikos was napping again, Alexios approached me with a grave look on his face. "I heard about what happened last night and this morning," he revealed.

"How?" I wondered. I assumed all along that he knew nothing about my life outside the classroom and the kitchen.

"I have my ways of staying informed about you," he replied. "I have known for quite some time that your mother is perpetual poison in your life."

"She is," I conceded, "but somehow I manage to survive."

"Survive, yes," he replied. "But you deserve so much more than that."

"I can have no more," I sighed. "You know that, Alexios. I am a slave."

"I intend to change that," he announced. "I have decided to talk with my parents and request that you be freed so I might take you as my wife."

"Your wife?" I repeated, unable to comprehend the implications of this disclosure.

"I love you, Graci," Alexios whispered. "I have known you for ten years, and along the way my feelings for you developed into something beyond friendship. I can't bear to see you serving this household as a slave when you should be free to enjoy beauty and contentment and abundance, all of which I can give you. I want to spend my life with you."

"I love you too, but more as a brother than a potential husband," I said frankly. "Besides, your parents would never agree to this. They expect you to marry someone of your class, certainly not a slave."

"And spend my life bored to tears by a woman I don't love, whom I cannot talk to about anything interesting, who is preoccupied with nothing other than the gold bangles she can sweet talk me into buying for her?" he countered.

Errikos shifted in his chair and opened his eyes for a moment. We looked down at our wax tablets and pretended to read. Soon he was snoring again.

"You're making a profound mistake." The words tumbled unbidden from my mouth. "Your parents will be so alarmed by your request, they will demand we never see each other again. To assure this, I will be sent away, forced into slavery under unpredictable circumstances. More importantly, don't let your unreasonable desires create a chasm between you and your family. I'm not worth it."

"Do you say this because you don't love me as much as I love you?" he asked. "If that is your intention, I'm not convinced."

"I would joyfully be your wife," I replied. "There is no better man in the world than you. But I am a slave and you are the grandson of one of the wealthiest men in Greece. What you want cannot be allowed. Only despair will result from your pursuing this cause any further."

"I don't believe you," he shot back at me, frustrated and angry. "You are wrong!"

"There is nothing more to say then," I replied. "I will pray you are successful and we can enjoy the rest of our days as husband and wife. I sincerely appreciate your desire to marry me. It is an honor I little deserve. If you receive your parents' consent, I will devote my life to keeping you blissfully happy."

Alexios stood up, lifted me out of my chair, drew me to him and kissed me on the lips. I was so surprised by his action, I stopped breathing. He pulled away from me for a moment. "You are supposed to breathe, Graci," he whispered. Then we kissed again, this time with an intimacy new to me. I opened my eyes to see Errikos looking at us. He winked at me then resumed his pretense of sleeping.

It was time for me to go. Alexios would talk with his parents that evening. Since I knew there was nothing I could do to convince him otherwise, I encouraged him to settle the matter before he became overly insistent and thus less convincing. Still, my heart sank. He wouldn't succeed.

He gave me one more hug and I was out the door.

I can only imagine what transpired. Alexios' parents locked him inside the walls of the estate to thwart any further access to me. I attended no more lessons.

I grieved for him more than for myself, though I missed him and Errikos tremendously. I silently cried myself to sleep every night for weeks. I wept for Alexios' broken heart and the fact that most likely he despised his beloved parents. But I refused to believe any of this was my fault, for it was not.

A month after the debacle, one of the slaves who served the family at their evening meal gave me the news that Alexios was sent away for an extended visit with family friends. When she saw he wasn't at dinner that night, she dawdled long enough to overhear that he would be gone indefinitely.

I should have anticipated what came next.

A few weeks later I was called out of the kitchen and taken to a private patio, where the merchant was standing with a visitor. "We have reached an agreement," he told me without preamble. "At first light tomorrow you will leave with my friend to serve in the kitchen of his estate. Meet us here with whatever belongings you want to take with you."

I wasn't even introduced to my new owner. There were no formalities, no attempts to soften the impact of this news. I may have been educated, but in the end I was still a slave without freedoms or feelings. I must be taken away permanently before Alexios was allowed to return.

I didn't mention to my mother what transpired. I rarely spoke to her anyway. If she knew about my departure and chose to acknowledge it, I would discuss it with her. Otherwise I would organize my meager belongings, wrap them in a square of cloth and go away quietly in the morning.

I slept little that night as I prepared to leave the only place I ever knew. I was neither sad nor relieved. I felt nothing. I was numb. Slavery had done its job.

At dawn I left my mother, apparently still asleep, without saying goodbye. The men were waiting. They chatted for a few minutes, bid each other farewell, and I started for the dock with the stranger.

On impulse I turned around to look one last time at the slice of land I once called home. Mother was watching me go. She glared at me then smiled cruelly. "Good riddance," her eyes screamed at me.

I turned toward the path before me and followed my new owner down the hill to the waiting ship. It was done.

∞ ∞ ∞

The man was a Roman senator named Appius Equititus Augustalis. He knew the merchant well, having spent vacations on his estate since childhood. This is what he recounted to me many years later.

Augustalis had completed an official visit to Greece. Having no particular need to return to Rome directly, he decided to visit his old friend and was thrust into the middle of a family both anxious and in mourning. Alexios had just been sent away.

His parents were doubly distraught. When they ordered their son off the estate, they were subjected to his anger and resentment. Never before had he behaved so disrespectfully. For eighteen years they cultivated his intellect, thoughtfulness, decency and social graces. But he had been corrupted by a beguiling slave girl and was no longer the son they loved so proudly and effortlessly.

"I worry that when Alexios returns, which he inevitably must do, we will have to endure this process all over again," admitted his father to Augustalis. "He is madly in love with this slave. I don't exaggerate. It's madness."

"Then there is only one solution. You must have her gone from the premises, never to be seen again," Augustalis counseled.

"But he will devote his life to finding her, he loves her that much," protested the father.

Augustalis paused, contemplating whether to enter the territory he was about to explore with his friend. He decided it was his duty to do so. Alexios' father and grandfather were both present. There would be no better time.

"Have you adequately considered the possibility that since Alexios seems to love her so deeply, he would be miserable with anyone else?" He stepped into it fully. "Would you rather have him happy with a freed slave as his wife or living another form of slavery, married to a woman he most likely deplores at no fault of her own?"

"I thought about that a great deal," the father replied. "My preference is to be more lenient. I love Alexios dearly. Despite his recent outbursts he is a remarkable young man. I hate to think he will be forced into a union he doesn't desire, hating his mother and me all the more for requiring such a sacrifice of him."

"Then why don't you reconsider?" asked Augustalis.

"His mother is adamant that this union is not to be," Alexios' father revealed. "She was opposed all along to allowing the slave girl to be tutored with him these many years. But I saw no harm in it. Now she is constantly reminding me that great harm has been done to us all as a result."

"Including to the slave woman, sooner than later," Augustalis noted.

"I know," admitted the father. "Think of Alexios' wrath when he finds out that his love has been sold to the highest bidder."

"You can't in good conscience let her be sold off to some abusive bastard who will rape her within ten minutes to prove he owns her," insisted Augustalis.

"Not all slaveholders are brutal," protested the merchant. "Look at us. We treat slaves quite well. And you, my friend, are more generous than anyone."

"That is because I see them as people, not beasts of burden," Augustalis observed. "And obviously you do too, or you never would have allowed her to receive an education."

Alexios' grandfather drew a sudden intake of breath. "I have an idea – a brilliant one if I do say so!" he exclaimed.

"Tell me," Augustalis urged.

"You will take her," the grandfather suggested. "She can serve in your household. We can then assure Alexios that she has been placed in the home of a friend, away from Greece, where she will be as respected as any slave could be. And you will have quite a prize, a comely young woman with a superb education who can cook the most delectable dishes on the face of the Earth."

"And you are willing to give up all that?" asked Augustalis.

"I have no choice," the grandfather said flatly. "It must be done."

"Well then, to help an old friend, let it be so," Augustalis agreed.

"We won't reveal to Alexios where she is," the grandfather stated, "and you must promise me one thing. You will neither free nor sell her. If you free her Alexios will do whatever it takes to be with her. And if you sell her I cannot assure my grandson that she will be in an exceptional home for the rest of her life."

"And you think he won't encounter her at my estate?" Augustalis asked skeptically.

"He knows very little about you," the grandfather confirmed. "More importantly, he is unaware that you arrived here unexpectedly after his departure. She will be safe with you and hidden from him. Now the promise. Can you commit to it?"

"I promise never to free or sell her," Augustalis vowed.

"It is agreed, then," affirmed the grandfather. "I will send word that Alexios should return immediately so he is gone from Rome when you arrive. It would be just my luck that you would cross paths on your way home and his way here. Please take the slow route back if you can."

"I have business to conduct on the way, which will create a delay and arouse no suspicions," Augustalis informed him. "We have a worthy plan, and I just acquired a slave sight unseen."

"Speaking of sight unseen, her only fault is that she wears clothes that hide all evidence of her extraordinary figure," commented Alexios' father.

"And pray tell, how would you know about that if she hides it so well?" Augustalis asked wryly.

"A man notices such things when a woman moves," he observed, "as my son no doubt witnessed probably for years."

"And do you know anything of her sexual experience?" Augustalis wondered.

"If she were anything like her mother, she would be lucky not to have become pregnant by now," the father noted. "But since she is the opposite of her in every way, I assume she is still untried. I heard no rumors that she was taken by force or gave herself willingly to anyone."

"Not even to your son?" queried Augustalis.

"He adores her too much ever to take advantage of her slave status," he responded. "And I am certain she never offered herself to him. Most likely he did nothing more than kiss her, he respects her so as his equal."

"There are worse things," Augustalis remarked, mostly to give the two men one more opportunity to change their minds.

"I know," admitted the father, "which gives me hope that eventually Alexios can settle down with an acceptable woman who will spark those same feelings once again."

"He is still young," Augustalis offered optimistically. "After all, how many of us have loved only once?"

"No one in this room," commented the merchant, glancing knowingly at Augustalis. "Thank you my friend, for committing to this arrangement. We reached a mutually beneficial conclusion. The gods sent you here at this precise moment. I pray they also bring my grandson back safely and in a more conciliatory frame of mind."

"It shall be so," affirmed Augustalis. "Rest assured we won't arrive in Rome until he is well on his way home."

Dinner that night was as eclectic and delicious as usual. Augustalis raved about each inventive dish.

"Your cook is a genius!" he exclaimed at the end of the meal. "Your dinner guests must all be vying to add her to their household staff."

"Actually the talented one is a slave, and a very young one at that," noted the grandfather. "Our cook gets the credit, but the flair behind these meals lies with a young woman who will be leaving us on the morrow. We can only hope she has taught the cook well enough so we can feast on decent fare after she is gone."

Augustalis made plans to talk with the head cook at his estate about the special responsibilities their talented new slave would assume. Uninspired, prosaic meals would be a thing of the past, and their dinner parties would soon become the most sought after invitation in Rome.

∞ ∞ ∞

I stood on the deck and leaned against the railing of the cargo ship, waiting for instructions from my new owner. He was nice enough when we spoke briefly the day before, but that didn't mean much. A kind face in public can mask someone quite sinister in private. I had no way of knowing for sure who my master really was, or how he would treat me.

But for some reason I trusted him. His brief interactions with me were more thoughtful than most. Perhaps it was his disarming gaze, at once open and discerning. Or maybe I was reacting to the irrefutable softness in his otherwise patrician voice. Then again, maybe I invented these perceptions to justify my fantasy of a better life in his household. I would find out soon enough.

I heard him talking with the ship captain. It sounded as if he was making special arrangements for my passage as well as his, but I couldn't tell for sure. I half expected to be shunted into the hold along with bolts of silk, burlap bags of peppercorns and boxes of jade beads, unable to see the light of day until we arrived at our destination. A slave could expect no better treatment than that, even from an owner with understanding eyes.

I had been in the water and by the water but never on it. I adjusted quickly, feeling my legs move with the rhythm of the vessel as it swayed with the waves. My fingers held tight to the wooden railing, like those of a child who is first learning to stand. In truth I was learning to stand in a new way, liberated from my mother's unwavering resentment.

I imagined myself taking wing with the seagulls gliding overhead. Although I observed them all my life, never before did I sense the freedom in their flight. Stout defenses that served me well yielded cautiously to tranquility. I tipped my head back, stretching my tense neck and shoulders, and exhaled my weariness.

"Even if I am journeying to equally hateful circumstances, I will have experienced this interlude," I though to myself. "I am no longer reviled by the woman who bore me, and I am blessedly unaware of what awaits me. I can always return to this moment, standing on the deck of a ship about to disembark, with nothing immediately ahead but open seas."

Lost in this unaccustomed reverie, I didn't hear my new owner approach. "Fortunately I secured separate sleeping accommodations for you," he announced, propelling me out of my daydream. "If the weather holds, you can spend most of your days on deck. It should be a lovely voyage this time of year, with calm waters and muted sun. We are on our way to my household in Rome. By the way, I am Appius Equititus Augustalis. You can call me Augustalis."

"I am Graci," I replied.

"Let me take your things, Graci" he offered. "I will show you to your quarters."

"Thank you," I answered, "but I can carry them. I have so little."

Augustalis led me to wooden steps leading below deck and climbed down ahead of me. I followed, holding onto the rope railing and barely keeping my balance as the boat pitched forward. We walked through an area allocated to four sleeping compartments, two on each side of the ship. Further back a hatch cover lay next to a hole in the slatted flooring, where a rope ladder dangled into a miniscule space below. It was barely large enough for a hammock.

"Your sleeping compartment may be in the bowels of the ship, but at least it is private," he explained apologetically.

"That's more than I expected," I replied. "Thank you for securing this spot for me."

I didn't reveal that I especially appreciated not being required to remain unescorted among questionable sailors and strangers in another part of the hold.

I handed my bundle to Augustalis, climbed cautiously down the knotted rope then reached for my belongings. The space was neither as small nor as uninviting as it looked from above. It was clean enough, and an opening in the hatch cover provided fresh air. Once I stashed my bundle in the wooden slots under the hammock, I climbed back out of the hold.

"Let's see what they are offering for the morning meal," Augustalis suggested. "There is no chance the food on board this ship will measure up to your creations. Most likely it will barely be edible. But at least it will ward off starvation."

I nodded silently and followed him aft. Lukewarm porridge, bland and watery, was being served. I accepted the bowlful that was offered to me and settled with my owner on a bench fastened to the interior of the ship.

"I hear you had an extensive education," Augustalis commented, then paused upon tasting his fare. "This porridge is even worse than I expected."

I decided to forego my assessment of the gruel. "My master was most generous," I affirmed. "I received daily tutoring for almost a decade, starting when I was six."

"Were you in lessons most of the day?" he continued.

"Oh no," I said. "I was in the classroom only briefly."

"And yet you learned languages and mathematics, literature and history?" he asked.

"I benefited from an exceptional tutor, and apparently I am a quick learner," I explained.

"When did you start working in the kitchen?" he pursued.

"When I was ten," I told him.

"You knew at that young age how to cook so innovatively?" he asked.

"I cleaned the kitchen and scrubbed floors for a few years," I explained. "Then one day when I was dusting the spice canisters, I was drawn to their unusual aromas. Without further consideration, I suggested to the cook that a new combination of spices might make her sauce more interesting. After she received compliments on the meal, she asked me for additional ideas. Eventually I was responsible for seasoning everything, inventing all the while."

"No one taught you any of this?" he queried.

"Everything I know about blending herbs and spices came from a source I can't identify," I admitted.

"I enjoyed every last one of the meals you prepared while I was visiting," he declared. "You have a rare talent."

"Thank you," I replied. "I am grateful my cooking gave you pleasure."

"It certainly did," he said appreciatively. "And I expect it will continue to do so for quite some time."

I took that comment as an indication I might work in the kitchen, good fortune indeed.

"I must prepare for a meeting I am attending in a few days," Augustalis remarked. "We will make one brief stop at the port of Syracuse for that purpose. Since you have no responsibilities, you can do whatever you choose for the remainder of the voyage."

"I would like to sleep," I commented.

"Very well," he agreed. "Slumber is exceptional on board ship."

After we consumed the porridge, which grew even less tolerable as it cooled, Augustalis walked me to my compartment below deck. I climbed into the hammock, covered myself with my threadbare wool cloak and fell asleep. Later I recalled hearing the hatch open occasionally, but that didn't awaken me. The rocking of the ship and the swaying of the hammock soothed my weary soul. I slept on and on.

Eventually a gentle voice roused me. "Graci, it has been almost two days since you have had anything to eat or drink," Augustalis whispered. "Arise for the evening meal."

"I'll be right there," I replied, clawing my way to the surface of wakefulness.

We ate in silence. Augustalis looked at me intently as if he were studying a moth that arrived with the prevailing winds and alighted on his toga.

"I began to worry after you went so long without emerging from the hold," he revealed. "At first I thought you misunderstood me and believed you were required to remain there, cramped and uncomfortable. But each time I checked on you, you were fast asleep. Since you didn't seem ill, I concluded you were simply exhausted."

"I still am," I admitted. "I won't be able to snooze my days away after this journey. If you don't mind, I would like to sleep until I can do so no more."

He continued to watch me closely. "Excuse my impertinence," he apologized in advance, "but did you share a room with your mother?"

"Yes," I responded, wondering why such a detail would matter to him.

"So you never had any privacy," he concluded.

"None," I said simply.

"I will give you that, and not just on this voyage," he declared. "I will make sure you have your own room in the slave quarters, even though that is usually afforded only to those who serve us for many years."

"I appreciate the offer, but please don't make an exception for me," I demurred. "Others have earned that opportunity. I haven't."

"Wouldn't you like to have a small space to call your own?" he asked quietly.

"I would," I assured him, a hint of enthusiasm poking through my caution.

"Then it is done," he stated. "Now that you have food in your belly, you can return to your hammock and your infinite need to rest. I promise not to awaken you for another day and a half."

After one more bout of extended sleep I was rejuvenated at last. Something else had occurred. Optimism, albeit a wary little cache of it, found a spot within me.

I was on deck one afternoon after we departed from Syracuse, exhilarated by the sea air and savoring the fact that I was required to do absolutely nothing. Augustalis approached me, leaning against the railing of the ship.

"We will arrive in Ostia tomorrow then travel to Rome," he observed. "You should know something about me and my family, along with the household and your responsibilities, before you are thrust into the middle of it all.

"First, Rome. You have lived on an estate in the country overlooking the sea. Rome couldn't be more opposite. It is an overcrowded city of almost one million people. Sometimes I feel I can get no air, it is so congested. Every imaginable language is spoken there, and myriad exotic delicacies can be had. Rome is at once a fascinating, sophisticated city and a terrible, oppressive one. You will experience both sides of it.

"I come from a long line of senators, governmental officials and military leaders. We grew wealthy not through our business acumen like the Greek merchant, but by handing down our fortune from one generation to the next and amplifying it through marriage. I was born into privilege and have expanded it as expected.

"I have a large home, walled and protected from much of the noise, dust and hubbub of Rome. A considerable number of servants keep the household running smoothly. I have a wife and five children, all of whom need a great deal of coddling.

"Because of my rank and the fact that we live in such a populated city, we have a staggering number of acquaintances and associates. We are constantly hosting dinner parties and large gatherings. Sometimes I schedule trips abroad not because they are essential, but because I must get away from the relentless requirement of entertaining others. My wife thrives on it; I am more reclusive.

"You will be assigned to the kitchen, where you will work at least twelve hours a day, six days a week. Our head cook is fair-minded, if somewhat protective of her authority. You will have to win her over. She will be told you were brought here because of your exceptional cooking talents. I will speak to her personally about this and let her know she is to give you free rein once you are familiar with how she runs things. I would ask my wife to do this, but she has no interest in such matters.

"I will request an escort initially to show you around the city and help you identify sources for the necessary herbs, spices and foods you are to prepare. You can expect to spend a number of months learning your way around Rome.

"You are free to explore the city on your own. The variety of temples and public events may interest you. But I warn you, don't try to escape into the apparently anonymous crowds. Rome runs on slavery, and an excellent system exists for finding and punishing slaves who attempt to take their own freedom. You will be far better served by making the most of your new situation. Are there any questions?"

I was at once reassured and intrigued by this man, who told me considerably more than I needed to know. I relished and valued every morsel of it.

"Thank you for your guidance," I said in gratitude. "I promise not to create any complications in the kitchen or elsewhere. As for running away, I have no loving family to return to, no happy memories to entice me to steal away to Greece. You have no worries there."

"Then it is understood," he replied. "I am heartened by your attitude and resilience. Your new life in Rome will be at least slightly better than the one you left behind."

"It will be more than slightly better, in great measure because of your fairness and respect toward me," I assured him. "I promise to be worthy of it."

∞ ∞ ∞

My new master's estate on the Palatine appeared modest enough from outside the walls, whitewashed clean and with little ornamentation. I should have expected something quite different based on the size of the property. It occupied the better part of a square block. Later I learned that owning such an expansive residence in Rome's most exclusive neighborhood was the mark of unfathomable wealth.

Once we were inside the enormous gate at the main entrance, I felt as if I had stepped into the home of the emperor. The interior courtyard was lush with fragrant blossoms and climbing vines, fountains, sculptures and private seating areas.

Augustalis asked me to wait there while he determined if his wife was home. I stood in the shade of a flowering plum tree and watched the bees buzzing from one succulent flower to another.

I also peeked discreetly into the rooms that opened onto the courtyard. Masses of marble paved the floors, ornamented the doorways and formed intricate mosaics and graceful statuary. The frescoes decorating the walls, everything from dramatic mythological scenes to tranquil rural landscapes, transported my mind to other times and places, real and imaginary. The silk covering furniture cushions and pillows burst with color at once exuberant and elegant.

Presently Augustalis returned by himself. "My wife is away with friends," he reported. "I will show you to your quarters, then tomorrow you can meet her and be introduced in the kitchen. In the interim you can rest and enjoy a good soak in the public baths. I will arrange for one of the servants to escort you there."

"Thank you for your kindness," I replied. "You must be weary from the journey, and yet you took pains to assure I am settled comfortably."

"It is the least I can do," he said lightly. "Besides, I want you to be in good spirits so your cooking is none the worse for wear."

Although the slave quarters were predictably plain and sparse, they were built more solidly than the rickety housing I lived in before. The walls were thick enough to afford a measure of privacy, the high ceilings provided good ventilation, and the doors were solid.

Augustalis showed me inside my room, which was noticeably clean. A narrow bed with a straw mattress occupied one corner. Pegs jutted from the wall to hold my clothing. A simple stool sat next to a rustic table with an oil lamp. On a ledge was a pitcher of water, a cup and a bowl.

I was ecstatic.

"Are you positive this is my room?" I asked.

"I assure you it is," Augustalis declared. "I sent a message ahead of our arrival and asked that space be prepared for you. Then when you were waiting in the garden, I found out which room was yours.

"I must attend to a few pressing matters before dinner. Someone will stop by to take you to the baths. Food will be brought down for you this evening. Then tomorrow you can begin teaching the cooks in the kitchen a thing or two."

"With all that I am, I thank you," I replied. "I will do what I can in the kitchen, and as soon as possible. If the herbs and spices I need aren't available, it may be a few days to gather them. I don't know my way around Rome yet."

"Of course," he nodded. "It will probably take you longer to win the confidence and respect of the head cook than it will to assemble what you need to start creating your delectable sauces. Now I must go. Rest well."

After Augustalis left I sat on the stool and looked around the room. Despite the noise of the city, it was quiet inside. Even so, aromas from the street insinuated themselves. I closed my eyes as unfamiliar smells, both rarefied and rank, assaulted my senses. "This will obliterate any lingering memory of what I left behind," I thought. "Good. There is not a whiff of sea air to be found."

I loosened the cloth tied around my few grubby garments and acknowledged I had nothing decent to put on after the baths. Worse, everything smelled of the dank cubicle in the ship's hold where I stashed my bundle. I was wondering where I could wash my clothes when a young woman, black as burnished ebony, arrived at my open door.

"Hello, I am Gaiana," she said amicably. "I was asked to bring you these tunics. I bought them this morning for you. Master said in his letter to his wife that you were about her height, and he requested that new clothing be procured for your arrival."

"I was just thinking that even a slave shouldn't be walking the streets of Rome wearing the rags I brought," I replied, relieved. "Then you appeared, sent no doubt by Athena the Goddess of Weaving. My name is Graci, by the way."

"I hope you like the tunics I picked out for you, Graci," Gaiana said. "I made the man at the stall in the Forum promise you could return them and select something else if you want."

"I'm sure they will be fine," I replied, holding up the two simple garments. "These tunics are well made and should last a long time. Thanks to you I have something fresh to slip into after my much needed trip to the baths."

"Bring a change of clothes, and we'll be on our way," Gaiana suggested.

Heading toward the public baths, I experienced a compelling sensation I had walked the streets of Rome before. Everything seemed familiar somehow. I didn't recognize the buildings or shops, but I understood the layout of the streets around the seven hills. Errikos must have described Rome to me in detail, though I couldn't recall when.

We arrived at the baths designated for slaves. What a luxury! The last time I had enjoyed anything like a bath was when I jumped into the sea. As I was stepping out of my clothes, Gaiana observed, "Those should be thrown into the Tiber."

I laughed. "Everything I brought is going directly there. Good riddance!"

"Was the place where you were before really bad?" she asked.

"The place itself was fine," I replied sincerely. "I was given an education and not required to work overly hard in the kitchen. My mother was the problem. She resented me from the moment I was born, and her feelings toward me grew worse as the years went by. It is a relief to be away from her hatred."

"I never knew my mother," Gaiana revealed. "I often wonder what she was like. But then I hear stories like yours from other slaves, and I believe I was better off growing up as I did."

"What happened to her?" I asked, easing into the refreshing water.

"My mother's family was captured in a raid by a neighboring tribe when she was a young girl," Gaiana explained. "She was treated so brutally she barely survived. She became pregnant with me by force and died in childbirth. The other female slaves raised me. When I was old enough to bring something in trade, I was sold. Now I am living in far better circumstances than I knew before."

"So we are both blessed to be here," I observed.

"Yes we are," she agreed. "Even though we have no freedoms and will die with nothing but our memories in our heart and calluses on our hands, we are better off than most."

"Augustalis seems like a good man," I commented.

"He's the best," Gaiana affirmed. "He never raises a hand to anyone, and he rarely utters a cross word except to his wife. She's the opposite of him."

"What do you mean?" I asked.

"Let me put it this way. She has little consideration for others, even her own children. She expects everything to be done for her, and when it isn't perfect she becomes vicious and rude," Gaiana revealed. "The slaves who take care of her clothing tell me she is seeing other men. They often find you-know-what on her fine silks."

"How sad," I replied. "Augustalis deserves a wife who loves and appreciates him. He must be miserable."

"I doubt it," Gaiana responded immediately. "Marriages among the upper classes in Rome are arranged based on wealth, not love. No one expects to love the person they marry."

I thought of Alexios and his ill-fated desire to marry me. Perhaps his situation was more unfortunate than the life Augustalis was living. Alexios wanted so much to marry for love, he fought with his parents for the right to do so. Apparently Augustalis did what was expected of him. I wondered if he ever loved another and fought for her as Alexios did for me.

"Tomorrow I will show you around the kitchen," Gaiana offered, interrupting my errant thoughts.

"You work there?" I asked, hoping that was the case. I liked her already.

"I do," she replied. "But I am only a helper. I don't do elaborate cooking. That is the responsibility of Eirene, the head cook."

"Is she good at what she does?" I queried.

"Yes, but we already heard you bring a particular magic with you," Gaiana commented.

"It's not magic, just experience," I observed. "Tell me, how will Eirene feel if someone new introduces fresh ideas?"

"So far she seems unconcerned," Gaiana reported, "probably because she can't believe anyone could create more delicious dishes than her own. If you can enhance the reputation of her kitchen, she would be happy to let you do so."

"I'm not sure how successful I will be," I admitted, "but I will try my best. Whatever happens, I will enjoy working with you."

I washed my hair and scrubbed my skin until it was as red as a sunrise the day of a storm. As I dipped in and out of the water, I imagined I was cleansing away the final remnants of my life in Greece. I prayed to the Goddess Aphrodite that Alexios would find love again and forget me. Then submerging myself once more in the water, I let him go.

I felt a glimmer of hope for what lay ahead. My mother's oppression was gone for good. I was serving in a household where I would be treated more as a person than an animal; where I would have a roof over my head and my very own room; where I could help create good food with the best ingredients; where I could even go to the baths to wash away whatever I no longer wanted on my body or in my mind and heart.

After a good long soak, I emerged from the baths and donned my new tunic. Gaiana and I talked about nothing in particular on the way back to my room. Growing more relaxed and tired, I welcomed one more night of rest before I began to work.

Fresh fruit, hearty porridge, brown bread and watered wine were waiting in my room when we arrived. I offered to share it with Gaiana, but she was

needed in the kitchen. I savored the food as well as my
privacy, drank the wine and fell asleep.

∞ ∞ ∞

Gaiana was outside my door early the next morning
to make sure I arrived in the kitchen when Eirene did.
She was already there, sipping a glass of honeyed water
as she reviewed what was left in the fruit and vegetable
bins. Whatever had lost its initial freshness would be
used to prepare meals for the servants and slaves. No
matter, even that was of better quality than what most
people ate from their porridge bowl.

Gaiana approached Eirene and introduced me.
"You come highly recommended by the head of the
household himself," Eirene told me appreciatively. "I
am looking forward to discovering the mysterious spices
you use so we can please Augustalis as much as you did
when he was in Greece."

"I'm not sure how mysterious they are," I replied. "I
simply created unusual combinations with whatever
herbs, spices and fresh ingredients were available. In his
enthusiasm Augustalis may have exaggerated my
talents."

"We will know soon enough," Eirene commented.
"I will show you around, then I would like you to take
an inventory of our spice shelves and herb garden.
Gaiana will help you find whatever we need in the
marketplace. I can't expect you to exhibit your expertise
to the fullest if you don't have the necessary ingredients,
can I?"

"I suppose not," I replied. "Unfortunately, I don't
even know the names of most of the spices I use. I

recognize them by their aroma. I won't know what to ask for in the spice stalls."

"You will just have to follow your nose, then," Eirene suggested merrily. Then she took me on a tour of the kitchen and bakery, which were large and well equipped.

"How many people work here?" I asked, amazed at the size of the food preparation area.

"That depends," she told me. "When just the family is dining, we need only four or five people, two or three to prepare the food and as many again to serve it. But when they are entertaining, which occurs frequently, as many as three dozen slaves and servants can be involved. This is one of the busiest kitchens in Rome."

"Then I'd better get to work," I said enthusiastically.

"Please do so as soon as possible," she replied. "I would like to feature your specialties at a banquet this weekend, and I doubt we have the spices and other ingredients you need."

"I'll take care of it," I told her confidently, ready to begin my new duties.

I quickly determined that the spice pantry was poorly stocked. What was there was so old and rancid, almost all of it had to be thrown out. Rather than creating a list of what I needed, I decided to replenish everything. If I didn't know the name of a particular spice, I could always make a note of the dish in which it was used. Whatever spices were immediately available would determine the fare I would prepare initially.

"I would like to replace what you have and add significantly to it, if that's acceptable to you," I reported to Eirene.

"Obtain whatever you need," she confirmed. "I don't want to be accused of economizing and thus limiting your creativity!"

I looked at her to ascertain if any resentment was hidden in that comment. Thankfully, it appeared to have been made in good cheer.

Gaiana and I began our search that afternoon in the herb shops, spice stalls and apothecaries scattered throughout Rome. Once again I had the distinct feeling I knew the neighborhoods where we could find certain rare spices, even though I could identify nothing more than their unique aroma. Invariably we discovered vendors with the freshest, most aromatic delicacies I had in mind.

"This is really strange," I commented to Gaiana. "I am guiding you around Rome and not the other way around."

"And I am doing nothing more than carrying your parcels," Gaiana laughed. "Goodness, they do smell wonderful. I'm getting hungry!"

After a few days I managed to find almost everything I needed. Cinnamon, cardamom and cumin, saffron and star anise, curry, cayenne and cloves, chili peppers and paprika, vanilla beans, anise seeds, nutmeg and juniper berries, fenugreek, turmeric, sumac, ginger and bay leaves filled the pantry with their unique aromas. Then, of course, there were fresh herbs in the garden that I could snip whenever I wanted: basil and oregano, tarragon and thyme, garlic and chives, parsley and mint, rosemary and lavender.

"Now you can create without restraint for the banquet on Saturday night," Eirene mused as she surveyed the shelves. Myriad pots, jars and containers were lined up in an order only I could decipher. But then, I was the one who needed to know precisely where everything was.

"Have you determined what you want to serve?" I asked.

"I am considering four fish dishes, roast pig and boiled ham as well as ostrich, turtle dove and flamingo. Then there will be the usual variety of first courses – jellyfish, sea urchins and the like – and fruit, nuts and cakes for dessert. I will select the appropriate wines. Where would you like to begin?"

"Let's start with the main courses," I replied. "How many people will we be serving?"

"About fifty," Eirene informed me. "It's just a small dinner party."

"Small?" I asked in disbelief. "How big are they usually?"

"Once a month there is a feast for at least twice that many," Eirene explained. "Then depending on celebration days, we may have three or four times that number of guests to feed, with hardly enough time to go shopping in between."

"I'd better get busy learning how to cook for the multitudes," I replied cheerfully.

"That should be easy," Eirene said with a hint of irony. "All you need to do is figure out how to prepare large quantities that taste as if each serving were individually created for the person about to savor it."

"Sounds like a worthwhile goal to me," I told her. "I will undoubtedly need your sage advice every step of the way."

Eirene managed the kitchen the way I heard Roman officers commanded their legions. Everyone had the capability and raw materials they needed to contribute their best. They also followed strict discipline and rules.

No wonder it was affectionately known as Eirene's Empire.

The first few sauces and marinades I prepared for family meals were not up to my usual standards. But the enthusiastic comments I received from the dining room convinced me not to fret. I could cook for fifty as well as five, and I would do so with every bit of flair I could summon to inspire me.

The day of the dinner party Gaiana was assigned to help me. She and I were a controlled storm of activity, finding new rhythms as we went along. I had no trouble adjusting proportions for large pots of sauces. Each one was subtle and inventive.

I rubbed the pork with rosemary and chopped garlic before it was roasted, then drizzled over the sliced meat a sauce made from the drippings, red wine and green peppercorns. I drenched the boiled ham in honey and stuffed it with figs and bay leaves. What I created to complement the fish dishes varied according to the taste and texture of the fish – everything from a sauce with bergamot, orange and saffron to a crushed olive and pepper paste. The roasted fowl were accented with sauces ranging from onion and sage to a slightly sweet mixture containing cinnamon and raisins.

I supervised the final preparation of the platters of food, drizzling fresh herbed olive oils on top and decorating them with fruits and flowers. "Those dishes are so beautiful, they should be captured in a fresco before anything is served from them!" exclaimed Eirene.

"I only hope the food tastes half as good as it looks," I replied.

Soon the servers were flying in and out of the kitchen, requesting additional quantities of everything I prepared. Although we had made enough food for half again as many dinner guests, we ran out of everything.

"This never happens," Eirene revealed. "We prepared more than what fifty of the most voracious guests would normally consume. Your talent with exotic concoctions woke up everyone's taste buds."

"I might have contributed a final flourish or two, but it took a full kitchen to make the meal," I responded.

Just then one of the servers ran toward us, her cheeks flushed. "Graci, they are asking to see you," she said excitedly. "The master of the household insists you present yourself so you can receive accolades from the guests."

I looked at Eirene. "Please choose a few others to accompany me," I suggested. "As I was saying, I didn't create the meal by myself."

"That is true, but they want to acknowledge your artistry," she said with a smile. "Go, go, and receive the credit you deserve."

I looked down at my tunic, which was splashed with sauce stains. The sides were smudged where I wiped my hands after measuring the spices with my fingers. My hair was in disarray, curls flying every which way. My brow was sweating. I was a mess.

The server was growing impatient. "I told Augustalis I would return with you immediately," she urged. "They are waiting."

Eirene handed me a wet towel, which I used to wipe my face and hands. Then she gave me a clean one to tie around my waist to cover the worst of the stains, and I followed the server into the dining room.

I had never been in the dining hall, which was fortunate. If I had known how exquisitely it was decorated and appointed, or how splendid the female guests' clothing, jewels and hairstyles would be, I never would have shown my face. But there I was, disheveled and discombobulated, in a sea of silk, gold and gems.

"Here she is, the immensely talented young woman behind the delectable dishes you enjoyed this evening," Augustalis cheered. "Graci, our guests want to toast you in person. They insist they never had a better meal in Rome, and some of them have indulged in banquets here for quite a few decades."

The guests laughed in approval. Then Augustalis raised his wine goblet, and everyone followed him in turn. "Here's to the first of many memorable feasts, prepared by the brilliant Graci and devoured to the very last bite!"

"Here's to Graci!" the dinner guests cheered in unison.

My cheeks turned crimson. I was mortified, praying I wouldn't be expected to speak. Augustalis turned to me, saw my embarrassment, and knew better than to invite me to respond. He smiled and nodded to me, indicating I could take my leave.

I lowered my head slightly to let everyone know I appreciated their acknowledgment, then turned and headed toward the nearest door. It seemed miles away. I felt everyone's eyes on me and speculated about stains on the back of my tunic that the towel didn't cover.

"The biggest problem with your being here, Graci, is that there are no leftovers for us to enjoy," laughed one of the more robust members of the kitchen staff. "Eirene, the next time you must procure twice as much as you think the guests will want, so we can indulge in Graci's treats when the party is over."

We were munching on bread and fruit when a servant entered the kitchen. "One of the dinner guests asked to offer his compliments to Graci in person, and the master agreed to it," she announced. "Graci, you will have to make one more appearance. But don't worry. The guest is alone in the dining hall. The master and his wife escorted the others out to bid them farewell."

I looked at Eirene, who nodded her approval that I could go. "I'll save you a bowl of dates," she offered, "in case he is long-winded."

Thankfully the towel was still tied around my waist. I hopped off the stool where I was sitting and prepared to leave once again.

"If he tries to convince you to serve in his household," Eirene called out to me, "remind him that you are already spoken for, and your master drives an impossible bargain."

Everyone laughed at her impertinence, and I found my way into the empty dining hall.

∞ ∞ ∞

He was standing with his back to the door on the other side of the room, as if he wanted to give me the opportunity to become accustomed to his presence before he turned to face me. He was exceedingly tall, with thick dark curly hair. The red senatorial stripe bordered his toga.

"An imposing figure," I said to myself. "Never fear. This is about accolades, not admonitions."

I was approaching the middle of the room when he turned slowly to face me. His gaze was piercing, even from a distance. I quite literally couldn't take another step. We stood still, staring at each other.

A curious heat began to rise from deep within my core. I had never before been attracted to anyone, but I supposed this was how it must feel.

"I don't want to alarm you," he said kindly. "If it bothers you to be alone with me, I can arrange for someone else to be here with us."

"It's not that," I replied. "I am a bit lightheaded. I must have made one too many sauces today."

"Each one was extraordinary," he commented, smiling.

"I appreciate your commendation," I replied, "but really, I was just one of many involved in the preparation of the meal."

"I know that, and they did their work superbly," he noted. "But you created something that affected me in a most unusual way. Every time I took a bite of a dish you embellished, it tasted familiar to me, as if I had enjoyed it many times before. Then when you appeared for the tribute you so thoroughly deserved, I felt as if I had already met you even though I most certainly have not."

"That is strange indeed," I replied, preferring not to reveal to him how recognizable Rome had been to me – or the quickening that arose in my belly the moment I saw him. "Maybe there is magic in the food."

"If so, I will gladly consume large quantities of it," he laughed. "I must remain on the good side of Augustalis so he continues to include me on his guest list."

He approached me as we were talking. Up close I could peer into his eyes. It was as if I were looking at a twin, and yet he was anything but that. We could not be further apart in appearance, background, experience or social class. He was on the top rung of society, and I occupied none at all. He was tall, dark and imposing. I was short and unremarkable.

He hesitated then revealed, "I feel as if I already know you. Intimately. Please don't misinterpret my motives. I am not trying to take advantage of you. I would never do that. But I am compelled to tell you that I have never, ever, reacted to anyone the way I have to you. And don't say it is your cooking, although I will admit it may have opened a doorway between us."

"A doorway?" I asked.

"Yes, a connection, a sense of knowing that defies all experience and reason," he replied. He looked at me searchingly to determine if I felt something similar and would dare admit it to him.

Here was a total stranger who declared something of immense import to him. And apparently it wasn't for the purpose of getting me into his bed. I didn't even know his name. But since he was a friend of Augustalis, he must be a good man, respectable and perhaps even respectful. I decided to take my chances.

"When you turned around," I began, willing myself to be forthcoming despite the inherent hazards, "I too experienced a kind of recognition, as if you were my twin and somehow we had been separated."

I drew a breath to apologize for my audacity. I couldn't have been more inappropriate, suggesting such similarity between us. He seemed not to be offended by it.

"I know all about you," he said quietly.

"Tell me what you know, then," I requested.

"You know absolutely who you are, and you approach every situation honestly," he declared immediately. "You are unusually intelligent and quick-witted. You are courageous, optimistic, self-sufficient and independent in the extreme. You are humble and wise, and you respond resiliently to whatever life offers you.

"All of this is true despite the challenging existence you have endured so far. It is evidence of your strength of character and your uncompromising integrity."

"You are describing a senator, not a slave," I replied noncommittally.

"But I did portray you accurately, didn't I?" he continued.

"Yes, I suppose you did," I admitted. "And I also suppose you described yourself."

"Proving that we are spiritual twins?" he asked.

"Proving that you are a perceptive man and a quick study, with a side of diplomacy thrown in for good measure," I noted, with more of an edge than I intended.

"So what are we to do?" he pursued.

"About what?" I refused to take the conversation where he might want to go with it.

"About this unprecedented situation in which we find ourselves," he replied.

"We do nothing, absolutely nothing," I insisted, leaving no room for negotiation. "You are a senator and I am a slave. You may attend dinners here and enjoy the food I prepare, but please don't try to see me or get to know me. It can end in no good."

"Do you really think so?" he asked, apparently unconvinced.

"I am certain of it," I said decisively. "Besides, I have no time for friendships, and you must be busy making sure the Empire expands ever farther and wider."

"It isn't a question of available time for either of us," he commented. "Perhaps you haven't yet heard that Augustalis gives his slaves a day of rest every week."

"He has been extremely thoughtful already," I replied. "I would never take advantage of his generosity."

"Augustalis is a man of exceptional goodwill," he agreed. "I am grateful you are in his care. If you were anywhere else, I would demand your immediate release."

I blinked at his comment, wondering why he would declare such a thing. He didn't know me. And then I thought, "It only appears we don't know each other. We are both keenly aware that is not true. Already you know him better than anyone you have ever met. Acknowledge that, at least. You must."

"I can't explain what unites us," I ventured. "Obviously, it is a force greater than either of us. We didn't overtly will our coming together. But destiny brought me to Rome, into this household where even the slaves are treated well. That same force guided you here on the first evening when my cooking could be tasted publicly, and most likely the only time I will be brought out from the kitchen to be acknowledged. We have now collided with each other. Infinite possibilities should await us at this particular moment, but there are none. We must pursue this no further. Neither of us deserves a life of torment as a result of unfulfilled desires or worse, unrequited love."

"But the love is not unrequited," he said simply, staring into my soul with penetrating, perceptive recognition.

"You can't possibly love me," I insisted. "Even if you somehow know me, even if you feel a bond with me, even if you have a desire to save me from my fate as a slave, it's not necessarily love."

"True," he replied softly. "But I know how I feel toward you, and most undeniably it is love. If you never love me that would complicate things, but it wouldn't alter my feelings for you."

"It would be more complicated if I did love you," I observed pointedly.

"Whatever you feel, don't try to shelter me," he warned. "I need no protection."

Something in that statement caused me to lose my composure. "Did it occur to you that I may be reeling from the recent changes in my life? That I am exhausted from trying to create dinner for fifty? That I am too confused to trust my feelings? And until I am more certain of what underlies my reaction to you, I will declare nothing? To do otherwise would be to dishonor us both."

"Oh, my dear," he whispered, reaching for me as I stepped away from him. "In my haste to communicate what I felt, I was thoughtless and disrespectful. I bungled things badly, and you may justifiably want nothing more to do with me. What can I do to make amends?"

"Give me time," I replied. "Until two weeks ago I spent my entire life within the boundaries of a country estate in a foreign land. I am adjusting to completely different circumstances in a large city. I need to put down roots first. Then perhaps I can develop a degree of confidence in what I am feeling and thinking. If indeed it is love, I will tell you so. Nonetheless, I am fully aware that even if we were to love each other more than any two people ever have, we cannot marry."

His face darkened with this reminder. "Let's not discuss possibilities or the limits thereof quite yet," he suggested. "I will give you time. Please send for me when you want to speak again."

"But I have no idea who you are!" I protested, smiling. "With all this talk of love, you might at least have the courtesy to introduce yourself!"

"I am Vibius Tetius Lucanus, Lucan for short," he replied.

"All right, Lucan," I said. "I will be in touch."

At that moment Augustalis entered the room. "Everyone was so ecstatic about the meal, I could barely get them to leave," he observed happily. "They kept giving me rapturous descriptions of one culinary creation after another. And it is all you're doing, Graci!"

"I take full responsibility if you choose to place it at my feet," I replied. "Speaking of which, I have been standing on them since dawn in an attempt to please, and they are reminding me of that fact. Good evening," I said, turning to take my leave.

"Thank your feet for their contribution to the evening," remarked Lucan spiritedly, "and be sure to put down roots as soon as you can."

As I was walking away, Augustalis asked him quizzically, "Put down roots?" I didn't hear Lucan's reply.

∞ ∞ ∞

I was so tired when I went to bed, I fell asleep instantly even though I half expected to toss and turn revisiting my conversation with Lucan. In the middle of the night while I was sleeping soundly, he appeared to me. If I had been awake, I would believe I could reach out and touch him. At first he seemed to hover over my bed. Then I heard him saying something to me telepathically.

"I promised to give you time, and my honor will keep me from visiting you during the day," he revealed. "But my willpower vanished as I sleep. I had to see you."

"How did you find me?" I asked, acutely aware of the strength of his presence and the clarity of his communication.

"I simply declared my desire to locate you," he said. "It was relatively easy, given that I know where the slave quarters are on Augustalis' estate. However, your actual location isn't all that relevant. We came together somewhere beyond the physical."

"So you aren't hovering over my bed as I sleep?" I wondered.

"No, I can't perceive you there," he explained. "You are meeting me above Rome."

"Shall I take this as an indication you are not a man of your word?" I quipped, only half in jest.

"I can't control where my consciousness goes while I sleep," he told me. "If I could I would respect my commitment to you even now. But my desire to communicate with you through the ethers has overpowered my slumbering will."

"Then I will treat this as an exception," I allowed.

We communed wordlessly for a moment, then without warning our spirits merged so completely I lost all awareness of myself as a separate person. Lucan and I were together as one. I welcomed this feeling. It was more natural than anything I ever felt before, asleep or awake. Even after our energies separated, a strong connection remained. We were two spirits unfathomably resonant with each other.

"We experienced this often before, which is why we recognized each other instantly," Lucan communicated to me. "Our oneness is greater than the lifetimes we are engaged in now, including the political and social structures that constrain who we are allowed to be. An inexorable pull to merge with each other defines us. All else is false drama, a Greek tragedy that everyone believes is real. Promise me you will remember what happened tonight when you awaken."

"I will try," I assured him.

"And I will hold you in my heart," he promised. Then he vanished.

I awoke with a start, overwhelmed by a feeling that someone was in my room. Then I recalled what had just occurred. It was real, not a dream. I fell back to sleep and didn't stir until well past dawn.

One could reasonably assume that since my existence as a slave was unbearable, I created this illusion as a means of escape. But my living conditions improved dramatically when I arrived in Rome. I was happier than I had ever been. I had no need to avoid my life by conjuring up a fictional flirtation with Lucan. Furthermore, if I needed an escape I would have fashioned one when I was in Greece, perhaps by meeting Alexios in my sleep. That never happened.

My nightly meetings with Lucan continued. Sometimes when I awoke I didn't remember the specifics, but I could tell we had been together. I was at peace, aware that a unique love defined me apart from the material aspects of my life.

Although I relished our ability to commune as spirits, I felt no great need to communicate with him face-to-face. Often during the day I could tell he was thinking about me, but still I made no attempt to see him again.

I took this as an indication that the love I felt for him existed mostly in the realms beyond my earthly existence. I believed I didn't love him as most people love another. I assumed the love he expressed the evening we met was simply a precursor to what we would experience in our sleep. Nothing more.

Beyond that, I was extremely busy. It's not as if I spent my days sitting in my room, brooding over how I felt about Lucan and calibrating how long I should delay before sending for him. I worked hard and fell into bed every night fatigued but fulfilled.

I was putting down roots, deep ones, understanding what relative stability could mean to a person. If I died an old woman in this room, a slave to the end, after having prepared tens of thousands of dishes for Augustalis' family and friends, it would be a good life. The future I envisioned for myself was eminently acceptable.

And it didn't include Lucan.

∞ ∞ ∞

One day five months after I arrived I was on my way to purchase supplies for the family meal that evening. It was a beautiful autumn morning, and I looked forward to spending it outside in the golden sunlight. I departed through the door to the slave quarters and started down the street, evaluating which vendors were most likely to have the freshest items I needed. I was oblivious to others on the street, pedestrians and shopkeepers alike. Suddenly I felt a hand on my elbow. I jerked it away and turned quickly, ready to fight back if a thief was accosting me.

It was Lucan.

"I apologize for this intrusion, but I couldn't wait another day to see you," he revealed. "I declined all invitations to meet Augustalis in his home or to attend his parties, for fear of encountering you by accident. I told myself that you deserve ample time to find your own way to me. I willed myself to be patient one more day, then one more day. But when I awoke this morning, I knew I could hold out no longer. So here I am. I will follow you as you go on your errands and carry whatever you purchase. You need not say a word to me. To walk by your side is enough."

I looked at this marvelous man, as ardent as he was dependable, and felt my heart overflow with love for him. I burst into tears. I cried tears of sorrow for my earlier life, tears of devotion toward this extraordinary person who had the courage to declare his love long before I could return it, tears of despair over the hopelessness of our situation.

Lucan pulled me against a wall away from the stream of passersby and drew me to him. He held me as I sobbed waterfalls, cloudbursts. I cried into his chest, leaning into him and experiencing for the first time how it felt to be utterly protected. That induced yet another torrent of tears.

Eventually the sobs turned into rivulets then stopped altogether. My cheek was pressed against an extremely soggy patch of soft fabric on the front of his toga. Pulling away from him and looking into his brilliant dark eyes, I said, "This will be the only time you offer to accompany me to the market. Look what I have done to your toga! It's disgraceful! And I can't blame it on pungent onions, since I haven't yet bought any."

"There's way too much fabric in these things," he replied casually. "I can always spare a square or two for you whenever you feel another thunderstorm coming on. Shall we head to the Forum? Should we check out the cabbages first or the cuttlefish? You may as well buy plenty, since you have your pack horse with you."

He gave me a quick hug and off we went. We were so relaxed in each other's company, it seemed impossible that I spent only a few minutes with him previously. Of course, that wasn't completely true. We met countless times in our sleep, if one could call that "meeting."

"Do you have time for a bite to eat?" he asked after I noted I had everything on my list. "Or do you need to head back and turn this pheasant into a feast?"

"I have some time," I replied.

"Good," he said. "I know of a place not far from here."

Lucan ushered me into a taberna with a private outdoor area in the back. We were shown to a secluded table in the corner. The proprietor surveyed us with the unconcealed gaze of a man assuming the worst about a senator and a slave. I pretended not to notice.

"The food here doesn't begin to measure up to yours," Lucan commented. "But at least it affords us a moment to relax and talk, and a chance for me to park your parcels and give my weary arms a respite."

"To think I was actually planning to haul everything back by myself!" I replied with feigned shock. "However did I manage until now?"

He ordered wine, bread, olives, cheese and dried fruits. When it arrived he poured me a glass of watered wine then placed food for me on a pewter plate. I had never eaten out before, nor had anyone served me for that matter.

Lucan raised his glass for a toast. "To Graci," he said softly, "the love of my life, the joy in my heart, the most spirited companion I will ever know, and the most discerning consumer of coriander in all of Rome."

"To Lucan, who had the effrontery to visit me in my sleep without an invitation, merge with me energetically on multiple occasions, insist that I recall as many of them as possible and then carry my bags to make amends," I offered in spirited tribute.

I paused, willing the words in my heart to be spoken. "I love you Lucan. I always have and I always will."

His eyes grew cloudy. "I thought I might never again hear you speak of love," he revealed. "I accepted that possibility, even though I knew your love would be the greatest gift I could ever receive. I am so grateful for this moment."

"As am I," I whispered, a smile erupting across my face.

He took my hand. "Let's not speak of anything else," he proposed. "I want to hold our love gently, to experience it here, now, with you."

We sat at the table, our fingers interlocked and our eyes diving into the complex caverns of each other's souls. No words were necessary. In that unobtrusive corner of the world there was nothing but our oneness.

∞ ∞ ∞

We made no plans. I never knew if he would be waiting outside for me when I left on my morning errands. His commitments to family and community were significant, and he had even less time to spare than I did. We cherished the simple pleasures of exploring Rome together while I shopped for the evening meal. We talked, laughed and fell even more deeply in love.

Our sexual magnetism grew more compelling as well, but we didn't act on it. We shared an unspoken understanding. Although we loved each other beyond imagining, not far in the background was our awareness that we could never be husband and wife. We were friends united in love. It couldn't be more than that.

Lucan was born into a patrician family, one of the oldest and most influential in Rome. Countless generations retained their wealth in the context of public service. Lucan was the oldest son and as such assumed the family's senatorial responsibilities. He was also actively engaged in the social and intellectual milieu into which he was born. He was as intelligent as he was unpretentious. He wore his status well.

As a boy and young man Lucan studied with a Greek tutor, learning the language fluently and reading books of philosophy and literature in the original. He mastered the Socratic method of inquiry. Although his acquaintances thought he was a stoic, he couldn't be categorized. He subscribed to no one philosophical system, being fascinated by them all.

Lucan's father was a strong *paterfamilias*, focused on upholding the traditions handed down by generations of powerful men. He was aware of his oldest son's capacity to step naturally into the roles that were expected of him, all except for one. Lucan refused to enter into an arranged marriage.

"I cannot marry someone I don't love," Lucan declared emphatically on numerous occasions. His father dismissed this notion, assuming Lucan was motivated by the need to have uncomplicated access to women a while longer.

Still it was odd. Marriage didn't stop such activity. In fact, sometimes it was more of a stimulant than a deterrent to promiscuity. What was behind Lucan's resistance? He couldn't possibly mean what he said. Hardly anyone in the upper classes married for love.

Although Lucan was introduced to many eligible mates, he showed no sign of relenting. "There's still time," thought his father. "After all, it's the woman who needs to be young for childbearing. Even old men can father sons."

Because he trusted his son ultimately to use good judgment, Lucan's father decided to wait him out. He was confident Lucan would recognize the wisdom in making the right match and finally agree to it.

Lucan was nearing his mid-thirties when we met. He was experienced with women, most of whom had been expensive companions provided by people intent upon ingratiating themselves to him. He accepted these gifts as much out of obligation as anything else. As beautiful and talented as these women were, he told me later that such encounters left him empty and oddly melancholy.

Then we met, and Lucan was forced to concede that the woman he had been waiting for could never be his wife. Nonetheless, he still refused to acquiesce to his father's unrelenting demand. There would be no arranged marriage.

We knew each other for over a year and still hadn't kissed. I felt his arms around me only once, when he comforted me while I cried the first day he met me on the street. We held hands on occasion, but even that was more casual than intimate.

Succumbing to our desires would bring us nothing but perpetual pain. We both knew that. The tradeoff for fleeting moments of ecstasy was simply not worth the cost.

∞ ∞ ∞

One morning Lucan and I stopped at the taberna for a glass of wine and a moment of privacy before I returned to work. He recounted to me a difficult conversation he had with his father the night before that ended with a threat. "How dare you fight me any longer!" he roared at Lucan. "You will marry, and soon!"

Whatever path Lucan chose, there would be a loss of love. If he went against his father's wishes, he would be rejected and perhaps cast out of the family. If he succumbed to his father's demands, he would spend his life in a loveless marriage apart from me.

"You know you must marry," I told him. "To postpone the inevitable will create such a rift between you and your father, it might not be healed even when you do agree to an arranged marriage. Then you will face a doubly unfortunate situation. It doesn't serve you to perpetuate this quarrel by hoping the impossible will occur."

Lucan looked at me incredulously. "If I didn't know you better, I would take your advice to mean your love doesn't matter, if in fact it still exists," he replied, clearly agitated.

"It doesn't matter, at least not in the ways you want it to," I replied as gently as I could.

"Meaning what?" he prompted.

"Meaning that our love can change neither the laws of the Empire nor the social norms your family has respected for generations," I observed. "I love you, Lucan, with all that I am. But that love is irrelevant in the eyes of your father and the Senate and every slaveholder in Rome."

"How can you be so dispassionate about a circumstance that defiles our love?" he asked in disbelief.

"I am not free to be your wife, even if you could marry me," I stated flatly. "I am owned by another who can determine everything about my physical existence, including whether I live or die. Augustalis is a good man, but he has never asked me what I want, nor do I expect him to."

"And so you find contentment in the smallest cracks and crevasses of life," Lucan noted quietly. "You have more serenity in your life than I have in mine."

"If because I am unencumbered I seize moments of happiness when they present themselves, then yes perhaps I am content," I admitted. "I have nothing to protect but my integrity. I have nothing to defend but the truth of my own spirit, which is the only part of me that is genuinely liberated."

"You are a slave, and yet in the ways that matter you are freer than I am," Lucan observed.

"I am free because I choose to be," I emphasized. "I insist on it. I could more easily be a victim in a ruthless, unfeeling, brutal world. Instead I preserve the aspects of myself that I can respect, and I do so passionately."

"I am also trying to respect myself," Lucan noted.

"I know that, but as I said it's not as easy for you," I commented. "If respecting yourself requires you to reject the social standards your family holds dear, you introduce a significant complication into your life and that of your father."

"Don't you also reject something?" he queried.

"I do," I replied. "I reject the notion that I am any less valid or worthy a person than someone who is freeborn. I reject the assumption that another can tell me what to think, how to feel, whom to love. I reject the belief that because I am a slave I have no spirit. I reject the idea that because I have no freedoms I don't know who I am."

Lucan was watching me with fascination as I spoke. After all the time we spent together, walking and talking and expressing our caring for each other in public as friends, he may not have truly seen me until now.

He took my hands in his and invited me into the well of his being.

"I have something to say to you, and I want you to hear it clearly," he said gravely. "It's an insight that just came to me, perhaps the most profound one of my life. And I have you to thank for it. My dearest Graci, I tell you this: I am more of a slave than you are because I allow my circumstances to define me."

I said nothing. I brought each of his hands to my lips and kissed them tenderly.

He got up from the table, walked around to my chair, lifted me out of it, pulled me to him and kissed me soundly. I put my arms around his neck, pressing myself against him. His hands explored my body through the thin tunic.

When I felt him grow hard against me, I kissed him with even greater urgency. A bolt of energy pierced the top of my head, traveled down my spine, entered my womb and sped straight to my heart. I was overcome by pure, perfect, pristine passion.

Lucan drew away from me slightly. He paused, I waited.

"Is there a large gathering tonight?" he asked.

"No, just the family," I replied.

"So you could be gone and not generate undue turmoil?" he queried.

"As long as Eirene receives what I purchased today, they will survive without me," I reported.

"And will you come with me if I take a room?" he proposed.

"I will," I whispered.

He nodded, turned and consulted with the owner of the taberna, who summoned a server to our table. Lucan handed him the packages and a generous payment. He provided an address and asked him to communicate the following message directly to Augustalis from Lucan: "Graci is indisposed and will be unable to work in the kitchen this afternoon. This is what she selected for the evening meal. She will be available tomorrow."

It was done. The young man sped off on what was obviously an important errand, and Lucan prepared to do the same. "I know of a place nearby where a relatively decent room can be rented," he said. "Would you mind remaining here until I have made the necessary arrangements?"

"I will anxiously await your return," I said softly.

After he left, I sat down in my chair and lifted a glass half filled with wine. "Receive your lover openly," I told myself. "The future is a chimera. Only this afternoon and evening and night exist."

I drank the wine and allowed myself to love.

∞ ∞ ∞

Lucan returned presently, more determined than I had ever seen him. He took my hand, left payment on the table, wrapped his arm around my waist, and we set off for the room he rented for the night.

The proprietor saw us enter and climb the stairs. Lucan slipped the key into the lock, opened the door, guided me into the room, closed and locked the door, then brought me to him. We kissed. We kissed for all the occasions when we wanted to do so but chose uneasy friendship instead. We kissed for all the star-crossed lovers separated too soon. We kissed because at that particular moment, with Lucan's back against the door and me plastered against him, there was nothing more indulgent for us to enjoy.

When we parted, I drew a deep breath then kissed Lucan impertinently on the tip of his nose. "That's just in case your nose feels neglected," I quipped.

"Actually, my nose isn't the only part of me that's feeling neglected," he said cheerfully.

"Then I must do something about that," I proclaimed.

"Indeed you shall," Lucan declared, sweeping me off the floor and into his arms then carrying me to the bed in a few long strides. It was barely large enough for us both, but that didn't matter. We wouldn't be far from each other anyway.

Lucan laid me on my back and edged onto the bed beside me. He was lying on his side, elbow bent, his head propped up by his left hand. His right hand explored my body lightly. I was fully clothed. His toga seemed voluminous.

"I have no idea how to get you out of that senatorial garment you are wearing," I commented, breaking the silence. "I fear if I try I will unwind it in the wrong direction and you will disappear in it, never to return."

"If you are in there with me, I would willingly and with forethought become lost in it," he mused. "But then my intention is to become lost in you, however we arrange to accomplish that."

"I have a suggestion based on no experience whatsoever," I replied. "Perhaps at some point we should get undressed."

"What?" he asked, feigning shock. "And spoil the fun of disappearing with you in what may be the best use of the senatorial toga discovered yet?"

"Then we can start with me," I suggested. "Never before have I been naked and wrapped in a toga, especially one reserved only for senators."

"If we're going to break with tradition, senatorial and otherwise, this is as good a time as any!" he exclaimed.

Then he rolled on top of me, and I was draped from head to foot in the folds of his toga.

"You forgot one thing," I whispered between kisses.

"And that is," he murmured.

"My nakedness is essential to the complete act of breaking with tradition," I replied. "Unless you are satisfied with halfway measures, in which case I will adjust my expectations."

"This is no time for compromise," he asserted. "It's all or nothing. With regard to attire, yours and mine, the only appropriate alternative is nothing."

Lucan moved off me, stood by the bed and dismantled the draperies around his body with impressive speed and efficiency. He doffed his under-tunic and was soon standing naked before me, his senatorial robe a pool at his feet.

"Most impressive," I said slowly, studying him all over, "and more imposing than you are otherwise, which is saying a great deal."

"That is because you keep staring at one particularly imposing appendage," he laughed, "or at least, I like to think it is imposing."

"In that regard you needn't be modest," I replied. "You are, of course, referring to your broad shoulders, which the draperies you usually wear conceal quite effectively."

"Actually, I was talking about my long, skinny legs, the likes of which one sees only in giraffes and a rare species of bird," he quipped.

He eased back onto the bed and spread himself along the length of me. I wondered how well we would fit together, since he was so much taller than I. We fit perfectly.

"And so, my love, now that you have done your due diligence on the senator, would you like to proceed?" he offered. "Or would you rather I return the key and escort you back to your room and your privacy?"

"If you even consider turning in the key before tomorrow morning, I will never allow you to carry my tomatoes and turnips again," I threatened.

"In that case, my only desire is to keep you well entertained until then," he vowed.

His hands roamed across my body with more urgency this time. I reveled in his touch. I closed my eyes and tried to memorize the moment, the better to recall it later.

"You have a singular advantage over me," he observed between kisses and caresses. "Unless you want to protect your modesty while I attempt to ravage your body, I suggest you let me help you out of that tunic. Besides, my toga is bereft on the floor by itself."

"Here's some diversion for it," I offered. I sat up, pulled off my tunic in one movement, tossed it on top of the toga, then remained still so Lucan could do whatever he wanted – gaze at me or touch me or devour me with his lips.

"You are magnificent!" he exclaimed, looking but not touching. "I thought I established with great precision what was hiding under that shapeless tunic, but I had no idea you were this beautiful."

"It's the one gift I got from my mother, and I've been determined not to squander it the way she did," I revealed.

"Have you been successful?" he asked, more than a little curious.

"Until this afternoon, yes," I assured him. "But what we are about to share is love. Nothing is being squandered."

"I will be gentle," he whispered. "Promise to tell me to stop whenever you want."

"I have an inkling neither of us will want to stop until we are so spent, we are capable of nothing but sleep," I commented.

"So we can awaken and begin again," Lucan added.

"Of course," I replied. "Why do anything else?"

Lucan drew me down onto the bed and began to run his hand, fingers splayed, slowly down my stomach to the curls above my opening, then lower still.

"I love touching you," Lucan murmured. "It's as if you have a secret garden, and you are allowing me the privilege of exploring it. Every layer of velvety soft skin, every fold, every inch of you is enticing. I want to know you here, so I can honor you each time we come together."

"Honor me however you choose," I whispered, "but also feel free to love me with abandon. All that I am is yours."

With that we were both undone. We made love for the first time, united with such passion I was lost to the world. I wanted nothing more than to stay joined physically with him indefinitely, irrevocably. How was it possible to lose myself so fully and yet feel so complete?

Eventually my awareness returned to my body on the tousled mattress in the rented room. I ran my fingers down Lucan's spine, grabbed his buttocks and gave them a playful squeeze. He was preparing to lift himself off me when I protested.

"If it is all the same to you, perhaps you could take up permanent residence inside me," I appealed to him, "for the night at least."

"I'll do what I can," he crooned, "but I don't want to suffocate you in the process."

"Impossible," I quipped. "Your toga is out of range, on the floor."

He laughed heartily then kissed my eyelids, my cheeks and my nose, lingering on my lips. I felt him grow hard again.

"You are a man of your word," I observed.

"Always," he whispered.

We loved and fondled, kissed and nestled all night, celebrating our togetherness, socially unacceptable though it was. If it was possible for me to love him even more, I did.

As the morning light poked through the shutters, I awoke in Lucan's arms, satiated and pleading with the sun to rise slowly.

"Graci," Lucan whispered, nuzzling my hair. "I am complete – with you, with our love, and with our lovemaking. I am finally the man I was striving unsuccessfully to become until now."

"To say that I love you is a paltry declaration of my feelings for you," I replied. "They are unfathomable, exalted, eternal, transcendent. Ours isn't a trivial love, one that will kick up its heels and die at the first puny challenge. It's enduring. And ultimately it's the only certainty I will ever know or need."

We dressed in silence. As he pulled me to him, I smelled myself – us – in the folds of his toga. He opened the door and we left the room. It too reeked of our lovemaking.

There was nothing to say as we walked to the slave quarters. We had loved each other and now, inevitably, it was time to part. He held me close and kissed the top of my head.

"You are with me always," he vowed.

"As you are with me," I replied.

Then I gazed deep into his eyes one more time, opened the door, stepped across the threshold and closed the door without looking back. I went straight to my room and burst into tears.

∞ ∞ ∞

"Wake up, Graci," came Gaiana's voice from outside my room. "You are needed in the kitchen."

I hopped out of bed, changed clothes and was on my way there still half asleep. I set to work selecting herbs for the roast meats and spices for everything else. No one asked me what I had been doing the day before, for which I was grateful.

Somehow I made it through the day. I was so tired that night, I fell asleep as soon as my body hit the horizontal surface of the bed. Lucan appeared immediately.

"I have been waiting for you," he said anxiously. "Thank the gods we can communicate with each other this way. I would die if that weren't possible."

"You would die?" I wondered.

"My spirit would die," he replied, "which is the worst kind of death, I think."

"But your spirit will always love me," I reminded him, "and where there is love, there is life."

"Perhaps," he said halfheartedly, "but I can't bear being shut off from you."

"You never will be," I assured him. "You will always have access to me this way, as long as I live. And afterward, who knows? It may be even better."

"That possibility I prefer not to contemplate," he replied. "For now, I just want to be with you as we are."

We merged into glorious oneness. It was different this time, a reflection of our having united physically in love. Eventually we separated, as I knew we must. I felt both blessed by our unreserved love and bereft that I could no longer experience it fully, nullifying all else.

"If I come to walk with you in the morning, will you be there?" Lucan asked.

"Yes I will," I assured him.

"Until then," he replied.

I awoke excited to be seeing Lucan again so soon. I longed to return to the rented room, even for a brief interlude. Then I dismissed the notion. He specifically asked to walk with me. That is what we would do.

He was waiting outside as I stepped into the street. I observed him with new awareness. He was strikingly handsome, with chiseled features, dark gray eyes and thick black hair. I recalled running my fingers through those curls and felt a sudden stab of emptiness.

"Those memories are better off forgotten," I told myself then thought, "Is he really as gorgeous as he looks right now?"

A quick assessment confirmed that he was. How could I have missed it before?

"Thank the gods for your ongoing need to peruse the markets!" he exclaimed. "I never thought I would so look forward to the process of produce selection. What is it to be today? Pomegranates and persimmons? Peppers and potatoes?"

"If alliteration alone qualified one as a poet, you would be vying with Vergil right now," I quipped.

"Vying with Vergil," he laughed, "as if that were not potentially potent poetry. I can see it now, the latest news making its way through Rome: 'Former genius in the kitchen takes her creativity elsewhere. Citizens mourn the loss.'"

He made no attempt to touch me, choosing instead to lead the way down the street. His stride was so resolute, I could barely keep up with him. Obviously he was committed to staying away from me and keeping the conversation light and affable. He was attempting to outrun me instead.

"You forget that my legs are not quite as long as yours," I called to him, breathless from the sprint I was running to stay at his side.

"Ah, yes, your legs . . . and mine," he said. "They are a study in opposites, to be sure. I'll slow down."

Establishing a more leisurely pace, he settled into dialogue of a different sort.

"How have you been?" he asked, inviting me to lead our conversation wherever I wanted.

"Tired and sore, blissfully," I replied.

"I have no doubt about that," Lucan admitted. "It was thoughtless of me to spend hours making love with you when it was only your first time."

"I seem to recall urging you on more than once," I chuckled.

"That you did," he affirmed. "Of course, it's not as if I needed any urging."

"You certainly didn't," I concurred. "You could have continued indefinitely."

"Still, I was grateful for the encouragement," he noted. "It kept me from feeling guilty when yet again I felt myself, shall we say, out of control."

"Promise me you'll never get that aspect into control," I countered, before I realized what I was implying.

We were approaching a cluster of marketplace stalls where we would be overheard if we continued our banter. He stopped and pulled me aside.

"What are we to do?" he asked earnestly.

"Love each other," I said simply.

He seemed exasperated with that response. I drew in a breath and prepared to explain myself when he replied, "I know that is the answer, the only answer, the ultimate answer to everything. I keep complicating the situation, loading onto it expectations and implications that serve only to compromise the truth of what we share."

"Would I be ecstatic if I could be your wife? Yes, absolutely, without question," I affirmed. "Do I love you more and better than anyone else possibly could? You can be assured I do.

"But we are required by the laws of Rome to accept our unfortunate fate as lovers. We are better served if we do so willingly and without regret. The sooner we accomplish that, the more quickly and easily we can return to what really matters, which is our love. I refuse to stifle it with anger against the forces that would destroy us if we put them at the center of our lives and our love. Please don't lead us into a trap from which we cannot emerge with our love intact."

"I appreciate your wisdom," Lucan acknowledged. "But I can't accept it."

"You have no choice," I observed. "You must recognize what is true in Rome, and also what is true in our love."

"But they are in conflict!" he exclaimed, frustrated.

"Not necessarily," I disagreed. "They are in conflict only if you allow legalities to take precedence in your heart over your feelings for me. If your love is paramount, not even prohibitions against our union can weaken or deny it."

"So you see no conflict?" Lucan asked, challenging my apparently relentless objectivity.

"I choose not to allow it to establish the context for my love," I explained. "I choose to love you first and foremost, with all my capacity to do so. Then if inconvenient rules made by stuffy old men intent on keeping their estates intact when they are handed down to their sons, happen to limit our opportunity to be together, so be it."

"I wish I had your equanimity," Lucan commented, shaking his head. "It eludes me."

"It eludes you because you grew up in the bondage of these rules," I explained. "I have lived in bondage, but it has nothing to do with what I would lose or whom I would disappoint if we found a way to be together. I have nothing to lose and no one to disappoint except you. And I won't disappoint you, because I refuse to stop loving you. Sorry, but you're stuck with my love, whatever happens in your life."

"So you are fine with the way things are," he concluded.

"I accept the way things are," I said flatly. "I would rather celebrate our love than decry the laws that keep us apart."

"Someone must decry and then overturn them," he declared. "Otherwise they will ruin even more lives, generation after generation."

"It seems you have just stumbled upon your calling," I noted. "You are a senator. Why not challenge the authority of the emperor and the Senate to create arbitrary decrees that serve the few at the expense of the many? Why not make Rome a republic again?"

"You know me too well," he acknowledged. "That has been my vision all along. I see no other purpose for being in the Senate, apart from pleasing my father. And if I refuse to marry, nothing else I do can possibly please him. So I return to the larger purpose for my life and the love I have for you. I can live for both of those."

"Without conflict?" I wondered.

"With much less of it," he said decisively.

"Then we are agreed?" I asked.

"Agreed in what way?" he probed, ever the debater.

"We are agreed to love without compromise or regret," I stated, "and to meet whenever we can for a morning trip to the market or a conversation while we sleep."

"Agreed," he replied, taking my hands in his and kissing each one tenderly.

We returned to our previous pattern of friendship, as if our night of lovemaking would not be repeated again soon, if ever. Were we to continue to experience physical intimacy despite our impossible union, the bonds of our love would eventually burst apart like a pod of seeds scattered in the wind.

Lucan busied himself in the Senate, challenging his peers to consider returning to a truly republican form of government. No doubt he felt like Sisyphus most of the time. He was once again a frequent guest at Augustalis' banquets, but I never saw him.

I developed a routine that suited me, shuttling from the market to the kitchen to the baths.

We continued to come together when we slept. Those encounters affirmed our love, even as my memory of our lovemaking lost its luster as days drifted into years.

We saw each other two or three times a month, always in public places. We talked of politics and philosophy, the latest ridiculous scandals and the simple, rewarding facets of our lives. If we drew judgmental stares from others, we were oblivious to them. We became a fixture in the Forum, the senator who treated the slave as his equal and not incidentally carried her groceries.

We were like an old couple enjoying tender companionship. Our time together was gentle. Our love was enduring. I was content, and as far as I could tell so was Lucan.

∞ ∞ ∞

I was in my room one day preparing to leave for the kitchen when a household servant knocked on my door.

"Graci," she called to me, "the master wants to see you at once. Please come with me."

"I'll be right there," I replied, then hurried to get ready. We walked to Augustalis' suite. He was reading at his desk when I entered.

"Graci, have a seat," Augustalis offered. I settled into a chair across from him.

"I have nothing but the highest praise for your service," he began. "You get along well with everyone, you work tirelessly, your creations in the kitchen continue to transport our guests into fits of ecstasy, and your personal behavior is beyond reproach. In the five years you have been here, I have thanked the gods regularly that I was allowed to bring you into this household."

"I am grateful to you as well," I replied. "I couldn't ask for better circumstances in which to live my life."

"You are omitting something," he responded.

"What?" I asked.

"The complete statement would be that you couldn't ask for better circumstances in which to live your life as a slave," he clarified.

"Yes, of course," I agreed, embarrassed at being corrected. "That goes without saying."

"Does it?" he challenged.

Augustalis was being uncharacteristically testy. Something troublesome must have precipitated my being summoned. I would find out soon enough. I chose not to respond to his question.

"I had a visitor today," he revealed. I tried to remain calm as I prepared for the worst. "Lucan's father is an old and dear friend. I have never seen him so agitated."

Augustalis paused. I looked at him directly, ready for whatever he was about to divulge.

"He is convinced that Lucan refuses to agree to an arranged marriage at this late date in his life – he is almost forty, you know – because he is in love with you," Augustalis revealed. "Since the two of you have been seen in public for years, he says he can only assume you are entertaining him frequently in private as well.

"Lucan's father blames you for his son's stubborn repudiation of an arranged marriage. He is also offended that Lucan has been consorting so openly with a slave. He asked me to disabuse you of any notion you and Lucan could ever marry and inform you that he will suffer Lucan's resistance no longer. Lucan is to be married within a month. The girl's parents have agreed to the union. Lucan has no choice in the matter."

I felt as if someone had just hit me over the head with an iron cooking pot. I became faint. Grabbing the edge of the desk, I asked, "Do you have some water?"

"Of course," Augustalis replied, pouring a cup for me from the decanter. "Take a moment to collect yourself, and we will continue."

Soon I was revived enough to resume the conversation. "I am fine now," I said. "Thank you for giving me a chance to regain my composure."

"Based on the way you reacted to this information, I can only assume you and Lucan are more than casual acquaintances," he observed.

"We are," I replied honestly.

"If you don't mind my asking, how much more?" Augustalis continued.

"We love each other," I replied. "We have since the first day I cooked for your guests and was invited to receive their appreciation. Lucan was in attendance that evening, and he sent for me after everyone departed. You may recall we were talking when you returned to the banquet hall after saying farewell to your guests."

"Are you saying you two fell in love that evening?" Augustalis asked in disbelief.

"It is more accurate to say we recognized each other then," I replied. "We knew each other somehow. Our love was inevitable."

Augustalis remained silent, allowing me to tell the story however I chose.

"I was aware at the outset that only sadness and misery would result from our becoming lovers since we could never marry," I continued. "Of course, Lucan understood that as well. We expressed our love in the context of friendship. He would meet me as I was leaving on my errands. We walked and talked, and he carried my purchases. Sometimes we had a bite to eat and a brief rest."

"And that is all?" Augustalis couldn't avoid the question.

"No," I said forthrightly. "One day without warning the boundaries of our carefully constructed friendship blew apart. Our self-imposed limitations vanished. Lucan secured a room and we spent the night together."

"I recall receiving Lucan's message from a servant who arrived with your parcels, saying you were indisposed," Augustalis told me. "But that was years ago. You spent only one night together in all that time?"

"Yes," I verified. "Under the circumstances it would have been too painful for us to continue. I must ask you, what can I do to help Lucan?"

"That is exactly what I have been wondering," he replied. "Only I have been thinking, what can I do to help Lucan and Graci?"

"I am unimportant," I said. "I want the best for Lucan and am willing to do whatever it takes, including never seeing him again, if that would make a difference."

"Spoken like someone who knows the meaning of love," he observed. "Unfortunately that is as rare as it is refreshing."

"Augustalis, I regret that you are in the middle of this insufferable situation," I declared. "How can I alleviate the burden of your current position?"

"Never fear, my dear," he said reassuringly, surprising me with this note of affection. "I rather enjoy the idea of dealing with two people inexorably bound by love instead of power and politics. Let me consider a few alternatives. I will send for you when I have decided what to do."

"Please remember that I will do anything to benefit Lucan," I said in closing.

"Understood," he said. "Now, I think you are needed in the kitchen."

He walked me to the door and opened it. The servant was waiting to escort me back. I had been in Augustalis' vast home only a handful of times, and its labyrinthine hallways remained a mystery to me. I never could have found my way on my own.

∞ ∞ ∞

Days passed and I heard nothing. Lucan was absent when I left on my errands. More troubling than that, I was unable to connect with him in my sleep. I tried to convince myself he was gone for good. His father, his lineage and his legacy prevailed. If that weren't already the case, it would be very soon.

One week after my meeting with Augustalis, I was called once again to his office. I prepared myself for the inevitable bad news. I assumed that a chapter in my life, the best one I would ever experience, was over. By the time I arrived at his suite, I was ready to accept whatever he had to say.

The servant knocked and Augustalis bid me enter. I opened the door, walked into the room and closed it behind me. Lucan was sitting opposite Augustalis at his desk. His back was turned to me. When he heard the door close, he stood up and held his arms out to me. I was unsure whether to simply take his hands in mine or allow an embrace. I let him decide.

He swept me into his arms and held me tight. I cried.

"Graci has a habit of sobbing uncontrollably every time I offer her an embrace," Lucan commented cheerfully to Augustalis. "It wreaks havoc with the stately nature of my senatorial garb. That's the main reason I resorted to friendship with her. No more soggy togas."

He hugged me again, sending waves of love that precipitated another avalanche of tears.

"I told you," he laughed. "A formal handshake, on the other hand, would elicit a consummately dry-eyed response."

I managed to collect myself and pull away from Lucan. He offered me the chair next to his. I sat down and he took my hand in his. This wasn't the encounter I expected.

"I engaged in extensive investigation and contemplation this past week, and gained a great many insights along the way," Augustalis revealed, launching into the matter at hand.

Lucan said nothing, and I wasn't about to interrupt.

"After I talked with you, Graci," Augustalis continued, "I asked Lucan to stop by for a visit. He responded to my questions exactly the way you did. In fact, the similarities between your comments were so uncanny, I would have thought you rehearsed your lines together.

"You both communicated the same thing to me, that you were willing to do anything and give up everything to benefit the other. The selfless love you share is extraordinary. I stopped believing such love could exist anywhere, especially in Rome. But here you two are, loving each other in the most unconditional and lasting way, then choosing to be nothing more than companions because of an anachronistic legal restriction.

"I did cover some additional ground with Lucan, however. I asked him if he planned to enter into the arranged marriage his father insisted he agree to, and he indicated he would not. When I challenged him, he assured me this was his final decision. I requested that he reconsider it and return in a few days' time. His answer was the same when he visited me again. That gave me much food for thought, almost as delectable as your creations, Graci.

"I asked myself this: What is more important, love or laws? Which aspect of the human condition do you believe in most fully, tradition or transformative change? When your days on this Earth are numbered, would you rather look back and say you convinced Lucan to marry a woman he didn't love and align himself with convention, or you did what you could to help love thrive even under the most unfortunate of circumstances?

"My heart guided me to the obvious answer to these questions. And thus I offer myself in service to the two of you and your love.

"I will continue with the details of my proposal, but first I must reveal a difficult complication. Graci, I didn't purchase you from your former owners. They asked me to take you away so that when Alexios returned, you would be gone forever. His father and grandfather were convinced if he ever discovered where you were and knew you had been freed, he would come after you even if he had married in the interim. Thus they asked that I commit never to free you from slavery. I regret having done so, but I am a man of my word and will not retract that commitment."

I looked at Lucan to see if he was surprised by this revelation. He wasn't. Augustalis must have talked with him about it already and explained who Alexios was. Interestingly, I wasn't particularly disturbed by what Augustalis told me since I never expected to be free anyway.

"Where does this leave us?" Augustalis queried, resuming his dissertation. "We have a senator who wants to remain so in order to change the laws of the republic. We have a slave who must remain so due to my code of honor. We have a restriction that disallows marriage between a senator and a slave even if she becomes a freedwoman. We have two people who love each other dearly in spite of it all. We have a crusty patrician who is becoming a hopeless romantic in his old age. Finally, we have that patrician's friendship with Lucan's father, which is about to be torn asunder."

"How so?" Lucan asked.

"I have decided to support your love in a number of ways," Augustalis announced. "First, I am sending the two of you to a seaside village where I have a modest private residence. You are to remain there together, anonymously, as long as you like. I will instruct my staff to care for your every need. If you prefer that they leave you alone and take a holiday themselves, that is fine. Graci, I will notify the kitchen staff that you have been called away, and I will inform Eirene that no questions are to be asked and no rumors allowed. Lucan, you can tell your father whatever you want.

"Then when you return, I have arranged for a well appointed apartment to be made available for your exclusive use. We will adjust Graci's responsibilities so she has ample time off to be with you, Lucan. I will manage the stories that circulate by planting a few of them myself. I haven't yet determined how I will explain the liberal way you will be treated, Graci, or the nature of your absences. But you and Lucan will be away long enough at the seaside to afford me the opportunity to revise my story at least a dozen times.

"Lucan, as for your father, I will tell him if he persists in trying to control your life, he will lose the best son a father could have. I will advise him to accept your refusal of an arranged marriage and never again broach the subject with you or anyone else. I hope he takes my counsel to heart. If he doesn't I will lose a good friend, but I will have done so in pursuit of a worthy cause."

I never knew my father, but that didn't matter. Another man equally my father had just offered a benediction approving my union with the man I loved.

Words escaped me. Unfortunately tears did not. Once again they were streaming down my face. Lucan offered me a corner of his toga. Augustalis simply smiled.

Lucan spoke first. "Augustalis, you have looked out for me since I was a young boy. I turned to you for advice at every pivotal juncture in my life, and you provided me with unerring wisdom. I decided not to seek your counsel regarding this conflict with my father because I didn't want to put you in an indefensible position. But he chose to do so.

"Now you know what is in my heart and in Graci's. You waited to make your offer to us until you knew for certain how I would answer my father's most recent demand. You were prepared to support whatever choice I made. You would also have done your best for Graci had I succumbed to my father's manipulations.

"In opposing my father, I have chosen to live as an unmarried man. The family lineage would stop with me were I to continue to assume the role of oldest son. I am prepared to offer that position to my younger brother, who already has two sons, and live a modest life thereafter. I am hopeful I can continue to retain my position in the Senate.

"Graci, I made this choice with no information about what Augustalis just proposed. I entertained no underlying intention of making you my lover, pursuing something beyond the few fleeting moments we spent together years ago in a rented room. What we share as friends is enough for me to defy my father one last time. You are enough for me.

"And so I return to my gratitude to you, Augustalis. You are offering us the closest thing to a marriage we could hope to have. You are blessing our union even if others will not. That means the world to me, not just because it affords me time with the woman I love, but also because your support is genuine and well considered. With all that I am I thank you."

My hand, warm in Lucan's, gave me the courage to speak.

"Augustalis, you honor us both with your caring and empathy," I began. "Your willingness to step off the path of tradition to create the time and space for our love is extraordinary. Without your intervention that opportunity would be forever withheld from us. You have redefined my life, which is irrevocably in your hands, and Lucan's, which is not. May the gods bless you always."

"And may love prevail," Augustalis affirmed.

We discussed logistics – when Lucan and I would be leaving, arrangements at the home where we would be staying. Then as the conversation was concluding, Augustalis grew melancholy.

"You know, I do this as much for myself as for you," he stated. "I entered into a marriage with a young woman I barely knew and didn't love. I did so mindlessly but also with the unfounded hope that our love would grow over time. We survive in the marriage only by spending most of our time apart and keeping up appearances in public. We have children, evidence of sex without love, and now there is neither.

"I tell you this because what connects the two of you is the opposite form of union. Your love is everlasting. It is still strong after many years despite your awareness that you can never marry and sire legitimate children of your own. It has remained steadfast even as you chose to limit your intimacy due to the heartache such encounters would cause afterward.

"Love should result in joy, not sorrow, and celebration, not condemnation. And even though I failed wretchedly at loving my wife, I love my children and I love the two of you. I find happiness in that and will celebrate it henceforth. I also intend to share in your joy, vicariously at least. Now make haste to accomplish your preparations so you can leave Rome as soon as possible, together."

Augustalis stood up, came around his desk, and embraced the two of us. We formed a circle with our arms around each other, strong, unified and unassailable.

"Graci, you have one more stop to make before you head to the kitchen," Augustalis said as we prepared to leave. "The servant will take you there."

"Thank you, Augustalis," I replied. "You are a most thoughtful and generous man."

"I am just someone who can recognize true love when I see it," he responded humbly, "and who has the means to help it blossom a bit."

Lucan embraced Augustalis one more time. "Thank you, from the bottom of my heart," he said simply. Then we left the room.

∞ ∞ ∞

The servant was waiting for me in the hallway.

"I will see you at the arranged time and place," Lucan said. "Until then, I will meet you where we go in our sleep." He gave me a hug and departed.

I turned to the servant and waited to find out where we were going. "We are to visit a shop not far from here," she informed me, and I followed her into the street.

114

We entered one of the most exclusive streets in Rome. I walked through it only infrequently, when it provided a shortcut to my destination. Rows of shops with every imaginable luxury and adornment opened onto the street. We stopped in front of a fashionable clothing store, breathtakingly expensive no doubt.

"Here it is," the servant told me. "The master made arrangements for you. They will inform you of them inside." She turned to walk away.

"Are you sure this is the right place?" I called after her.

She nodded in the affirmative, not looking back.

Tentatively I stepped through the door. Arrayed within the shop were designs made of ethereal linen, diaphanous silk and luxuriously heavy brocades. If that weren't enough, trays of exquisite gold jewelry were arranged tastefully around the room. A woman looked up from an elegant desk, stood and approached me.

"You must be Graci" she said graciously. "Welcome. Augustalis wants me to prepare you for your journey. Here is what I have in mind. This afternoon I will take you to my private baths, where you can relax and receive the best massage in Rome. The oils are exquisite. Then we will return here. You are to select whatever clothing and jewelry you desire, with my assistance regarding which colors and fabrics best complement your features. Tomorrow you have an appointment with a hairdresser and another visit to the baths, followed by a manicure, pedicure and massage. Then we will go shopping for sandals, aromatic oils and perhaps a special gift or two for your beloved. The third day has been set aside for the final fittings and, of course, a bath and a massage."

Earlier in the day I prepared myself for the worst, that Lucan was about to marry another and I would never see him again. Now I was going to be groomed and outfitted for a journey to the sea with him, where we would have the use of a private residence for as long as we wanted. A voice within me protested that this couldn't be happening, and another one welcomed these gifts. I opted for the latter.

The only predicament I faced over the next few days was my reluctance to be sufficiently indulgent with what I selected for myself. My wardrobe never before consisted of more than three well-worn tunics and a tattered cloak. One tunic I would wear, one would be drying after having been washed, and one I saved on the off chance I needed something that was neither stained nor damp. My sturdy leather sandals were scuffed and grimy.

The idea of having even one special tunic astounded me. I was expected to select at least a half dozen of them, plus warm cloaks for the evening, matching sandals, gold bangles and an array of sensuous accoutrements.

"You must have something made from this silk," the shopkeeper insisted, holding a swath of emerald green fabric to my face. "It highlights your brown eyes and the copper in your hair. And this ethereal layer of gold chiffon is perfect with it. I can see you in the evening by candlelight, glorious and sparkling in this combination."

"Glorious" and "sparkling" were two words I never thought would describe how I looked, and yet in her hands that seemed possible. When the green and gold outfit was completed and I tried it on, I glittered for the first time in my life.

"You may resist my next recommendation," she noted, "but I must make it anyway. Try this matching torc and bracelet with it."

She handed me a heavy necklace made of two half circles of woven gold, with a hinge in the back and two lion's heads that came together in the front. Their eyes sparkled with small emeralds. The bracelet was of the same design. Opening the torc to place it around my neck, she was startled when I suddenly ducked out of her way.

"I knew it," she commented good-naturedly.

"It isn't the extravagance that has caused my reaction, but rather the idea of having two lions choking my throat," I explained. "I can't put that on."

"I understand," she replied, returning both pieces to the display case and bringing forth a delicate gold and amber necklace. I loved it, and she was more than satisfied.

We went shopping for gifts I could offer Lucan. In one shop specializing in antiquities from Britannia, I discovered two items for him. Both were made of solid gold, and one in particular was extremely costly. I demurred. But when my companion reminded me that Augustalis insisted no expense be spared, especially with regard to what I gave Lucan, I bought them both.

The first item was a goblet nestled in a hand-carved wooden box. Encircling the outside of the bowl were four bands of Celtic knots. It was a superb piece of craftsmanship, and I was overtaken with chills when I held it.

"There is power and mystery here," I commented. "I don't know why, but Lucan is supposed to have this."

I also selected a tiny, intricate gold chain tucked inside a leather pouch. I had a similar sensation when I placed the chain in the palm of my hand. It too was meant for Lucan.

A large trunk was packed with my new clothing, accessories, gifts and refined delicacies such as candied fruits and nuts, massage oils and bath scents. It also included an ample supply of ground willow leaves and pennyroyal to prevent pregnancy, provided by the best herbalist in Rome. "He can't keep up with the demand," my guide observed sardonically.

I decided not to leave without talking to Eirene and Gaiana. They were both so helpful and loyal to me, it seemed thoughtless not to let them know what was about to occur.

I approach them when we were alone in the garden on the afternoon before I was to depart. Drawing them toward a rosemary bush in the far corner, I whispered, "I am leaving tomorrow for an indefinite period of time. I know I can trust you, so I have decided to explain where I will be going and with whom. I don't want you to worry about me."

"We already know," Eirene told me. "When Augustalis summoned me to explain you were being called away, I guessed immediately what was occurring. He confirmed it, but only after I gave him my assurance no one else would know."

"I have been aware for years that you and Lucan are in love," Gaiana inserted. "I see you together all the time at the market. And as much as you try to appear to be just casual acquaintances, it is obvious something else is going on. It is written all over your faces."

"And neither of you said a word to me about this?" I asked.

"It was better to let you think you were fooling us," Gaiana chuckled.

"Augustalis is the kindest and most thoughtful man in Rome," Eirene observed, changing the subject. "He is one of the wealthiest and most powerful as well. No one can tell him what to do or think. His actions with regard to you and Lucan are typical of him, though in this case he is challenging society more than usual. I admire him for that and won't break our confidence. No one will know where you are or why you left."

"You can count on me to keep this to myself," Gaiana assured me. "I can't abide the gossip that occupies the minds of many slaves. If I hear them repeating any slanderous stories about you, I will squelch them immediately."

"I will be back, though I'm not sure when," I replied. "Keep the kitchen buzzing happily until my return, and don't let the spice pantry go stale!"

"We can't blend spices with the same subtlety that you do," Eirene commented, "but you have taught us a great deal about how to sense what herbs and spices are needed. No one will go hungry or uninspired in your absence. Peace and joy to you and Lucan."

I cooked for a large banquet that night. The combination of excitement over my impending journey with Lucan and my desire to please Augustalis stimulated my creativity. Everything I prepared was delectable.

As I was organizing the spices one final time before I left, a server announced that I was wanted in the dining hall. I followed her there. Deafening applause met me at the door. Augustalis was standing, holding a goblet of wine aloft.

"To Graci," he toasted, "whose creations feed our spirits as much as our bodies, and whose love is evident in every morsel she prepares."

Hope, 120 AD

The guests cheered and toasted me. Lucan, sitting next Augustalis, did so as well, beaming with delight.

PART TWO
EUPHEMIA AND AUGUSTALIS

The next morning I awoke early and took my time preparing to leave. I donned a new ankle-length tunic for my travels, the most modest one I purchased. It featured two layers of linen in light blue and aqua, the sheerest one on top, clasped on the right shoulder with a gold buckle. I draped the matching woolen cloak over my arm in case I needed it for warmth later in the day.

The trunk I packed for the journey seemed more like a treasure chest to me. It contained a rainbow of folded tunics, each one with a complementary cloak, in hues ranging from honeysuckle and magenta to periwinkle and emerald. Four pairs of sandals were included, more than I ever had, along with a parasol, a fan and wickedly fragrant oils. Gold and bronze jewelry – necklaces, armlets, anklets, brooches, earrings and hairpins – were packed in individual silk drawstring bags.

Recalling the rough tunics that served me until that morning, I was surprised I could adjust so easily to my new attire.

I left the slave quarters and followed the street to the main entrance of Augustalis' estate. The carriage was waiting for me. As I approached it, a servant nodded in acknowledgement and helped me inside. The sun shone so brilliantly, it took my eyes a moment to adjust to the dark interior of the carriage. I saw the outlines of an empty seat covered in soft cushions and settled myself there. The carriage door closed.

Lucan's arms swept me into an ardent embrace. He pulled me to him and kissed me eagerly. I kissed him in return, holding back nothing. As the carriage made its way through the bustling streets of Rome, we couldn't be seen. Our privacy was absolute. I gave myself over to his kisses.

My hand roamed across Lucan's body, acquainting myself more intimately with him. I felt him through the folds of his toga. He was as hard with his desire as I was wet with mine. Complete union was all we wanted. We came together with urgent passion.

"How I have missed you there!" I whispered.

"And I, my love, have desired nothing but to feel myself surrounded by you," he groaned in response.

The carriage jostled through the streets, creating just enough movement to excite us continuously. I thanked the gods, and the distracted praetors, for the disrepair that caused the carriage to heave and jerk erotically. It was beyond stimulating.

"I seem not to have lost my desire for you," Lucan chuckled. "At this rate we will be completely spent by the time we get to the sea."

"In which case we will have no choice but to rest so I can ravish your body once again," I murmured seductively.

"Speaking of ravishment, I haven't done enough of that to yours," he declared.

Lucan raised my tunic over my head, undressing me in one purposeful movement. "I have missed these," he whispered, cupping my breasts in his hands and massaging them with tender care.

"You can stop that the day after tomorrow," I crooned. "Until then, I will let the carriage do its work to keep you perpetually aroused while your hands explore me wherever they want."

"Wherever?" he asked spiritedly.

"My body is your playground," I replied. "Every curve and crevice exists for your pleasure. And mine as well, of course."

"Of course," he replied before he kissed me in all the right places.

After much delicious, delirious lovemaking, I collapsed onto his chest and into his arms. I was incapable of moving a muscle.

"How does it feel being pinned down by a rag doll?" I asked.

"If you are referring to the part of the doll that is soft and hot, I'd say that it is the greatest aphrodisiac in the world," he replied contentedly.

"Let me know when that aphrodisiac loses its potency, and I will give you a respite," I quipped.

"Let's see, that will be in about three or four, make that five or six, hours," he retorted.

"Suit yourself," I told him. "I am more than happy to let you keep me right where you want me."

"Which is by my side, on my lap and in our bed," he announced.

"Agreed," I chirped happily.

It was a joyful journey. We found every possible way to make love in cramped but blessedly well cushioned quarters.

We arrived at Monte Circeo spent, ravenous and ready for a nap. Lucan rearranged his toga, I donned my tunic, and we prepared to disembark.

∞   ∞   ∞

The household staff waited at the main gate to greet us. As we stepped into the light of day, I noticed Lucan's toga was missing the red senatorial stripe. We would be anonymous here. No one would know he was a senator and I was a slave.

We met the caretaker, the cook, the housekeeper, the gardener and two assistants whose purpose was to assure we were comfortable and lacked nothing. Lucan addressed them graciously, and I thanked them for making the villa ready for us.

It was spring, the day of the equinox in fact, and everything was already in full bloom. Fragrances from shrubs covering the mountain and gardens within the villa filled the air with evidence of succulent new growth.

The home Augustalis described as modest was actually an expansive, elegant villa rustica. It was situated similarly to the one I knew in Greece, on a ridge overlooking the sea and not far from a beach. The architecture was informal but gracious, with beautiful frescoes decorating the walls, intriguing mosaics set into the floors and large rooms opening onto porticos along the front to catch the fresh breezes that prevailed throughout the year. If that were not enough, an atrium opened to abundant light and air.

Our suite was bright and spacious, with a private portico overlooking the sea. The furnishings and frescoes featured seascapes in pale colors that enhanced the luminous palette just outside.

The bed, perched on a marble pedestal, looked as soft and encompassing as swans down. It was covered in soft linens and pillows in a riot of colors, most inviting for lovemaking.

The caretaker brought our trunks into the bedroom. I placed my clothes and accessories in a wardrobe decorated with exotic wood veneer and laid Lucan's gifts on a small table inlaid with an intricate garland of tortoise shell and ivory. Like everything else in the villa, it exhibited superb craftsmanship.

"All unpacked?" asked Lucan, walking up behind me and putting his arms around my waist. He kissed the back of my neck then nipped my ear lobe.

"I am ready to remain here for a long while," I sighed contentedly.

"Good," he said, turning me around to face him. "We should have a nap on that very inviting bed, followed by a long dinner spiced with our usual meandering conversation, then return to bed replenished and revitalized so we can make love all night and into the dawn."

"Then nap and make love some more tomorrow?" I asked playfully.

"If you insist," he replied. "I may be able to accommodate your wishes if I try hard enough."

"Never fear, my dear. You are perpetually hard enough," I retorted.

The first week we left our room only for meals and strolls in the garden and on the beach. The servants seemed unfazed by our behavior. They allowed us our privacy and were unquestioningly available whenever we needed them. They went about their work with only minimal intrusion from us.

Eventually we were ready to spend more time outside the bedroom than in it. We began exploring the grounds around the villa and nearby Monte Circeo, which featured an amphitheater and several fine buildings situated along lagoons. But mostly we walked on the beach, barefoot and hand in hand.

The villa was well stocked with everything from locally grown food, olive oil and fine wine to the best literature.   Augustalis had a significant library containing rare Greek and Roman writings.

"I read many of these, but others are unfamiliar to me," I commented.

"You are better read than I," Lucan noted. "We both had Greek tutors, but yours was superior to mine. Then again, he was dealing with a more intelligent and motivated student."

"I was motivated," I agreed. "The short time I spent each afternoon with Errikos was the joy of my life. I loved to learn, and reading took me to places unavailable to me otherwise."

"All because Alexios insisted you join him during his tutoring sessions," Lucan observed.

"We would play outside during his afternoon break," I recalled. "At first we chased butterflies together, but then he began to teach me reading and calculation. I caught up with him quickly, at which point he decided I deserved to be educated. He convinced his parents to let Errikos tutor me for a brief period every afternoon. This went on for years, even after I began working in the kitchen."

"Sounds just like him," Lucan commented.

"You know him?" I asked in surprise.

"I do indeed," he replied casually. "Actually, we are good friends. He used to accompany his father when he visited mine. Although I was older than Alexios, I wanted to practice speaking Greek with him. We got to know each other that way and have kept in touch ever since."

"Did he ever tell you about me?" I pursued, intrigued by Lucan's revelation.

"Yes he did, on many occasions," Lucan reported, offering nothing further.

"Did you know about the conflict with his parents over marrying me?" I continued.

"I did, in fact," Lucan revealed. "His father sent Alexios to our house to get him away from you."

"He was with your family?" I exclaimed in disbelief.

"His father deduced that since my own father was adamant about the necessity of arranged marriages, our home was a safe place to park Alexios until they determined what to do with you," Lucan explained. "I was profoundly affected by his description of his parents' insensitivity to his feelings and their rejection of the woman he loved. I had resisted my father before, but after the long days and nights I spent consoling Alexios I was determined to hold out for love."

"Little did you know you would hold out for the same woman Alexios loved," I observed.

"I couldn't conceive of such a fate," Lucan recalled. "But I was well aware that the pain and anger Alexios experienced were needless. He is such a good man, he deserves to be happy."

"He is an exceptionally good man," I agreed.

"Tell me, Graci, did you love him?" Lucan queried.

"No, not really," I admitted. "I didn't know what love was until I met you. But I did respect him immensely, and I had great affection for him. I admired his ability to see me not as a slave, but as someone with the capacity to learn. If his parents had allowed us to marry, I would have been quite content with him. But I couldn't love him as I do you.

"And now I have a question for you. When did you know I was the slave girl whom Alexios' parents rejected and his grandfather handed over to Augustalis?"

"I heard about you before we met," Lucan revealed. "Alexios' father sent a message requesting he return home immediately and informing us that Augustalis was bringing the problem slave to Rome. Oddly, he happened to mention your creativity in the kitchen."

"So when you saw me that first night after I was introduced to Augustalis' dinner guests, you knew I was the woman Alexios loved?" I conjectured.

"I did," Lucan admitted. "I also knew you were the woman I loved, and my concerns for Alexios quickly faded into the background."

"Have you been in touch with him since then?" I pursued.

"We communicate frequently," Lucan replied. "He knows I haven't married and am keeping busy in the Senate."

"And he has never been back to Rome?" I inquired.

"His family is making sure he doesn't return," Lucan informed me. "Beyond that, I haven't invited him here."

"Augustalis knows all of this?" I asked, delving further.

"He does," Lucan confirmed, "which makes him all the more determined to keep his word to Alexios' grandfather. We have presented quite a dilemma for him."

Lucan hesitated then spoke. "Graci, you probably want to ask if Alexios ever married. He did not, and he still longs for you. He would feel heartbroken and betrayed if he knew we were lovers. I hope he never finds out, but I also believe the day will come when he does."

"How sad," I sighed. "I wish him love and happiness, not love and misery."

"As do I, my dear," Lucan replied, enfolding me in his arms.

More than a month passed, and still we had no inclination to return to Rome. Lucan drafted a note to Augustalis asking for confirmation that we could remain a while longer. He received a simple message in return: "Stay as long as you want, but please don't drink every last amphora of good wine!"

My monthly flow had come and gone, an indication that despite our almost nonstop lovemaking the first few weeks, the herbs successfully prevented my pregnancy. I was optimistic that under our more reasonable sexual activity, once or twice a day, I could prevent conception every moon cycle.

That was a relief to me, although Lucan expressed unabashed willingness to include a child or two in our lives. I kept taking the herbs.

To say that the days we spent together were idyllic is to capture only a small facet of our experience in the villa by the sea. We were so consumed by each other and the union we were celebrating, all other considerations vanished. Rome seemed a thousand days away, her petty politics and patrician powerbrokers a distant echo from the past.

We found ourselves in each other. Our love was so compelling, so irrevocable, we gave up any notion that we could live without it.

Our passion became more complete and also more comfortable. We grew accustomed to achieving such a state of ecstasy, we were transported beyond our bodies. Nothing held us back. We learned to ride the wave of climax almost indefinitely.

We experienced no reticence – nothing but joyful fascination as we touched and tickled, caressed and kissed every surface from the top of each other's heads to the tip of our toes. We created new positions for making love, discovering what the other most enjoyed and what stimulated the sweetest orgasms.

Almost as marvelous as our lovemaking was our sleeping. Every night Lucan would tuck himself behind me, draw me close to him, wrap one arm over my waist and bring his hand up to cup my breasts. I fell asleep with his warm breath in my hair and my womb wet with his seed, contented as never before.

∞ ∞ ∞

As with all ecstasies, this one came to an end. We received word from Augustalis that Lucan's father had taken ill. Lucan was being summoned to Rome and his father's sickbed.

Lucan and I decided it was best for me to remain at the villa since we didn't know how long he would be gone. If he was needed in Rome for only a few days and I already started back to work in Augustalis' kitchen, we would be unable to resume our retreat. We were blithely hopeful Lucan could return to the seaside shortly after being reassured that his father's health was restored.

A week later I received notice from Augustalis that he would be sending the carriage in two days' time to bring me back to Rome. The missive contained no further context. As I packed our trunks, I noted with regret that I hadn't given Lucan the gifts I selected for him. He had brought something for me as well, which he placed on the table with them. We were so persuaded that ample time stretched out before us, we hadn't even considered exchanging our gifts.

As I held Lucan's gift for me, I experienced a quality of remembering similar to what I felt when I first saw him. It was an ancient, intricately carved sandalwood box. Something jingled inside when I shook it. To avoid the temptation of opening it, I nestled it among the garments I packed for him.

Everything was in order when the carriage arrived. I thanked the servants, who had treated us with unceasing kindness during our stay, and bid them goodbye. After the trunks were loaded onto the carriage, I was on my way.

The ride back was bittersweet. There I was, alone, in the compartment where Lucan and I made love all the way to the villa. Every rut in the road and resulting bump reminded me of the seductive bliss we experienced together. More frequently, though, I thought about my beloved and what he must be experiencing. I expected the worst, but even that didn't prepare me for the news I received upon my return.

∞ ∞ ∞

As I stepped down from the carriage I saw a servant waiting by the front gate, ready to take me to Augustalis' suite. My queasiness signaled that the news was not good.

"Come in and more importantly, welcome back," Augustalis said in greeting. "I missed you. Everyone missed you. I kept telling myself the sacrifice I was making when I faced yet another unexceptional meal was worth it, since it was for the sake of love. But really, my dear Graci, no one else's cooking can compare with yours. Some of the dishes that came out of the kitchen after you left were barely edible – dreadful. By the way, how was your time at the sea?"

I told him in some detail how delighted Lucan and I were with his home and how well his servants cared for us. "It was an extraordinary experience, with endless joy spilling over from one day to the next," I recalled. "Augustalis, you gave us a gift we will carry in our hearts forever. Thank you. Bless you."

"I am heartened to hear that because Lucan returned to face the fury of his father," Augustalis revealed. "He had a minor collapse, probably no worse than a mild fainting spell, and parlayed it into an apparently life threatening spectacle. That gave him the excuse to call Lucan back to Rome.

"Not surprisingly, almost immediately after Lucan arrived his father's good health returned. Clearly that was the plan. He announced that what his son had done with you was so heinous, he was reconsidering Lucan's place in the family. He also told Lucan he would never succeed in his efforts to defy him."

"That man is despicable," I cried.

"It gets worse," Augustalis warned. "Lucan's father proclaimed he would be disinherited if he didn't agree to the marriage arranged for him earlier. Lucan would be stripped of his place in the Senate, thrown out on the street without a denarius to his name and have his birth removed from the lineage. His parting words were, 'If you want that slave so badly, then become one yourself. It is what you deserve for desecrating the family name.'"

"This is dreadful!" I exclaimed. "How can he threaten such vengeance?"

"He believes he has ultimate power over all family matters, and any form of opposition must be quashed," Augustalis said with obvious distaste.

"Lucan came to me immediately, in a rage," he continued. "He was ready to disappear from his father's house and walk away from the life he led. I tried to reason with him. I devised every imaginable compromise solution, but none of them was workable. His father's disapproval of every alternative was inevitable. Lucan became more insistent that the only tolerable option was to turn his back on his family. I asked him to reconsider his choice and return the next day to talk with me.

"He has been here every afternoon since then. Each day he seems to be reacting less to his father's desire for revenge and more to his sense of duty to make a positive difference in the world. I didn't lead him there; he arrived of his own accord."

"At least Lucan is maintaining a modicum of reason amidst the threats," I observed.

"Of course, you were integral to our discussions," Augustalis stated. "He tried to convince me to free you so that when he was out from under his family the two of you could marry, move to the country and live a simple life. Since he would no longer be a senator, the sanctions against your marriage would be lifted. I reminded him of the commitment I made not to free you and said I intended to honor it. Then he became furious with me for being as stubborn as his father."

"How unfortunate, after all you have done for us," I sighed.

"As you know, Lucan has no need for great wealth," Augustalis noted. "He is humble and unassuming, which makes him such an eloquent and effective champion of the people. Rome needs him in the Senate to resurrect a republican form of government. More than anyone, Lucan can do this. It is his mission.

"It is also his destiny to love you, Graci. And therein lies the impasse. If he is to have a larger impact in the world, he needs to remain aligned with his family and in the Senate. If Lucan is to love you, he must forfeit his family and his purpose.

"But he must not!" I insisted. "He can't let me stand in the way of the important contributions he is here to make. His vision and leadership are essential. Already he has built extensive credibility in the Senate."

"I agree," Augustalis replied. "But he loves you with all that he is. The very core of his being cries out for you whenever he considers succumbing to his father's demands. He would die of a broken heart without you, but I cannot agree to your freedom."

"He shouldn't center the rest of his life around me," I urged.

"That is Lucan's decision, and I will support whatever he chooses," Augustalis declared.

"But nothing he chooses can be wholly appropriate," I cried.

Augustalis was silent, considering what to say next. "I want to apologize to you as I did to him, for ever suggesting that the two of you withdraw to my villa. It was a grave mistake. I took overt action in conflict with the wishes of his father. Perhaps more than his son's resistance, my intervention inflamed his anger and fueled his overreaction.

"Now we are facing an untenable situation. Neither alternative is optimal. I hoped, wrongly I fear, that you and Lucan could love each other while he remained influential in the politics of the Empire. Unfortunately his father has successfully thwarted such an outcome. I deeply regret putting you both in this position. I am sorry, Graci."

"There is no need to apologize," I said softly. "Lucan and I could have declined your offer to retreat to your villa. But we did so willingly, and I don't regret it for a moment."

"You are far too forgiving," Augustalis said with sadness and a touch of weariness in his voice. "I am the cause of this trouble, and I accept responsibility for it."

"I recall being in a similar situation when Alexios asked his parents to free me so we could marry," I commented. "I begged him not to make that request since I was certain they would rebuff him and worse, send me away. They behaved just as I predicted.

"The difference between then and now is that I didn't love Alexios. We were dear friends and I admired him greatly. But because I wasn't blinded by love, I could see the situation clearly and anticipate what would happen. When you made your proposal to Lucan and me, I could view it only through the eyes of love."

"And I could see only the potential of your love," Augustalis observed.

"Everything you hoped we could experience occurred when we went away together," I assured him. "If I never see Lucan again, the love we shared and the oneness we created will remain in my heart. No one can take that away from me, even if they take Lucan. You gave us the opportunity to love each other with the profound innocence, hope and passion of newlyweds. And that is an unfathomable blessing."

"I listen to you and realize once again what a perfect match you are for Lucan," Augustalis revealed. "You are like twins who think alike and see the world the same way. Despite the difference in your upbringing and privilege, you are replicas of each other."

"Interestingly, when we first met I remarked that we were twins," I recalled.

A knock came from the door and Lucan entered the room. I sprung from my chair, ran to him, and we embraced. He took a deep breath then exhaled slowly.

"Take a seat and let's have another conference," Augustalis suggested.

"Lucan, you cannot walk away from your family," I blurted out. "You have your whole life ahead of you, and you must do the greatest good with the privileges into which you were born."

"So you would see me marry and sire children by a woman I don't love, honoring the wishes of my father and desecrating our love?" Lucan asked incredulously. "How can you say such a thing? You can't mean it. And if you do, then you couldn't possibly love me."

I looked to Augustalis for reassurance. I had completely bungled our initial conversation, and I regretted it at once. Lucan deserved the opportunity to speak his mind before I proposed anything or offered my opinion, and I had taken that away from him.

"May I suggest neither of you say anything in the heat of the moment that you are certain to regret later," Augustalis advised.

"Wise counsel," Lucan commented appreciatively. "I have been so overwrought lately, I can't trust what I say or how I say it."

"As long as you speak your mind and refrain from judging Graci when she speaks hers, we may make progress this afternoon," observed Augustalis.

"Duly noted," Lucan agreed, somewhat calmer.

"We now have the opportunity to talk through the current situation in the privacy of this chamber," Augustalis stated. "We will take whatever time is necessary to achieve a conclusion you both can accept.

We can resume the conversation tomorrow and the next day if necessary."

Addressing Lucan, Augustalis stated, "I brought Graci back to Rome because I believed that without her voice, you would be unable to make a choice that serves you both. I acknowledge this is your decision and yours alone. But Graci is a part of you now and deserves to be heard. And so here we are. I will serve as moderator when needed and stay out of the way otherwise."

Augustalis sat back in his chair, looked thoughtfully at us both and prepared to remain silent. I was hesitant to speak after the way I botched my opening comment.

No one said a word. The hush was almost unendurable. How could Lucan and I have arrived at this place of separateness and suppression, willful or otherwise, after the oneness we knew so recently? It was tragic, a testament to the power of lovelessness over love.

"I am reluctant to say anything since I may well utter words I regret later," Lucan admitted. "Ultimately the decision may be mine alone, but I consider it Graci's as well."

"I already stated how I feel," I replied, hazarding his wrath one more time. "Lucan, you may romanticize about a simple life with me in the country, but you have no experience living off the land. You are an intellectual, a scholar, a senator. You weren't meant to do manual labor and eek out a subsistence living. That is not what you came here to do."

"I came here to be with you," he protested. "And if bowing to subsistence living enables us to stay together, so be it."

"But being with me isn't possible," I replied. "I can never be freed."

This time it was Lucan who looked pleadingly to Augustalis for help. No doubt he was hoping I would be allowed to live with him, even if I couldn't become a freedwoman. Augustalis offered no such conciliation.

"This is horrific!" Lucan stormed, rising from his chair and walking over to a doorway opening onto the courtyard. "We are getting nowhere with this conversation. Augustalis, thank you for arranging it, but I think I should leave before the chasm between Graci and me grows even wider."

Lucan's use of the word *chasm* sent a dagger through my heart. We were unable to communicate with each other and incapable of providing mutual love and support. I felt hopeless and frustrated. If Lucan's father had been there, I would have scratched his eyes out.

"Lucan, I love you," I said gently. "The only truth in my life is my love for you. Whatever happens, that love will not change. I am incapable of anything but loving you. My words come from that place of love, which is unconditional.

"Your father may love you, but it is conditional. He demands that you live out your role as his son on his rigidly defined terms, not yours. You have been brought so low by his vile temper and his despicable manipulation, you believe my love is conditional as well. Worse, you accuse me of not loving you at all. You can't possibly think that of me."

Lucan turned and walked back to his chair, then sat down.

"Your love is everything you say it is, Graci," he replied. "And my father's love, or lack thereof, is as you describe it. What a painful betrayal of the son by the father!"

"Or the daughter by the mother," I replied. "I'll match you on who has been abused more, you by your father or me by my mother."

He blanched.

"I have become as despicable as my father, wallowing in self-pity and protesting my victimization," Lucan observed dejectedly. "I daresay the person I am now may need to be relegated to a small plot of land in the middle of nowhere. I deserve to have no credibility in the Senate, or anywhere else for that matter."

"You are being too hard on yourself," I insisted.

"Tell me, Graci, how did you endure your mother's incessant resentment, jealousy and even hatred and not become an angry, abusive person yourself?" Lucan asked.

"I always believed a benevolent force cared for me even when she didn't," I replied. "And that turned out to be true. When she refused to feed me her milk, another slave shared hers with me. When I was old enough to learn, Alexios insisted I be tutored. When I was about to be thrust out of Greece, Augustalis arrived unexpectedly to bring me here to meet you. I have an abiding faith in this force, and it has never abandoned me.

"I endured my mother's insults without allowing them to circumscribe me. I experienced her loathing without assuming I was vile. I saw her jealousy and understood it was a reflection of her need to be taken by men in order to feel loved."

"Just as my father needs to control me in order to feel powerful," Lucan noted.

"True," I replied. "Your father wants you to believe he is omnipotent. But he is unworthy of his power because he is not benevolent. Acknowledge who he is but don't react to it. The moment you do, he owns your decision.

"I recognized every flaw and foible my mother possessed, but I never gave myself over to her limitation. I refused to align with it. And thus I was saved from it."

Augustalis shifted in his chair. "She is a wise woman, Lucan," he declared, "and you would be well served to take her words to heart."

"That is exactly what I am doing," Lucan replied. "I recall remarking to Graci that I was more of a slave than she because I allowed my circumstances to define me. I enable my father to control me every time I react negatively to his demands. For half of my life I have rebelled against his rules, which then enabled him to occupy a central position in my existence. I live in opposition to my father. In a twisted way it is his life, not mine.

"I was born into privilege and power. The privilege I care little about. The power matters a great deal to me because I can use it for the advantage of the people."

"I couldn't agree more," Augustalis affirmed.

"The Senate has been corrupted by the same power I inherited at birth," Lucan noted. "It is composed of men who have lost their way, who posture, play politics and accomplish virtually nothing. I am disgusted with the constant machinations that occupy everyone's minds. It is a waste of intelligence and experience. Absolutely no benefit comes of it.

"I can remain repulsed by the Senate, as I am by my father, and enable my fellow senators to justify my own hopelessness. Or I can refuse to believe their selfish, narrow-minded ways will prevail. I can use my life and my power as an advocate for the greater good."

"That is what you were born to do," I declared.

"I can see myself as a catalyst for change in the context of the Senate," Lucan noted. "The path would be convoluted. Roadblocks would be erected every step of the way, but I might just persevere.

"With that said, knowing I could never again be with Graci would cause me the deepest despair. Such ill fortune would annihilate my spirit. It is not enough for me to know our love is eternal. I must also have Graci in my daily life. Regretfully, I am required to choose between an immense love and an equally immense purpose."

He looked at me searchingly. I returned his gaze with an infusion of love, saying nothing. I couldn't make the choice for him. He didn't expect me to do so, but he looked for direction from me. None was forthcoming.

"Perhaps you should continue this discussion in private," Augustalis suggested. "I have little wisdom to offer. If you decide to be together, I will be as flexible as I can be within the bounds of my commitment regarding Graci. If you select a different course, I will support you in other ways. Whichever path you take, Graci will always have my care and protection, and you, Lucan, will have my unqualified assistance.

"Now I leave the two of you to your conversation. I will be in the next room reading. Please let me know when you are ready for me."

Augustalis selected a volume from his desk and closed the door behind him.

"Are you angry with me?" Lucan asked. "You refuse to say anything. That is so unlike you."

"I am silent because I don't want to obstruct your decision or influence your thinking," I explained. "I want to refrain from guiding you, inadvertently or otherwise, in a direction you may regret later. I couldn't bear knowing you held me responsible for your unhappiness should that come about."

"And you think you aren't already responsible for my unhappiness?" Lucan asked, suddenly angry.

"No, I do not," I said steadily. "I have made you happy. Your father has made you unhappy. I refuse to be responsible for the position your father has put you in, either by contributing his seed for your conception or his fortune for your perpetuation."

"Then you are writing me off," he concluded.

"Quite the contrary," I replied. "I am offering you the latitude you deserve to carve out your destiny. It is the least I can do, given how little latitude I have to create my own."

"So you won't help me make this choice, even though you love me?" Lucan asserted.

"I won't help you choose precisely because I love you," I countered.

"Then we have nothing more to talk about," he said curtly, standing up and preparing to leave.

I wanted to rage at him for being so obstinate and protect him from feeling so vulnerable. I longed to offer my body to him to affirm our oneness. But he was separate from me now.

He was leaving. My heart was torn in two. "Lucan, I will always love you," I called after him. And then he was gone.

I sat in the chair, so stunned I could neither move nor speak. The man I loved just left me. He was hurt, resentful and unable to receive my love. The impossibility of our love had finally taken its toll. We were split apart.

I knocked on the door to the room where Augustalis was waiting. He could tell from my face it was over. I willed myself to maintain my composure.

"He is gone from this room and from my life," I said. "Take care of him as you would a son, and please help heal his wounded heart. Thank you for all you have done. I will be fine."

My voice cracked with those words. Rather than detaining me, Augustalis allowed me my pride. I left with no protest from him. I made it to my room just as the tears and my monthly blood started to flow. My grieving began.

∞ ∞ ∞

Excruciating sadness haunted me after that day. When my trunk arrived from the carriage, I put it in a corner of my room and covered it with a cloth, unopened. The sight of it was more than I could bear. I may be strong, but I had my limits. And I had reached them, every last one of them.

Lucan didn't attempt to communicate with me in his sleep. That was fortunate, for I couldn't have withstood the pain when I awoke after such communion.

I set about allowing the loss to overtake me, aware that the only way to arrive on the other side of it was to grieve without restraint.

I didn't berate myself for what I said during our confrontation in Augustalis' office. I had spoken from my heart, and because of Lucan's torment, he heard my words as a statement of love sacrificed. If I regretted anything, it was that he was in such an untenable position.

I reviled the contemptible laws that kept us apart. Arranged marriages were financial mergers, not sacred unions. What could possibly be sacred about forcing two people together to consolidate power and accumulate an even greater fortune?

Patrician society in Rome was perpetuated for centuries by the denial of love and in many instances the defilement of it. I struggled to forgive not just Lucan's father, but also the selfish purpose the demands he made on his son were meant to achieve.

When I was tired or morose, my thoughts went to the people who attended Augustalis' parties and ate the food I worked so hard to create. At times I was assaulted by rage. I wanted to say to them, "How dare you take me for granted, you who have obliterated any chance I might have for fulfilling love? You have wealth but are without conscience and humanity. I serve you only because I have no choice. I make your food only because my enslavement requires that I work for nothing, so you can lead lives of leisure and luxury. In no way can I honor you."

During my last encounter with Lucan and Augustalis I claimed to have learned a great deal, but it eluded me now. I was resilient, but sometimes when I grew tired of being brave and alone, it took all my strength to keep from trying to escape the Roman society I so deplored.

Somehow I managed to endure my more tempestuous emotional upheavals, and eventually I admitted to myself that I was free to live in either contentment or despair. Whichever I chose was not a function of my slavery. Nothing inhibited what I believed in or how I created meaning in my life.

Bondage didn't prohibit me from reaching deep within myself to embrace my fundamental divinity.

Thus I moved through yet another rite of passage, transcending once again the impulse to resist the constraints that surrounded me. I rediscovered what I knew before, which was that I should acknowledge but not be brought down by the limitations forced upon me.

The baths were my saving grace. I gave the water my sadness and pain then let it envelop me until utter peace replaced the unwanted dregs I brought with me. I usually went by myself, since the solitude was healing as well. The baths cleansed me in more ways than one, rejuvenating my body and renewing my spirit.

I spent most of my spare time in seclusion, though in truth I had little of it. When I wasn't cooking, I was exploring Rome for an expanding collection of spices from across the known world. I gathered an assortment superior to what was found in even the best spice shops, and I invented ever more subtle combinations of flavors and aromas.

My work in the kitchen and my daily trips to the market helped me emerge eventually from the terrible sorrow that clutched at my heart whenever I thought of Lucan. I stayed busy because my work required it, not because I wanted to avoid the anguish. Over time my heartache evolved into a dull sadness, which I assumed would be with me to my dying day.

Lucan accepted no more invitations to social gatherings given by Augustalis. And it goes without saying that he no longer accompanied me to the market.

Thus I continued day after day, month after month. Gradually I emerged from the oppression of my lost love and began to think of myself just as Graci, not as someone whose heart was broken.

Around the time when my joylessness was replaced by more predictable tranquility, I was summoned to Augustalis' office. My stomach pitched and turned at the prospect that Lucan might be there. I was relieved to see he was not.

"Come in, Graci," Augustalis said heartily. "You look well. And since your cooking has never been more delectable, I can only assume you are no longer as miserable as you were earlier."

"I am feeling better," I replied, refusing to go into further detail.

"I asked you here so I could inform you of what happened with Lucan, if you want to hear it," Augustalis continued. "If not, I understand. There is no need to reopen old wounds that have hopefully started to heal."

"Please tell me what you know," I responded. "I am not as fragile as I once was, thank the gods."

"Very well then," Augustalis agreed. "I have news that I thought might interest you. Shall I proceed?"

I nodded yes.

"Lucan married the young woman who was chosen for him, the one he rejected before your visit to the sea," Augustalis informed me. "He did so quickly, within weeks of our last meeting here. She is now pregnant.

"His father set them up in a lavish home of their own, which Lucan cares nothing about. He treats his wife with respect and deference. He seems to feel a measure of compassion for her, since her situation is no better than his. But he makes no pretense of loving her.

"I am no longer in touch with his father, and I rarely see Lucan. I stopped inviting him and his wife to banquets here, partly because he refused every request and partly because I don't want you to worry about an unfortunate accidental meeting."

"Thank you for that," I inserted.

"Lucan has become inactive in the Senate and seems not to be pursuing the greater good that once inspired him," Augustalis disclosed. "But then, he has had a lot to adjust to, and he is neither as feisty nor as tough as you are."

"I am not all that tough," I objected.

"From my perspective you are, Graci, and I take neither your spiritedness nor your strength for granted," Augustalis replied. "No doubt the past months have been the most difficult ones of your life, and that is saying a great deal. You are an even more remarkable woman than I thought, having come through them."

"I feel more regretful than remarkable," I commented.

"That is understandable," Augustalis assured me. "If you would like to take another respite by yourself, somewhere different of course, I would be happy to send you there. You have demanded a great deal from yourself lately, and you deserve time to heal the soreness in your soul at a deeper level. This is the least I can do since your heartache is very much my doing."

"I appreciate your offer, but my heartache is completely my own doing," I replied. "I am capable of coming out of it given time. You need not assure my full recovery by sending me away."

"Well, if you ever want to go anywhere, just let me know," he reiterated. "I have an appalling number of residences, some of which I never get to from one year to the next."

"I will remember that," I told him. "And when you see Lucan again, please give him my love with your thoughts but not your words."

"That I will do," he replied. "By the way, I have something for you. It is a small volume that tells the story of Vespasian, one of the commanders who conquered Britannia and then later became Caesar. For some reason his biography made me think of you. I would like to give this to you to enjoy during those infrequent moments when you have nothing to do. It is a compelling tale of a complex man."

"No doubt I will appreciate it," I said, accepting the volume from him. "Does it have a happy ending?"

"It does indeed," Augustalis promised, a twinkle in his eye.

"Good, then I won't be crying myself to sleep," I quipped.

Vespasian's biography rekindled my love of reading. I finished the volume within days then read it a second time. As always I felt free when I accessed the ideas and philosophies, stories and treatises of others.

When I imposed upon Augustalis to allow me to borrow additional volumes from his library, he gave me access to his entire collection. I especially loved narratives in the original Greek. They took me back to my daily interludes with Alexios and Errikos, reminding me of the gift they both were to me at that otherwise vulnerable time in my life.

I thought about Alexios often, not out of any desire to substitute him for Lucan, but rather to acknowledge my gratitude to him. Not only did he make my childhood bearable, but he contributed to my adulthood as well. Thanks to him I could read everything on Augustalis' shelves if I wanted. And if I finished them all before I died, I would simply start over again.

A firsthand account of a prophet in Jerusalem named Yeshua especially intrigued me. Written by one of his followers, it contained stories of this remarkable man and his beloved Mary of Magdala. I became so engrossed in their story, I felt as if I had gone back in time and was traveling with them.

When I asked Augustalis if he had any other volumes documenting the life of Yeshua, he replied that he did not. Then promptly the next afternoon eight manuscripts were delivered to my room, "for my own private collection" as the accompanying note from Augustalis indicated. Each one presented a distinctive account of Yeshua's life as told by an individual who accompanied him. I was so drawn into their narratives, I would read well into the night and all too frequently get little sleep.

The philosophy preached by Yeshua provided a source of abiding contentment for me. He spoke eloquently of love, forgiveness and compassion. He reminded people that they carried the spark of their Creator within them and need not look to priests in temples to access it for them. He was a servant priest, not a patrician with servants, and as such he spoke to my spirit.

Two years passed since Lucan was married, and I prayed he was doing well. I hoped with all my heart that he was happy and satisfied.

∞ ∞ ∞

One morning I was returning from the baths. Another slave was assigned to do the shopping for the day, and I had time to refresh myself early.

"Is that you, Graci?" a man's voice called out in Greek to me. I turned to discern the source of this unexpected greeting.

"Alexios!" I exclaimed, walking rapidly toward him and hugging him excitedly. "What brings you to Rome?"

"Business," he replied. Then he looked me up and down, quite thoroughly in fact. "You smell of fresh flowers."

"I just left the baths," I explained. "I create oils infused with the fragrance of various blossoms, which I use liberally afterwards. I probably smell like an entire flower market at the moment."

"It is so incredible to see you again, I am at a loss for words," Alexios admitted.

"Words aren't necessary," I interjected. "After so long, where could we possibly begin a conversation anyway?"

"We could begin anywhere," he commented. "You look well. Are you happy?"

"I am quite content," I assured him. "I have taken up reading in my spare time. I am making my way through my master's extensive library. Each time I open another volume, I bless the day you made it possible for me to receive such a superb education. I was unaware at the time what a lasting contribution you made to my life."

"You were a more exceptional student than I," Alexios noted. "You kept me involved in my studies. Otherwise I wouldn't have learned half as much as I did."

"I am glad I contributed a little something to balance the scales," I told him. "Looking back on that time, I can easily convince myself that the benefits were all going in one direction, from you to me."

"It was the opposite, actually," he stated. "May I walk you to your quarters?"

"That is probably not a good idea," I replied. "I don't want to cause any more trouble for you than I already have. You are better off not knowing where I live."

"I already know where you live," he said simply.

"You do?" I asked, surprised.

"About a year ago I accompanied a business partner who was dining with Augustalis in his home," he explained. "The moment I tasted the food, I knew you were the genius at work in the kitchen. Afterward as I was thanking Augustalis for his hospitality, I asked if perchance you served in the kitchen. He confirmed that you did then asked how I could have identified your cooking so precisely. I told him a bit of our story, though not all of it, of course. He invited me to meet with him the next day, and I agreed.

"I had no idea he knew my father and grandfather. After he recounted his friendship with them, he told me everything that happened after my parents sent me away. He also affirmed his intention to honor his commitment never to free you, emphasizing the fact that you and I could never marry."

"Augustalis was in an untenable situation," I noted.

"He was, but he agreed to it," Alexios observed. "I was offended initially. But as we talked it was obvious he cared a great deal about you. He took a keen interest in making sure you were comfortable and happy. I concluded that my grandfather placed you in extremely good hands, and I told Augustalis as much.

"He commented that you are an extraordinary woman, and it is a travesty you were born into slavery. I reminded him that the real travesty was his perpetuation of your bondage. He didn't disagree. Then he thanked me for enabling you to receive an education. We parted amicably, and I committed to myself not to seek you out. I haven't, though I knew all along where you lived."

"Thank you for that, Alexios," I replied. "It has made things easier for us both. This may be impertinent of me, but I must ask it anyway. Did you find someone to love?"

"No I didn't, and I never married," he revealed. "Instead I have been pursuing my grandfather's business, traveling much of the year to negotiate trade agreements far and wide. At first he put me in charge of smaller transactions. But as I gained experience, I took on more significant responsibilities. Now grandfather is thinking of retiring, and I am assuming greater leadership. My father shows no interest in the business. The acumen of a merchant seems to have skipped a generation."

"And my mother?" I hadn't thought of her in a long time, and now it seemed imperative to learn how she was doing.

"She died recently of complications from a brutal beating by a man she saw on occasion," he reported. "I thought of getting in touch with you to let you know what happened, but I decided it was better to leave things as they were."

"Alexios, you have always been so considerate and caring," I said earnestly. "I can never repay you for all the ways you look out for my best interests."

"I often wondered what would have happened if I had listened to you and not gone to my parents to inform them I wanted to marry you," Alexios admitted. "Each time I consider it, I realize we are both leading better lives than we would have otherwise. Yes, I was rash and impetuous, and I might have known I couldn't defy my parents on such a critical matter. But I was honest and gave them an opportunity to honor my request. Predictably, they chose not to do so.

"Now here you are with all of Rome at your feet, under the protection of one of the most munificent patricians in the city. And I am traveling everywhere, meeting interesting people and experiencing one adventure after another. Life is good."

"It is indeed," I agreed.

I had been so engrossed in our conversation, I didn't realize Alexios escorted me home. We were standing outside the door to the slave quarters.

"How did you know?" I asked.

"I made a few inquiries," he said with a smile. "You didn't think I would discover you are serving in Augustalis' household then leave it at that, did you? I have been watching out for you all along. But today when I happened to see you, I couldn't resist the temptation to speak to you."

"Being with you again has been lovely, just like old times," I replied. "Except that we aren't chasing butterflies, since there are none to be had in this city."

"Take care of yourself, Graci," he urged as I opened the door to go inside.

"I will, Alexios," I affirmed. "Peace be with you."

I went to my room and sat on the bed, staggered by what just occurred. It was one thing to see Alexios again. But to find out he was aware of where I lived and chose not to contact me out of consideration for my welfare, was extraordinary.

He hadn't changed a bit.

∞ ∞ ∞

My conversation with Augustalis and then Alexios got me thinking about the various kinds of love. It is such an ambiguous way to portray relationships. Alexios and Augustalis were both expressing their love toward me. Yet I didn't see it as such because I wasn't in love with them. I recognized love only in the context of my lover. Lucan may be the love of my life, but Alexios and Augustalis were my loving protectors.

I explored every volume I could find on the character and spirit of love. I also revisited my manuscripts of Yeshua's teachings, searching in particular for his commentary on love. Here are key insights I discovered along the way.

Love defies description, although well-meaning people have tried in every conceivable way to represent it. Even I, an average person with an ordinary mind, am attempting to do so now. I am writing on the nature of love not because I can but because I must.

Love is the creative impulse behind all that exists. Everyone and everything begins in love and returns to love. That is the one certain aspect of our being. If we emerge from the seed crystal of love and travel back to our home in love when we die, then everything in between can also be the manifestation of love.

Unfortunately it is not.

The human condition is fraught with all but love, or so it seems. People pursue ends that serve their own selfish interests rather than selflessly benefiting others. Generosity is uncommon, as is compassion. Forgiveness is rare, judging and vengeance are not. And in the end one can become so beaten down by lovelessness, it is easy to believe love exists only infrequently.

That is a dispiriting way to live, one I have consciously chosen not to pursue. And yet I wonder.

Could it be that my mother and Lucan, the two people who might have loved me the most, loved me the least?

When I was born my mother experienced a double measure of sadness, a child she didn't want and the death of the baby's father. I forgave my mother for not loving me. What else was I to do? Rage at her in righteous disgust every time she came to mind and thus corrode my ability to love?

I can't alter the circumstances of my birth, and I certainly couldn't change my mother. I accepted the former and forgave the latter.

As my capacity to forgive my mother deepened, I felt more empathy for her terrible fate. I understood how she lost her way. And from that compassion a spark of love for her was kindled inside me. It is still only a spark, but it is better than no love at all.

When I heard of her death, I was relieved she was liberated from a life in bondage that she didn't cause and could never accept. She has returned to the love from which she was created. She is all love now.

Why did I choose to love and forgive someone who couldn't love and forgive me? The answer is simple, yet it took me years to uncover it: Love must spring forth from the sheer desire to love. If one is waiting for reciprocity, love remains elusive. If it derives from the desire to be loved, it is conditional and therefore limited.

At the risk of appearing to have an ulterior motive for loving, which I do not, I assert this. Loving is more rewarding and uplifting than its opposite. I love loving. Lovelessness is a constraining, unfortunate way to live.

Thus in the context of my mother, I refer to love and not the lack of it. Why dwell on what was deficient when instead I can focus on the love I felt for her eventually?

My consideration of love with regard to Lucan is a different matter altogether. Our love was mutual and instantaneous. It was our destiny to meet, recognize each other and come together physically and spiritually to achieve the oneness our love made possible.

After our last encounter in Augustalis' quarters, I wondered if I fantasized that my relationship with Lucan was more profound than it actually was. If the love were authentic, how could our relationship end so abruptly? Wouldn't the love compel us to remain together whatever the cost? And since no such compulsion was in evidence with either of us, one could assume the magnetic attraction we felt was more lust than love, a fire burning bright but short-lived.

My coming together with Lucan was an inexorable impetus to achieve oneness. Even before our sexual union we formed a natural complementarity with our values and viewpoints, preferences and perceptions. We were like two halves of the same entity, not identical but close.

To deny my love for Lucan would be to turn away from my own deepest essence. My love for him is a fountainhead within me, the one certainty I have in an otherwise uncertain life. My capacity to love him whatever the condition of our togetherness is what I know to be most true about myself.

My love is ferocious, not weak. It makes me strong, unwilling to give up who I am to achieve something outside myself. It enables me to clarify what matters to me, which is my ability to love, which is unassailable.

Then again, I wonder if my stubborn refusal to damn Lucan and my equally obstinate insistence that I will love him always is not just an attempt to hang onto something meaningful in a life devoid of meaning. Am I grasping at this love so I will have something to live for, even if it is a memory growing ever more distant? Is it weakness instead of strength that causes me to believe so profoundly in my love for Lucan?

I doubt it. My heart feels the glow of love, even though I haven't seen my lover for years. I can tell when he is thinking about me. It feels like an extra log thrown on the fire within me, warming me once again. I don't doubt his love, even though he married another and dismissed me from his life.

Lucan's acceptance of an arranged marriage had nothing to do with me. It didn't represent a rejection of who I was in his life or a denial of his love for me. Rather, it was evidence of the indefensible situation in which we both found ourselves. He chose the most appropriate course available to him.

But didn't Lucan's actions squander and maybe even desecrate the great blessing of our love? Isn't love supposed to be cherished as the most precious gift one can receive? And if so, how could either of us reconcile the fact that we weren't together?

I recall my initial statement when Lucan entered the room for our last meeting. I told him he should marry the woman his father selected for him. He was furious, declaring if I loved him I could never utter such words. I stated what he couldn't bring himself to admit. And once the words were spoken, they couldn't be taken back. I created the inevitability of his marriage by voicing what demanded to be said, and what he could never express.

We both made the choice for him to marry. We did so not as two people, but as one. We held the same thought, as we did so often before. Either of us could have asserted the inevitable, and the other would have recognized its authenticity, painful though the implications were.

One might deduce that I was more courageous than he. But I think not. He couldn't bear to hurt me with the message he knew he must deliver before the end of our conversation. So I did it for him instinctively at the beginning. The least I could do was set him free to live his life as he must. It was the ultimate act of love, not the denial of it on his part or mine.

I wish him well. I also wish him love. I hope he has grown to love his wife and cherish his children. I pray he has forgiven his father. I hope he has also forgiven himself, though there is really nothing to forgive.

Thus were my thoughts about two people central to my life. My mother couldn't find space in her heart to love me. And although Lucan loved me with all his heart, the conditions of our togetherness were irretrievably at odds.

I rarely considered an existence configured any differently from the one I knew. It was comforting to be assured I would remain in Augustalis' appreciative household, where I had my own private room and a great deal of latitude. Life was good.

∞ ∞ ∞

Seven years passed since I had seen Lucan. Eirene was slowing down, and I assumed more responsibility in the kitchen. Since I had trained others to cook the way I did, my work involved more supervision than anything else. I rarely did the daily shopping, though I still ventured out to replenish herbs and spices and discover new ones.

I was planning the menu for a dinner party a few days hence when a servant arrived with a message that Augustalis wanted to see me. I followed her to his quarters.

"Welcome, Graci," he said enthusiastically. "I am receiving accolades from Eirene about your management of the kitchen. She insists that if you get much better at it, she can convince me she should retire. You continue to impress one who is very hard to please. But then, you did that from the day you arrived."

"Eirene and I are similar in our approach, although I tend to be more involved in the details than she – not always a good thing," I replied. "I haven't yet been able to detach myself from the final round of tasting and spicing."

"Actually, I invited you here for another purpose," Augustalis informed me. "Lucan is in the next room. He asked if he could meet with you. I told him that was entirely up to you. If you don't want to have any contact with him, you can leave before he sees you. His intention is to honor your privacy if that is what you choose."

"Do you know why he wishes to see me after so many years?" I asked.

"He simply wants you to know he is doing well and make sure you are too," Augustalis replied. "I tell him repeatedly you are flourishing, but he wants to verify that for himself."

"In that case I will talk with him," I consented without further consideration.

I took a deep breath and entered the room where Lucan was waiting. He was standing in an open doorway looking out at the courtyard. I took deliberate steps toward him, willing myself not to falter. It had been so long since I was in his presence, I had forgotten what he could do to me even with his back turned. He pivoted to face me.

He was older and even more imposing, but still as handsome as ever. He met my gaze. Myriad competing sentiments were evident on his face, reflecting my own turmoil. The magnetism was still there, along with profound sadness and a wide swath of regret.

"Hello Graci," he said tightly, holding back his emotions.

"Hello Lucan," I replied, refusing to assert myself further into the conversation.

"Augustalis wasn't exaggerating when he told me you are thriving," he observed. "You radiate peace."

"My life unfolds in many blessed ways," I concurred. "I approach each morning with gratitude and each night with a sense of meaning. And you?"

"I am succeeding in my own way," he affirmed. "I am married and have three children, two boys and a girl. Another one is on the way. I love having them around. They are such bright spirits, open and ready for anything. I am turning out to be a good father – better than my own, at least."

"And your wife?" I persisted.

"She is a wonderful mother to our children," Lucan revealed. "They are at the center of her life, which is great for them and for her. She and I are making the best of a marriage neither of us wanted. Respect between us has grown over the years, as has a measure of affection. But I don't love her. I cannot."

Having no response to that, I stood where I was, silent. A wave of detachment came over me, calming my heart despite Lucan's presence.

"I came to apologize for being so unkind the last time I saw you," he declared earnestly. "My behavior was inexcusable. The fact that I treated the woman I loved, and still do, so callously is appalling to me. I have regretted my words and actions every day since then. I want you to know how sorry I am for blaming you for my misfortune and for good measure, accusing you of not loving me. My reaction that afternoon was unforgivable."

"There is nothing to forgive," I assured him. "We both spoke in the heat of the moment, a most difficult moment I might add. I said what I did that day because I had to, for both of us. I spoke your truth as well as mine – preemptively, unfortunately – and gave you no alternative but to hear it. My intention was to liberate you from any obligation toward me. Instead I bound you to an outcome that may not have been of your choosing."

"Oh, my dear Graci, how I have missed you," he said, throwing his arms around me and holding me close. I recognized the smell of him through his toga, and an acute longing pierced my well-protected heart. Still I remained composed. No tears threatened to burst forth from my eyes. Then I pulled away.

"Shall we try sitting instead of standing while we talk?" I suggested, selecting a chair far enough away from the others that he couldn't hold my hand.

"What have you been doing with your life?" he asked, trying to sound casual and succeeding miserably.

"Oh, the usual," I replied a bit too offhandedly. "I still spend most of my time in the kitchen. But I have taken up reading again and am devouring the manuscripts in Augustalis' library with as much appetite as his guests consume my food. I love my literary explorations, along with going to the baths and creating new concoctions with my expansive, expensive spice assortment. It is a small life but a good one. I am happy."

"I can tell you are," Lucan confirmed.

"Are you . . . happy?" I asked.

"I will answer that with a qualified yes," he replied. "Under the circumstances I am as happy as can be expected."

"What would make your life more fulfilled?" I continued. That question arrived unbidden. I had no idea it was there, then suddenly it was out in the open.

"Do you really want me to answer that?" Lucan queried.

"It was thoughtless of me to ask such a thing," I apologized. "You need not dignify it with an answer."

"But I will," he said. "My life would be more fulfilled if I could spend every day and every night with you. My life would be more fulfilled if my children were our children. My life would be more fulfilled if our conversations and companionship stretched out until the end of this lifetime and far beyond that. My life would be more fulfilled if you were not a slave who can never be freed and I were not a senator responsible for the maintenance of a family legacy. My life would be more fulfilled if love actually prevailed over everything that would annihilate it, and if it brought joy instead of heartache."

I wanted to say, "Love does prevail," but I knew now was not the time for that. Lucan needed to reveal everything he couldn't say the day we parted.

"I make love out of obligation, not passion, to a woman who deserves more than that from me," Lucan declared. "I awake in the middle of the night grieving over the loss of you. I rail wordlessly at my father for forcing me into a life of perpetual ambivalence. I can't be fulfilled without you. I can't be happy without you. And so I remain slightly fulfilled and slightly happy, but never joyful and certainly never ecstatic.

"I told myself I wouldn't end up complaining to you, and here I am doing exactly that. You must find me an intolerable boor."

"Nothing about you is intolerable, and you needn't berate yourself for speaking honestly," I asserted. "Isn't that what you came here to do? If not it would be a complete waste of your time and my good intentions. So speak honestly and I will listen."

"I stayed well informed about you since I stormed out of here," he revealed. "I couldn't live with myself if I hurt you irreparably. Two sources were critical in this endeavor. One you can guess, and one may not be obvious to you."

"One is Augustalis, and the other I can't identify," I replied.

"Alexios," Lucan said.

"Alexios? But how?" I asked.

"He came to see me a year after I was married," Lucan explained. "He attended a dinner here and discovered you were working in the kitchen. Then he met with Augustalis and learned the terms of his grandfather's agreement with him. Knowing I was acquainted with Augustalis, he came to see me the next day to ask my advice regarding whether he should ask him to reconsider his refusal to free you.

"As his story unfolded, I became increasingly distraught. To protect you as well as my friendship with Alexios, I didn't intend to tell him I knew you. But I was still grieving over having abandoned you. I couldn't contain my emotions. After Alexios recounted everything to me, instead of convincing him Augustalis would never go back on his word, I told him my own story."

"How did he react?" I pursued.

"At first he was angry and resentful," Lucan recalled. "But as we talked, the fact that we both faced identical family challenges brought us together again. He chose not to marry, traveling constantly in order to maintain an adequate distance from those obligations. I did the opposite. Implausibly, we both loved you, but neither of us could marry you."

"*Implausible* is the correct word for it," I interjected.

"Somehow our friendship survived that conversation," Lucan observed. "True to form, when it was almost over Alexios asked me what he could do to help alleviate my misery. I requested that he provide me with a second perspective on how you were faring. I trusted Augustalis to tell me the truth, but he is a bit out of touch. A lot could pass under his nose unnoticed.

"Alexios has been using creative ways to keep track of you when he is in Rome, everything from conversations with Gaiana to watching as you pass by on the street. He insists he does this for himself as much as for me."

"It wasn't an accident, then, that he saw me on my way back from the baths," I commented.

"No it wasn't," Lucan confirmed. "Although he did admit afterward that once again you managed to spoil him for anyone else."

"I certainly hope not," I countered. "I want him to be happy, not comparing everyone he meets with an overblown idea of who I am. Even I can't measure up to his fantasies."

"I daresay you can," Lucan objected, "and they aren't overblown at all. You might think this strange, but Alexios and I actually had a conversation comparing our perceptions of you. They were almost indistinguishable except for your infinite capacities as a lover, which I discreetly omitted. No, Graci, you are still the same girl he fell in love with and the same woman I have loved since we met. That won't change.

"You deserve to be loved by at least two good men, and you are. Augustalis loves you as well, but more as a daughter. So you have the appreciation and adoration of three good men. That should be ample love for one amazing woman."

"Your love is more than enough," I affirmed. "Thank you for caring so much you sought assurances that I survived the trauma of losing you. It was cataclysmic. I won't pretend otherwise. For months I was more of a ghost than a person, but over time the ache in my heart subsided. Only then was I able to consider the character and quality of love, and ultimately see it as a blessing.

"The love we share is such an incalculable gift, it need not fit into an acceptable structure to be genuine. Although our love faced unfortunate external constrictions from the beginning, those barriers don't invalidate it."

"Nor will they ever," Lucan declared.

"Look at us," I continued. "We survived an excruciatingly difficult parting after a transcendent time together. We haven't seen each other for years, and you are married with children. Still our love is as enduring as it was before. To denigrate it by denouncing the forces that keep us apart is to miss the point, which is that we love each other and always will. This isn't about whether we can be together as husband and wife, or escape for short trysts, or live on a patch of land in the country."

"A tryst would be tempting," Lucan interjected.

"Not tempting enough for the heartache afterward," I countered.

"I agree, though the temptation remains," Lucan admitted.

"After we parted I sensed your love," I recalled. "It was palpable. I could tell when you were thinking about me lovingly. We remained together, even though it wasn't face-to-face."

"Do you have any idea how much this conversation leads me to love you even more?" Lucan asked.

"Yes I do, for I feel the same way," I replied then paused. "Now what?"

"Perhaps we could meet more regularly as friends," Lucan suggested. "I am about to reengage in the Senate after relegating it to the periphery of my life since my marriage. I would love to discuss with you the controversial initiatives I am launching. I plan to involve Augustalis in those conversations as well. If you have the time and inclination to participate with or without him, I welcome it. Your intelligence and insight would be invaluable to me."

"I wanted to ask you how things were going in the Senate, but since you hadn't brought it up, I thought better of it," I admitted. "I am pleased you are returning to your larger purpose, and I will gladly do what I can to be helpful."

"What can I do for you?" Lucan asked.

"I would be grateful if you could purchase whatever volumes on the prophet Yeshua come on the market," I told him. "Years ago Augustalis gave me a few manuscripts, which are almost worn out from constant reading. Anything you can find in Greek or Latin I would gladly accept."

"I will place a standing order for every manuscript the better booksellers can acquire. The packages will be sent directly to you," Lucan promised.

"Wonderful!" I exclaimed.

"Do you want to see Alexios on occasion?" Lucan inquired. "He would appreciate spending time with you."

"I would like that as well," I confessed. "Just have him leave a message for me when he is in Rome, and I will arrange to meet him."

"We have come a long way," Lucan observed. "Here I am offering to help you get together with another man who loves you dearly, and I am not the least bit jealous. That is quite a statement about the love you and I share, and the affection we both have for a mutual friend."

"We have indeed come a long way," I acknowledged, "and there is further still to go. Thank you for having the courage to be here today and for giving me a choice about whether to talk to you. It has been an enlightening and reassuring encounter. Take care of yourself and let me know when it would be helpful for us to talk again."

I got up from the chair, walked over to him, took his hands in mine, brought them to my lips and kissed them. He started to rise, but I didn't want to risk an embrace. I could tell he, too, preferred not to hazard a hug. I shook my head to indicate he need not walk me to the door. I entered the next room and closed the door quietly behind me. Thankfully Augustalis had departed. Then I wept.

∞ ∞ ∞

I was to meet Alexios for what I thought would be a casual conversation. He had been traveling a great deal. But then, he was the most peripatetic person I knew.

"How is it that you keep looking better and better?" he asked when he saw me.

"Perhaps it's my mysteriously mongrel heritage," I laughed.

"Seems more like a rare pedigree to me," he quipped.

"We'll never know, will we?" I bantered back then thought better of it. I didn't want to thrust our meeting into the chasm of my past, or ours for that matter.

We entered a taberna across the street and sat at a corner table. He ordered a small jug of a most excellent vintage.

"Special occasion?" I queried.

"We'll see," he replied noncommittally.

We talked about nothing that would warrant such expensive wine. Then mindful once again of the difference between us, I thought, "My extravagance may well be his daily fare."

"I have a hypothetical question for you," he began. I knew from his altered tone this was why we were meeting. "If you were freed, would you consider marrying me?"

"That is about as hypothetical as you can get," I declared, "given that your grandfather convinced Augustalis never to satisfy the first part of your question."

"But if it were to happen somehow," Alexios persisted.

I paused long enough to signal to him what my answer was likely to be. "Thank you, my dear sweet Alexios," I replied. "But I couldn't do so. You know the reason why."

"But Lucan is married, and only one thing will change that, which I don't wish on anyone," he noted.

"I am not holding out for Lucan," I revealed. "I never thought I could marry him."

"If you were freed, you would rather remain alone than marry me?" he clarified, sounding neither surprised nor defensive.

"That is true," I said simply.

"Oh, Graci, will I ever understand you?" he asked.

"I doubt it, since I hardly understand myself," I admitted.

"So it is decided," Alexios said with finality. "No matter how much time passes or what occurs in the interim, you would never consent to being my wife. I have just one more question. Would you have married me earlier if my parents had allowed it?"

"Yes, absolutely," I assured him. "We would have been extremely happy together. But I am not the girl I was then. I love another now, and that won't change. I would never dishonor or disrespect you by marrying you when my heart belongs to Lucan. You are too dear for me to do that to you."

"Despite the exquisite irony in that statement, I understand what you are saying," Alexios confirmed. "I guess I will just have to settle for friendship with the most fascinating woman I know, the grown up butterfly chaser. You are still chasing them, you know, but they are of a different sort now. They are facets of your own spirit, free despite your bondage."

"You know me well," I affirmed. "Alexios, how can I thank you for being such a steadfast sentinel in my life?"

"Perhaps this is a repayment for something you did for me, so long ago we have no memory of it in this existence," Alexios conjectured. "I have a sense that is so, and whatever I do for you in this life or the next would never be adequate. Let's just enjoy who we are now and what we share. Then only the best of the gods' blessings will come to us both."

"May it be so," I vowed, knowing it already was.

Afterward I wondered if Alexios had information about his grandfather's possible change of heart that might have prompted our conversation, but I released the thought. There was no use speculating. Acceptance of my position in life served me well. I had no reason to alter it.

My collection of manuscripts about Yeshua the prophet grew rapidly after I asked Lucan to procure additional volumes for me. The more I read, the more palpable was Yeshua's presence in my life. It was as if I could hear him talking directly to me. I read so many first-hand accounts containing his quotes and detailed descriptions of his incomparable existence, at times I felt as if I too had known him personally.

I kept my interest in his teachings private. I talked to no one about what I was reading or how the material affected me. Instead I allowed myself the consummate contentment of studying a few passages before bedtime then going to sleep with them on my mind. Invariably I slept peacefully, confident that whatever my outward existence held in store for me, I was loved in the realms of divine grace.

Lucan gathered around him a small group of senators willing to risk their fortunes, reputations and the wrath of their colleagues by creating a plan to return Rome to the people. Marcus Aurelius was Caesar, and he was more willing than previous emperors to support such a cause. Lucan hoped that when he created significant enough backing for this change in the Senate, Marcus would declare the return to a republican form of government. The advocacy of influential senators might well convince the emperor to initiate such a change during his reign.

As Lucan pursued this cause, he became the man I knew in the beginning, unfailingly realistic with a tinge of hope. We met on occasion to discuss his progress. Although I had neither the background nor the political acumen to contribute to his thinking, talking through the issues with me seemed to help him. Over time I learned enough to be more of a participant and less of a sounding board during our conversations.

Lucan's wife gave birth to five children, all of whom enchanted him. His oldest son was maturing in ways that made his father proud. The other two were following in their brother's footsteps, naturally and without the competition that often affects siblings. His two daughters had obviously learned how to charm their father. When I joked with him about the bills they would run up when they became old enough to require silk and gold, he revealed he had already set aside funds for such extravagances. He was an indulgent father, and his children gave him considerable joy in return.

We had been through a great deal separately and together, and now we were settling into a comfortable if infrequent pattern of meeting as friends with a shared purpose. I had no expectations beyond that. He was relatively at peace, as was I. I would never have predicted this at one disastrous juncture in our relationship.

∞ ∞ ∞

Almost a year passed since I last saw Alexios. I had no idea where he was in the world. Britannia? Spain? Africa? Egypt? Judea? I prayed he would be safe wherever his ships took him.

When Augustalis summoned me to his suite, as usual I was given no information about the purpose of our meeting. I knocked on the door and entered. Alexios was there, beaming.

"Come in, Graci, and have a seat," Augustalis said exuberantly. Alexios stood up and offered me a chair.

"I am in receipt of extremely interesting and unexpected information," Augustalis commenced. "Alexios arrived with it about a week ago, and we have been discussing how to proceed. Before we go any further, we thought it might be wise to involve you in our deliberations. Let me explain.

"Alexios' grandfather had a change of heart and is rescinding his requirement that I never offer you your freedom. In a sealed letter to me he confirmed that the decision is entirely up to me now, and he supports whatever I choose. He also indicated he has received verifiable reports that I have steadfastly honored my original agreement with him."

I kept my composure despite being overwhelmed by the news. "Alexios, this is your doing. How did you accomplish it?" I asked.

"When I saw you last and inquired whether you would marry me if you were freed, it was both a proposal and a hypothetical question," he explained. "Whatever your answer, I was confident I could take steps to help you.

"If you had said you would marry me, I planned to ask my grandfather to reconsider his requirement that you never be freed. I have spent my life proving I am devoted to his business and worthy of taking it over when he steps down. He knows I will be responsible whatever my personal circumstances. If I appealed to him to let me marry you, I am confident he would have agreed to it. He would then require my father to approve of the marriage as well. A letter would be prepared for me to deliver to Augustalis requesting that he set you free so we could marry.

"If, on the other hand, you indicated you would decline my offer, I could explain to my grandfather that there was no danger of my ever marrying you, and thus the sanction against your being freed could be lifted. I informed him years ago of your feelings for Lucan, so he had ample background on the matter. Under the circumstances my story would be credible to him."

"You are ever my guardian," I said with all my heart.

"I want no more than you deserve," Alexios asserted. "When I was in Greece attending to business between voyages, I told my grandfather you wouldn't marry me even if you were freed. Then I convinced him to release Augustalis from his obligation so he could make his own choice regarding your future. A few weeks later he handed me a letter to deliver to Augustalis dispensing with all obligation. I was so pleased with his decision, I hugged him until he insisted I stop. Apparently I was cutting off his air supply.

"And so, Graci, it is now within the purview of Augustalis to determine your future. I have unlocked the door. We will see if he opens it."

"I never allowed myself to contemplate such a possibility," I admitted, my voice quivering. "Just knowing the restriction is no longer on Augustalis' shoulders is a relief to me. He has been carrying an imponderable burden of commitment, which he honored despite the difficulties it presented. You have freed us both, even if nothing else changes."

"I was relatively certain that either way my grandfather would agree to remove his restriction," Alexios admitted. "Thankfully he had the wisdom to recognize the appropriate course of action and the character to follow it."

I turned to Augustalis and stated, "Please know that just because the requirement has been nullified, I assume nothing more. I am blessed to be serving your household."

"I have no doubt you mean what you just declared," Augustalis admitted, "which makes you one of the most decent and enlightened people in this city of decadence and inhumanity. I have come to know you quite well over the years, Graci – not as well as Alexios does, but certainly with enough insight to make a confident choice regarding how your life might unfold.

"First let me say I deplore what Rome has become. Half of its citizens are slaves. Most work is done on their backs, and they are cast out when they become sick or are no longer useful. The wealthy, and I fall squarely in that group, have nothing to do but engage in excess. They do no work and have become too lethargic even to read. They are obsessed with hedonistic pleasures of every sort. I find it disgusting and terribly unfortunate."

"I can vouch that in my extensive travels I have encountered no place as misguided as this city," Alexios concurred.

"I own slaves, which makes me no better than others of my class," Augustalis stated. "But I hope I treat them with more respect and dignity than they would receive anywhere else. I believe I do. That doesn't excuse my choice to hold people in bondage, but it does assuage my conscience a bit.

"One of the greatest dilemmas I have faced since I brought you here is that although I grew to care for you deeply, I could never grant your freedom. I cursed myself for agreeing to the required terms when I took you into custody. Of all my slaves you are the one to whom I would most readily confer freedom, but that option was denied to me. More significantly it was denied to you."

I was barely breathing, anticipating what might be forthcoming.

"Thanks to Alexios and his grandfather, who is discerning enough to know that things change and decisions made in haste deserve to be reviewed," Augustalis resumed, "I now have the freedom to bestow your freedom. Henceforth you are a freedwoman, Graci. Congratulations!"

"With all that I am, I thank you and Alexios and his dear grandfather," I replied with deep emotion. "I can't fathom what it means to be free. I was born a slave and expected to die as one. This is a stunning shift in what my life holds for me. It is inconceivable, really, and will take some getting used to. I can't wait to discover what lies ahead."

I managed to say this before tears erupted from my eyes. Since Lucan was not there to offer me a patch of his toga, Alexios handed me a small cloth napkin from a tray on Augustalis' desk. When I had stopped crying, he commenced the conversation.

"We made a few arrangements to help you adjust to your freedom," Alexios announced. "Shall I continue, Augustalis?"

"Please do," he nodded.

"I purchased an unpretentious home for you not far from here," Alexios divulged. "The deed is in your name and will remain so until your death, at which time it will revert to me provided I am still alive. The property has guest quarters where I will stay when I am in Rome. Were I not to make use of the house, I am relatively certain you would refuse this gesture. So yes, I will benefit from the purchase of the property."

"It doesn't need to be in my name," I protested. "I can maintain it while you are gone and earn my keep that way."

Augustalis smiled at Alexios. "I told you she would object," he commented wryly.

"It is too late for protestations," Alexios declared. "I signed the documents this morning. You are now a freedwoman with property, Graci, both much deserved and a long time coming."

"A thousand times, thank you, dear Alexios," I replied with as much caring as excitement.

"With regard to earning your keep, there will be none of that," Augustalis insisted. "I am paying for your household help. You are not to lift a finger unless, of course, the urge to cook overtakes you every now and then, especially when I am invited to dinner."

I was about to demur again, but instead I responded graciously, "Thank you, Augustalis. That is most generous of you. After living in one room for so long, I would be overwhelmed trying to take care of an entire house."

"You will have slightly more than one room now," Augustalis observed, "and the help is absolutely essential. After all, you will want to protect Alexios' investment."

"Absolutely," I smiled.

"There is one more thing," Alexios remarked. "It concerns your living expenses. You will need funds to restock your spice cabinet and perhaps purchase a tunic or two. Lucan established an account in your name that you are to draw on as needed. The initial sum is substantial and will be replenished regularly. You will never be lacking in resources for your daily requirements. You need not work another day in your life unless you are pursuing a labor of love, which is perfectly acceptable."

"This is all really true!" I exclaimed. "Pardon me, but I am only beginning to assimilate the incredible announcements you just made. I am eternally indebted to you both."

"No more than we are to you," Augustalis replied. "And now to celebrate this occasion, I had an afternoon repast prepared. Let's adjourn to the courtyard for a bit of sun, fresh air and a glass or two of wine."

It was a delightful meal, and simple it was not. Augustalis asked the kitchen staff to acquire the most succulent, extravagant morsels available anywhere: smoked seafood, marinated meats, mouth-watering desserts and magnificent wine. We talked and ate until dusk.

"There will be no more kitchen duty for you," Augustalis declared. "I informed Eirene that you wouldn't be there today. Tomorrow I will explain why, with the not insignificant addendum that you are no longer serving this household. Now off to your room for a good night's sleep so you will be ready to move into your new home tomorrow."

"All I have is a trunk and a rather large collection of manuscripts, which won't be difficult to pack," I replied happily.

Alexios explained when and where he would meet me, and I prepared to leave.

"Throughout my life you both have given me opportunities to grow and express myself, even as a slave," I acknowledged. "And now you are enabling me to do so even further, in the context of my freedom. I love you ever so much. Bless you."

I arrived at that meeting a slave and left a freedwoman, and it was all their doing.

∞ ∞ ∞

For the first time since I returned from the villa by the sea, I opened the trunk containing the clothing I took on that trip. It smelled of the fragranced oils I packed along with everything else. The aroma transported me to that interlude and the transcendent oneness I experienced with Lucan. It seemed like time out of time.

I vacillated over whether to bring the trunk with me to my new home and finally decided to do so. I felt no more need to avoid those memories. And besides, my suddenly transformed life required a change of clothes.

Also in the trunk, tucked away among silken tunics and soft woolen cloaks, were the gifts I chose for Lucan and never gave to him. The opportunity to present him with these tokens of my love had come and gone.

I requested another trunk where I packed my volumes on Yeshua. They were like old friends – familiar, comforting and always there when I needed them.

I cleaned my room, made sure everything was in place and settled in for a long sleep. This was my last night in Augustalis' home and my initial one as a freedwoman. Tomorrow I would be a different person. Or would I?

That night for the first time since we left for the sea, Lucan came to me in my sleep. It had been so long I thought I was dreaming instead of communing with him.

"Congratulations, my love," he said, radiating joy. "Thanks to two people who love you dearly, you have been freed from the bonds of slavery. I am happier than I have been in years. No, that is not true. I am happier than I have ever been. Your bondage was a travesty from the beginning, as it is with everyone born, sold or captured into slavery. At last you are free."

"I am indeed, although I haven't experienced much change yet," I replied. "No doubt that will occur when I leave this household and move into one of my own. Even then, having a home instead of a room, and one that doesn't belong to someone else, is a foreign concept. Alexios has given me so much."

"Yes he has," Lucan affirmed. "He is unhesitating in his desire to help you and unconditional in his caring. Reciprocity is not relevant to him. I can learn a great deal from him. He is far more enlightened than I and more thoughtful as well."

"But you are providing for my daily needs," I reminded him. "Without that I would be cooking again in someone else's home to support myself. They might not be as kind and generous as Augustalis. I would be free but in worse circumstances than before. You saved me from that fate."

"It's the least I can do," Lucan replied. "I wanted to buy your house, but Alexios insisted if word got out that I had done so, everyone would assume you were a kept woman. And as he so astutely observed, since neither you nor I would enjoy the benefits of such an arrangement, we'd best not risk the rumors."

"Thank you for being with me tonight," I responded, preparing to let him go. "Tomorrow is truly a new dawn."

"Graci, your freedom is mine as well," he said lovingly. "I have been captive in my own self-imposed bondage, resentful and victimized. No one forced this on me, as your slavery was imposed upon you. I did it to myself. When Augustalis told me he had permission to free you and decided to do so, it felt like shackles had been torn from my soul. His choice unlocked my heart."

"I am overjoyed to hear this!" I exclaimed. "Oh how I love you."

In that instant we merged as one. We remained in a state of limitlessness love for a long while, revitalizing our unified spirit. Such was the true gift of my freedom, the capacity to love in this way, to join with my beloved even if it was only as we slept in our separate houses. I was free, as was he. I was home, with him.

When we parted, we were no longer the people who came together in spirit earlier that night. Our touchstone was our unfettered love and the oneness that derived from it.

I awoke immediately after he left. Yes, I was liberated from slavery. Equally important, Lucan and I were also released from the spiritual bondage to which we had surrendered our power and optimism.

Then a realization descended upon me like the volcano over Pompeii. I loved Lucan with all my heart from the moment I met him. But my heart had self-imposed restrictions.

It said to me, "You can love him, but . . . ." What followed that last word was crucial. "You can love Lucan, but don't plan on spending your life with him. You can love Lucan, but you can never be his wife. You can love Lucan, but your togetherness will be only temporary. You can love Lucan, but in the end he must serve his larger purpose, which requires him to do his father's bidding. You can love Lucan, but if you expect that love to bring you perpetual happiness, you will be sorely disappointed. You can love Lucan, but really, friendship would be less painful."

I loved him, but it was always in the context of the constraints we faced. I didn't love him with a heart full of limitless love, although I told myself that was so. I loved Lucan within the bounds of self-protection, not joy and abundance.

If instead I told myself, "You can love him, and . . ." I could then affirm, "You can love Lucan, and in doing so you can transcend the worldly restrictions that would otherwise define your life." Or, "You can love Lucan, and in every moment the joy of that love enables your spirit to soar." Or, "You can love Lucan, and your oneness remains strong and steady." Or, "You can love Lucan, and knowing it is unconditional allows divine love to flow to you and through you."

As I was lying in bed contemplating this new understanding, an even more powerful insight penetrated my heart. Lucan was correct when he declared that if I loved him, I could never recommend he agree to an arranged marriage to fulfill his legacy!

He was saying in essence that if I truly loved him, I would argue vehemently for a life with him, however impossible or impractical it might be. But I did the opposite, under the pretext that because I loved him I was liberating him.

How could I have been so misguided?

When I returned from the sea to the punishing alternatives Lucan and I both faced, the joy we shared was ripped away. In its place was my haunting certainty that our togetherness would be both transient and painful. So I struck it down. In a moment of sorrow and weakness, the undercurrent of enslavement that coursed within me overpowered my love for Lucan. It was a tragedy of my own making.

No wonder Lucan stormed out of the room after my insistence that he marry another. No wonder he chose not to see me for seven years. I slammed and locked the door on our love to protect my vulnerable heart. I gave him no choice but to enter into a loveless, if respectful, marriage. In the interim I remained stubbornly self-sufficient, convinced I had done the noble thing.

I told myself that my love for Lucan was the consummate expression of my ability to render slavery irrelevant in my life. But that was a fabrication. I was in bondage after all to our hopeless situation. Worse, my own slavery had slain my ability to love freely.

That is the truth, declared as clearly as I can state it.

Lucan visited me as we slept that prophetic night, and as we came together the chains around my heart finally fell away.

Afterward, half awake and half in meditation, I received life-altering revelations about what held me back until that moment. I couldn't enter into my new life as a freedwoman still in spiritual if not physical bondage. To be truly free I must recognize and release what confined me – imprisoned me, really – since my birth.

I remembered being a small child needing my mother's love and experiencing only rejection. I felt profound compassion for that little girl. I recalled growing older, no longer dependent on my mother for my survival yet still desiring her love. I recollected becoming independent of my mother, almost but not quite impervious to her abuse. Even then I longed for a mother who loved me. Aware of the futility of that desire, I did what was necessary to survive. I fortified the wall around my heart.

I wondered about my inability to see Alexios as anything other than a brother or a friend. No doubt the lack of love flowing from me to him was a function of my history with my mother. Although he loved me unhesitatingly and defied his parents when they refused to agree to our marriage, I felt almost nothing toward him. My ability to love was suffocated by my mother's abuse and her constant reminders that I would always be a worthless slave. Even Alexios' steadfast devotion couldn't kindle a tiny spark within my heart.

Throughout that night I reviewed my life with a new perceptiveness. A veil over my inner knowing had been lifted, and I was able to see myself clearly for the first time. The vast sorrow within me began to dissipate.

I forgave and released, cried and cleansed, swept away the storms in my spirit and filled myself with light. I would take nothing with me into the dawn of the new day, and the beginning of my new life, that I didn't absolutely choose to keep.

Bondage in all its forms would no longer demarcate who I was.

Freedom in all of its manifestations would become my reality.

∞ ∞ ∞

By morning I was ready to depart. I surveyed the small space I called home for over half of my life and gave thanks for the refuge it provided me. Then I placed fresh stalks of lavender on the bed and left.

Alexios was waiting for me. He had a cart ready for my trunks and a strong slave to remove them from my room, load them for transport and take them to my new residence. I was both excited and apprehensive about moving into my own home. I hoped it was small and unassuming, since I needed so little space.

"You look fantastic!" Alexios commented as we made our way through the streets. "Freedom becomes you."

"Actually, I got very little sleep last night," I reported. "I was busy letting go of every aspect of my former life that I don't want to drag into my new one."

"No wonder you are so radiant," he noted. "Congratulations on being the architect of your real freedom from slavery."

"Thank you for understanding that," I replied. "There is the freedom others grant to you, and then there is the freedom you grant yourself. After receiving the former I engaged in the latter, quite thoroughly I might add."

"Here it is," Alexios announced, unable to contain his excitement.

"Where?" I asked. We stopped in front of an enclosed domus too grand to be mine. It was only a few blocks from Augustalis' estate on Palatine Hill. Aristocratic residences in that neighborhood were exceptionally crafted and extremely expensive.

"Here," Alexios repeated, inserting a heavy iron key into the gate. When it swung open, he held his hand out for me to enter. On the other side of a vestibule was an immaculately maintained central courtyard featuring ornamental pools and a profusion of flowers. My first thought was that I could spend endless days in this very spot, reading and pruning and meditating.

"Alexios, this is too much for me," I objected, embarrassed at his extravagance. "You can't possibly put the deed to this home in my name."

"But I have, and it won't be undone," he replied merrily. "Graci, you are already overwhelmed, and I haven't even shown you the inside!"

He took my hand and led me to the main reception room. Two couches facing each other were covered in cushions of every hue. Their bronze end supports were carved into the head of a horse and the bust of Cupid. Comfortable chairs and small tables completed the seating area.

"What a relaxed place to sit and talk," I commented. "And this dining area is so inviting, I can imagine a good meal and scintillating conversation lasting well into the night."

"With you involved, it will be more than merely a good meal," Alexios quipped. "Come, let me take you to your suite of rooms."

"Suite of rooms!" I exclaimed, overjoyed. "You have transformed my life, and I promise to embrace it with every last shred of my liberated heart and soul."

The suite consisted of a large bedroom with an adjoining sitting room and a library. On the other side of the bedroom was a bathroom complete with a sunken white marble tub and a mosaic floor featuring Neptune accompanied by frolicking nymphs.

Gossamer sea green linen curtains complemented the aquamarine, cream, gold and turquoise bedcovers and pillows. Tables inlaid with silver, ivory and glass accented the seating areas and frescoes. Intricate mosaics on the floors highlighted scenes from Greek literature and mythology. I recognized Agamemnon and Cassandra immediately, so powerfully was their story brought to life. Not a hint of ostentation marred the expertly crafted rooms and furnishings. I would be comfortable here.

In one corner of the bedroom was a shrine with bronzes of Lares, spirits of the ancestors of the house, and Venus, goddess of love. Silver plaques of Jupiter and Genius to protect home and family hung on the wall above the shrine. An oil lamp glowed in honor of the gods and goddesses safeguarding my new nest.

I thought of Yeshua and invited him to join the congregation of spirits. All were welcome.

Alexios interrupted my reverie, explaining. "My suite is on the opposite side of the courtyard. I have furnished it with everything I need. It is a relief to have my own place to stay whenever I am in town."

He showed me around his quarters. The suite had the same configuration as mine, but the furnishings were massive and masculine, exactly his taste. Ancient artifacts he brought back from his travels throughout the Empire were everywhere. He was a citizen of the known world, and he celebrated its diverse cultural histories.

"Finally, I will show you the guest rooms, vegetable and herb garden, staff quarters and last but not least, the kitchen, pantry and bakery," he offered. "I won't subject you to the hypocaust, although I assure you after my close inspection that you are now the proud owner of a superbly constructed central heating system. It will keep the house, and not incidentally your bath water, at a perfect temperature."

"No more chilly winter nights?" I asked playfully. "How will I ever survive?"

We finished the tour of the house, during which I met the staff of five. I didn't need five people to take care of one house. But this was Augustalis' doing, and I was resolved not to object. Each one was well spoken and anxious to know how I could be served. I suggested we discuss it later in the day.

"Tell me how you found this place," I inquired of Alexios as we explored the garden.

"After we talked when I was here last, I was determined to convince my grandfather that he should release the restriction he imposed upon Augustalis," he recalled. "I was also confident that given the choice, Augustalis would grant your freedom.

"For years I considered purchasing a residence in Rome. It is such an active crossroads for trade, I wanted to set up a portion of my business here and not travel quite so much. Then it occurred to me that perhaps one location could become a residence for us both.

"I happened upon this estate as I was perusing the neighborhood. The owner, an elderly widower with no heirs, was preparing to move permanently to his country villa. The moment I stepped into the courtyard, I knew this place would suit my needs.

"I offered to buy it along with whatever furnishings he didn't want to take with him. We agreed on a price, and I gave him ample time to move out. Since I spend my life negotiating trade deals, I am accustomed to making expedient decisions.

"After my grandfather gave me the letter for Augustalis, it occurred to me to put the house in your name when I completed the purchase. I wanted you to feel secure in your new life, and that starts with having a home of your own. The previous owner took most of the furniture from his suite and left everything else. I spent a few days selecting what I wanted for my quarters, and it was done."

"You make it sound so simple," I remarked, "but I know the trouble and expense that were required."

"Really it was no trouble," Alexios assured me. "This was the only property I looked at. And as for the expense, I made my grandfather's business appreciably more successful and profitable than it was before. Money isn't an issue."

"How can I ever thank you?" I asked, knowing I could never repay him.

"Your gratitude, my dear Graci, is more than enough," Alexios assured me. "I need only to know you are living here happily. That is ample recompense for me."

"My happiness has already taken up residence in no uncertain terms," I reported. "In fact, I feel a major burst of joy coming on. Shall we retire to the shade of the courtyard for some joy-filled refreshment?"

"Unfortunately, I have to leave for a meeting with a new trade partner," Alexios replied. "But I will return in time for dinner. It may not be as delectable as your dishes, but it should at least be edible. And don't you dare wander into the kitchen to help because you discover you have time on your hands! Settle in, explore the place, take a nap and I will see you later."

"Good advice from a perpetually perceptive man," I laughed.

I had taken a luxurious bath with fragrant oils and donned one of the tunics from the trunk when a servant knocked on the door to my suite.

"You have a visitor," he said softly through the door.

"Who is it?" I queried.

"He gave me no name," the servant replied.

It occurred to me that only two men besides Alexios knew I was here. Either one would be a pleasure to see. Besides, I was refreshed, relaxed and ready to entertain my first guest.

"I will be there shortly," I said. "Please ask him to wait in the reception area."

I retrieved three gold bangles from the trunk, slipped them on my wrist and made my way to the foyer. Lucan was standing there, looking uncharacteristically uncomfortable.

"Welcome, Lucan!" I greeted him as I swept in. "Can you believe this? I hope so, because I cannot."

"Seeing you glide in here wearing that particular tunic sent me directly to those weeks we spent by the sea," he noted. "Only you are here, with your freedom, in your own home, looking positively stunning."

"My slave clothes are being burned as we speak," I announced. "And the tunics I packed in the trunk when I departed from Augustalis' villa were my only other alternative. It's good to see you, Lucan."

"I can't tell you how good it is for me to be with you here," Lucan effused. "I could hardly wait to come by. How about giving me a tour?"

As I showed him the house, he commented on numerous amenities that escaped me on my initial explorations with Alexios. It was an exquisite home, made with the best materials and superb artistry.

"This residence is known for its sophistication and impeccable taste," Lucan noted. "The former owner is a man of great wealth and impressive modesty. He had this home built for his wife, whom he loved dearly, as they were growing older. She was in ill health, and he wanted her to have a serene sanctuary."

"How do you know so much about this property?" I asked.

"I live just around the corner," he revealed. "I used to stop by when it was being built. The owner and I talked whenever he happened to be here supervising the construction. He was a remarkable man, gracious and engaging, the consummate gentleman. After he and his wife moved in I visited them occasionally. What an extraordinary couple they were, still deeply in love after forty years of marriage."

"So you don't need to be shown around," I observed.

"Not exactly," Lucan admitted.

"Did you have anything to do with Alexios' finding this house?" I asked.

"He found it on his own," Lucan assured me. "But having visited me often, he was fully aware I lived close by."

"Hidden agenda, perhaps?" I teased.

"Anything is possible," he admitted.

"Shall we sit, then, and recount our blessings as old friends?" I offered.

"I prefer sitting and celebrating your much deserved freedom," Lucan asserted.

"That, too," I agreed as we entered the receiving room.

"It's hard to believe this beautiful home I watched being built is now yours!" Lucan exclaimed. "No wonder I took such an interest in it. I wanted to be sure it was done right, though I certainly didn't know why. This room is lovely. Can you imagine a more inviting space for entertaining guests?"

"And who might those guests be?" I asked, unaccustomed to the idea of socializing.

"Well, let's start with the one who presented himself uninvited this afternoon," Lucan replied. We settled into the two couches, and a servant arrived with a silver platter of exotic foods and a carafe of red wine.

"I had these sent over this morning, in case the kitchen hadn't yet been stocked for afternoon conversations with friends," Lucan revealed. "No doubt you will be taking inventory in the pantry as soon as I leave."

"Or tomorrow, if I am feeling particularly lazy," I laughed.

"I want to explain how you can access an account with funds I set aside for your living expenses," Lucan declared, changing the subject. "A monthly payment will be made to you along with additional funds should you need them. I also established an ancillary account so you need never be concerned about supporting yourself. You have done enough work for more than one lifetime."

"I am grateful for your thoughtfulness and generosity," I said with all sincerity.

Then as I was preparing to go on, Lucan interrupted me. "Love is what underlies my actions, Graci. I prayed for an opportunity to care for you somehow. But there seemed to be no direct way to do so as long as you were in bondage as a slave. It pleases me to do this for you as an expression of my love."

Tears were welling up inside me. The man who spoke those words was the one who came to me in my sleep the night before. His penetrating gaze expressed his own experience of our reuniting. Still we remained where we were seated, as if held there by an invisible force as powerful as the one that made our merging possible.

I cried. He sat looking at me with such empathy, I cried all the more.

"It looks as if another soggy toga is in our future," he said, breaking the silence. He bounded across the room, sat down beside me, swept me into his arms, offered a length of his toga and whispered, "Go ahead and sob all you want. My toga and I are at your disposal. It's a good time to release, let's see, how many years' worth of tears?"

"I lost count," I muttered through the ensuing waterfalls.

"Well I didn't," he replied, holding me closer. "Cry a few tears for me while you are at it." Then he brought my head to his chest. His arms enveloped me in a comfortable embrace. He was ready to remain there for the duration. And so was I.

Every time I emerged from a torrent of tears and regained a semblance of composure, he kissed the top of my head, which launched another waterfall.

"It seems that the top of your head is allergic to my kisses," he chuckled. "Perhaps I should try something else. The tip of your nose?" At which point he planted a flutter of kisses precisely there.

If kisses on the tip of one's nose can be erotic, these were. They went straight to my core. I felt as if I were back in the carriage with him, ready to make love in every conceivable way, only this time without the cramped quarters and rutted roads.

I pulled away from him, just far enough to look into his eyes. All I could see in them was love, the same love that brought us together initially. If anything changed it was that our love was even more profound than before. I let his love flow to me then spill over as tears of joy. He found a dry spot on the front of his toga, and I had another good cry.

"If I didn't know you better, I would deem this meeting to be an utter disaster," he mused. "But then, I do know you almost as much as I love you. And I have determined from extensive experience that the most unequivocal way you express how glad you are to see me is when you present my toga with a river of tears. Actually, there are other ways you show me you are glad to see me, but under the circumstances I am content to accept your tears as a token of your ardor."

I wanted to take him to my room and make love with him for three days, at least. But Alexios would be arriving, and Lucan had a wife to go home to, and it wouldn't necessarily be the most perfect experience for either of us. After so long I was unwilling to settle for less.

"I can barely keep from ripping those flimsy silk layers off your body and loving you right here in plain sight," he admitted. "And if my lips stray to yours, there will be no stopping me. I leave it up to you. You are free and I am married. I am perfectly willing to treat my marriage as almost everyone else in Rome does – an accommodation requiring no commitment of fidelity. Though you must know, when I married I told myself I would break my marriage vows only with you. Thus far I have broken them with no one."

There was so much to say to him, and yet nothing to say at all. I took my time, willing myself to speak truthfully.

"Last night, when you visited me in our sleep," I paused, and he nodded in recognition, "a most profound thing happened. It wasn't just that you came to me after not having done so since your marriage, or that we merged into sublime oneness once again. That alone would be blessing enough.

"But afterward I experienced a transformation and a revelation. The transformation was like a rebirth into a new freedom to love you, one I previously withheld from myself. There were no barriers to my love for you, no shackles around my heart to protect me from the pain of our impossible, hopeless, desperately problematic love. I was able to love you with every particle of my being, and all those particles vibrated with the power of my love."

"That is more than I deserve," Lucan whispered, "but I accept every bit of it."

"Then a revelation arrived," I continued. "I realized you were correct when you told me that tragic day in Augustalis' office that if I loved you I would never urge you to marry another. I believed all along that your statement was an overreaction to the terrible dilemma you faced. But you were correct. I didn't love you, at least not as I do now. I loved you sincerely but not wholly, for my slavery limited my ability to love."

"You loved me as much as you were capable of loving at the time," Lucan observed. "I could say the same for myself."

"I never anticipated being freed from bondage," I said. "But you know that. Until yesterday my life was framed by my slavery. What I experienced as unconditional love was subtly and yet significantly conditioned by the lovelessness from which slavery derives. Coupled with my mother's rejection, I built an impenetrable barrier around my heart. I couldn't really love you.

"You said to me once that you felt you were more of a slave than I was because you allowed circumstances to define you. Well, I allowed my slavery to define the degree to which I could give and receive love. I wasn't capable of loving you in the way you deserved. For that I am infinitely sorry."

"Oh, my darling Graci," Lucan replied, holding me close. "I was in my own bondage to my family's legacy and my father's demands of his oldest son. Just as the law allows people to be bought and sold as slaves, it enslaves others by the requirements of inheritance. Granted, it is enslavement brought on by wealth and privilege, but it limits freedom nonetheless.

"I was as bound by my father's expectations and my own fears of who I would be if I were disinherited, just as you were bound by Augustalis' commitment to Alexios' grandfather. And now we have both been freed. You are no longer a slave, and I am no longer under my father's rule."

"Why aren't you?" I asked, surprised.

"My father died a month ago," Lucan disclosed. "Despite my sadness at losing him, I felt liberated from his iron-fisted control over me. I am the patriarch of the family now. Although that means little to me, it has brought a degree of self-determination unavailable to me earlier.

"The financial account I set up for you is from a small one my father held in trust for me, to be made available upon his death. It is only fitting that those funds go to you, so you can live in comfort."

"You came to me last night because of your own liberation," I realized.

"Mine and yours," Lucan replied. "It was time for both of us to experience each other without restraints."

Just then Alexios burst into the room. He registered no surprise at seeing me nestled into Lucan on the sofa.

"Don't move, you two," he said casually. "You look eminently comfortable and happier than I have seen either of you since . . . . Hmmm. You are happier than I have ever seen you. Do I detect an onslaught of unfettered joy about to descend upon the room?"

"*Unfettered* is the operative word for many things," Lucan commented jovially.

"I daresay if it gets out of hand, I might have to reconsider my plans to sail to Britannia next week," Alexios retorted. "It would be difficult to leave such exuberance."

"Then by all means, stay," laughed Lucan. "With you adding your own unfettered joy, Rome might develop a terminal case of goodwill and generosity. It's worth changing your plans to see what happens."

"Unfortunately I can't delay," Alexios replied. "Just this afternoon I completed arrangements with Rome's largest exporter of olive oil to trade his product for bronze and iron. Far be it from me to keep the Empire from profiting from its conquests."

"Or you from your own cargo ships," Lucan quipped.

"Precisely," Alexios responded sardonically.

It was fascinating to watch Lucan and Alexios converse so amiably. Although I had known them both a long time, I had never seen them together. They were like brothers, enjoying each other's company. Incredibly, their friendship survived the peculiar fact that they loved the same woman.

Then another insight presented itself to me. Whereas Alexios' love was an expression of his desire to assure I was cared for, Lucan's was born of oneness that transcended lifetimes. They were different manifestations of love, harmonious rather than competitive.

"Shall I leave you for the evening?" Alexios offered. "Or would you two like to join me for dinner?"

"I must depart shortly," Lucan noted, "but we would be happy to share some of this repast with you. We haven't touched it."

"I can't imagine why!" Alexios chuckled, and we dug into the assortment of delicacies Lucan provided. Everything was superb, and the wine was extraordinary.

"Here's to freedom!" Alexios cheered.

"And a roof over my head," I added.

"And everlasting love," Lucan chimed in.

"And everlasting love," all three of us repeated, toasting in high spirits.

We chatted informally, as if this were something we did often. I had a compelling sense of family with these two men. It went way back, long before this lifetime, and perhaps forward even further.

∞ ∞ ∞

I spent the next few weeks getting to know the servants, helping them learn what I desired of them, stocking the shelves in the pantry and establishing routines that worked for everyone. One by one they expressed how much they appreciated my respectful treatment of them. I explained that I was only recently a freedwoman, after which they inevitably replied, "But how could that be? You know how to read and calculate numbers."

My response was the same to each of them: "I have been fortunate indeed."

Since Lucan referred to the fund his father left him as being small, I assumed the account he set up for me would be adequate but not extravagant. I wasn't interested in extravagance, anyway. My needs were minimal.

When I met with the man in charge of the account in order to withdraw funds for food and household goods, I asked how much was available. He told me the sum, which was shockingly large. I assumed it was my annual allotment.

"It is your monthly allocation," he clarified, too supercilious for my taste.

"I couldn't spend that much in six months, let alone one," I told him.

"You'll just have to try," he said dryly. "I don't want Lucan to reprimand me for withholding anything when he sees the total growing inordinately each month."

"Another gold bangle might reduce the balance sufficiently," I mused. I didn't need to spend it on reading material, since the library in my wing of the house had shelves of manuscripts unknown to me.

"You'd need to purchase eight or ten of them a month, I'm afraid," he replied. "Perhaps you should learn what every Roman woman of privilege knows, which is that there is plenty more where that came from."

How odd, I thought, to have too much money to spend. I would let it accumulate, and if Lucan wondered why I wasn't enjoying it more I would remind him of how much I love simplicity.

I invited Eirene and Gaiana for a visit. The day they were to arrive, I felt strangely uncomfortable. My old clothes were long gone, and the only garments I had to wear were much too fine. I selected the least impressive combination, made sure the food being prepared would be a special treat and waited to greet them in the courtyard. They arrived early, just as I sat down on a bench.

"The gods be praised!" exclaimed Eirene. "I'm so happy for you, I think I'll burst!"

That was all it took for my self-consciousness to vanish. The three of us hugged and chatted away like long-lost sisters.

"Guess who got your room?" Gaiana asked as I was showing them around the house.

"The one who deserves it the most, of course," I laughed. "I hope you didn't come across too many cobwebs when you moved in."

"There were no cobwebs to be found," Gaiana replied. "But the most unusual thing happens at night while I am sleeping. I feel as if a kind, loving man is visiting me, though I have no one in my life like your Lucan."

"It's probably the spirit of someone you have loved, who continues to cherish you," I suggested.

"You speak with such confidence, I can only assume you and Lucan used to meet that way," she observed.

"We did at first, but not after he married," I revealed. "Then during my last night in that room, he returned in his sleep to visit me. It was a wonderful gift. I am so glad something similar is happening to you."

"If you keep this up, one of these days you will run off with him, whoever and wherever he is," Eirene chided Gaiana good-naturedly. "We will check on you only to discover you have disappeared."

"If I do, you will know I am blissfully happy," Gaiana laughed.

"And you aren't now?" Eirene asked, pretending shock.

"Not blissfully so," Gaiana retorted.

I had an enjoyable afternoon with my two friends. We reminisced and celebrated the many years we scurried around in the kitchen together. It was a sisterhood of the highest order, and I was thankful they were still in my life.

As they were leaving, I said to them, "We should do this often. Please come back soon."

That comment was met by an uncomfortable silence. Gaiana looked down at her feet, and Eirene was searching for what to say.

"You forget we are not free to visit whenever we want," Eirene said. "But as often as we can arrange it, we will happily accept your invitation."

"In the spirit of the moment I was inconceivably thoughtless," I apologized. "I would love to see you both, any time."

An impenetrable barrier existed between those who were slaves and those who were free to live their lives as they chose. An agreement between two men had kept me in bondage, and a third man enabled it to be rescinded. A letter and a subsequent choice set me free. That was the only difference between Eirene and Gaiana, and me.

During my bath that night I scrubbed away another layer of residue from my enslavement, a tenacious one that caused me to question my worthiness to be freed. It seemed so arbitrary. Decisions by others enabled my freedom. Similar ones were not forthcoming for Eirene and Gaiana.

I pondered the paradox. Just because they didn't deserve to remain in slavery was no indication I didn't deserve to live otherwise. I was worthy of it, and so were they, even though I was free and they were not.

I slept that night more at peace than ever. When I awoke, I had a new understanding of my freedom. The tides of my bondage ran deep and were mostly hidden. I needed to let them rise to the surface so I could acknowledge and release them. It was my responsibility to keep exploring the depths of my enslavement. My freedom would be gained one layer at a time.

In the end I was the only one who could set me free.

∞ ∞ ∞

I had been in my new home a month. I was about to leave on a few errands when a servant announced I had a female visitor. No name was provided. I assumed it was a neighbor presenting herself after having decided that even though I was only a freedwoman, I didn't represent a significant decline in the social status of the surrounding area.

I met her in the courtyard. "Welcome," I said cordially. "I am Graci. What can I do for you?"

"That question has quite an involved answer," she replied. "May we go inside?"

"Certainly," I agreed, turning to the servant and requesting that light refreshments be brought to us in the sitting room.

My guest was a striking woman, obviously from the upper classes. She had the self-assurance of one who grew up with wealth and experienced even more of it in adulthood. I wondered what complicated story, or possible complication, she was planning to reveal to me. We settled ourselves and I waited for her to speak.

"I am Euphemia, Lucan's wife," she stated.

My cheeks flushed and my throat went dry. Rather than saying anything in response, I nodded in recognition.

"You have seen him since you moved in here?" she inquired.

"Once, the afternoon I arrived," I told her. "He stopped by to welcome me, and then he, Alexios and I visited for a while." I wanted to imply the truth, that we were not engaged in a tryst that day.

"And you haven't been with him since?" she persisted.

I was beginning to feel she was interrogating me without my permission. I half expected her to accuse me of myriad infamies, seductions and perhaps even a few depravities. Such is the predilection of the jealous wife. I considered asserting she should ask her husband instead of me. But I found a reservoir of grace instead.

"No, he hasn't returned," I replied.

"I thought not," she commented. "I could tell by the way he has been acting."

"What do you mean?" I asked.

"Distracted and very much like a man in love with someone else," she revealed.

I wanted to say, "And that is different from before?" But again I refrained. I hadn't yet discerned her purpose. I wasn't sure if she intended to confront me or confide in me.

"I've known all along that he loved you," she continued. "I was informed of your journey to the sea right after Lucan was initially told to marry me. At the time I was relieved you went off together, since I hadn't met him and wasn't inclined to marry.

"Then his father called him back to Rome under the pretense of illness and served up his ultimatum. Lucan and I were unexpectedly thrown together. Neither of us was ready for that turn of events, but for different reasons."

"Understandably," I inserted.

"Before we were married Lucan requested a private meeting with me," Euphemia recalled. "We had attended a few celebratory banquets together but spent no time alone. He explained how much he loved you, the terrible impossibility of your situation and why he agreed to marry me. I told him my father forced me into marriage as well, and I wanted it as little as he did.

"Then he did a most remarkable thing. He said that although he may never be able to love me, he would respect me and be as devoted as he could. He also committed to being faithful to me. His fidelity would be a confirmation that marriage without ideal love could still exhibit caring and compassion."

"He gave you all he had to give, which was considerable," I commented.

"Yes it was," Euphemia concurred. "Finally, he acknowledged the necessity of having children, which would require us to make love. He told me he would be affectionate if not rapturous.

"I was too young to appreciate the implications of his revelations, but over time I understood him to be a man of paramount integrity. He never grew to love me, and our experiences in bed were without ardor. But he has been a good husband and an extremely devoted father."

"Do you love him?" I inquired.

"If you are asking whether he is the love of my life, the answer is no," she replied. "Unlike him, it's not because I love another. I don't know what it means to be loved passionately, by Lucan or anyone else. There is no spark between us. We are companions and parents to five children, nothing more.

"And so I come to the point of my visit. I am releasing Lucan to you so you can be lovers once more. I am telling you myself because if you were to hear it from Lucan, you may not believe it to be true."

"Why would you do such a thing?" I questioned.

"I have seen a changed man in the past two months," Euphemia replied. "His father's death was a huge relief to him. I hope you realize the spirit in which I say this. Then soon afterward you were granted your freedom. That second change altered Lucan's outlook entirely. After he visited you here he was in a kind of reverie. I could tell his mind and heart were constantly with you.

"In all the years of our marriage, he never allowed that to happen. I knew he loved you, but he sequestered his feelings. His love was locked away somewhere in his soul. He rarely accessed it, for to do so would only remind him of what he sacrificed with our marriage. I finally comprehended how much he relinquished when he surrendered to his father's demand. I also came to terms with what I forfeited, which was my independence."

"You both experienced unfortunate deprivation," I observed.

"What we sacrificed is appalling," Euphemia affirmed. "Now after having five children, Lucan and I both feel we have done our duty to our families. We haven't made love in years. Since neither of us cares to be physical with each other, I would rather reach an overt agreement with him and be done with it.

"I intend to create my own suite of rooms in our home where I can practice my music. I have turned my back on that great love for too long. I want to sleep alone, spend time in solitude and choose when I interact with the children. It matters not how often I see Lucan. Once a day or once a week would be fine with me."

"You can finally live your life on your own terms," I noted.

"Yes, finally," she agreed. "Please understand I am not angry or resentful, nor do I feel rejected by Lucan. He has taken pains to ensure that isn't the case. It is time for both of us to be happy. I want my privacy, he wants to be with you, and neither of us wants to be with each other."

"Your equanimity is extraordinary," I remarked.

"It was a long time coming, and recent events ushered in the perfect solution for all three of us," Euphemia noted. "This conversation was destined. I haven't suggested anything yet to Lucan. I wanted to talk to you first. If you welcome this arrangement, I will let him know that as far as we are both concerned he can stay here every night if he so chooses. I hope he remains involved in the lives of our children, but they are growing up and need their parents less, anyway."

"I'm convinced you are speaking from the heart," I stated. "If I thought otherwise I would never agree to it. But I can hear the truth in your words. You are proposing a solution that would serve all three of us."

"What I have told you couldn't be more genuine," Euphemia assured me. "As for keeping up appearances, all of Rome talks about Lucan's fidelity. It is quite the exception, you know. They would understand if he returned to you now that he can.

"I am prepared to inform my parents that they dare not denounce Lucan or me when word gets out he is seeing you, which it inevitably will. I will tell them if they do so, I will communicate far and wide the details of my father's infidelities, though that would be news to no one. He is infamous."

I really liked Euphemia. She reminded me a lot of myself. If she weren't the wife of the man I loved, we would most certainly become friends.

"You and I are so similar despite our divergent beginnings," I remarked. "You act on your convictions, a woman of integrity in a city that reifies the opposite. I understand why Lucan speaks so highly of you, and with such affection."

"And I am gratified to know he loves such an accomplished, gracious woman. I only wish," she stopped mid-sentence.

"Wish what?" I encouraged.

"Wish you hadn't been required to endure something as terrible as slavery," she said sadly.

"It was terrible, although I didn't acknowledge how devastating my bondage was until after I was freed," I admitted. "Still, it was no worse than what your families required of you and Lucan. The blessing of your marriage is that the two of you selected kindness over abuse and respect over disregard. You are perfectly matched."

"No, you and Lucan are perfectly matched," she said without a hint of malice. "He and I were merely smart enough to know we must make the best of an arrangement neither of us wanted."

"Euphemia, you say you don't love Lucan, but your coming here today is the consummate act of love," I observed. "It may not be the romantic love many believe is the most legitimate kind between a man and a woman, but you love him nonetheless."

"I do love him the way one loves a loyal friend or a devoted mentor," Euphemia replied. "He has been good to me, and I hope I have reciprocated adequately. Now it is time for us to start a new chapter in our lives, one we choose rather than one chosen for us. I couldn't be more pleased for all three of us."

"Nor could I," I affirmed. "May you find great joy in your solitude and your music, and may you never forget what a generous gesture this meeting represents."

"I haven't played the cithara in years," she noted, "but perhaps when I have regained a measure of skill, I will invite you for a private concert. Then maybe afterward you can meet the children."

"I would be honored," I replied sincerely.

There wasn't much more to say. She told me she would discuss this with Lucan as soon as possible, after which I could expect his absence to come to an immediate halt.

"Very immediate, since he lives just around the corner," she chuckled.

On the chance Euphemia's conversation with Lucan occurred sooner than later, I prepared for his arrival. I took a quick but thorough sponge bath, applied my favorite fragrance and donned a simple robe that opened down the front and tied at the waist. I put away the manuscripts and other items strewn about my suite.

When everything was in order, I met with the manservant in charge of overseeing everyone's duties. I explained to him that I was expecting a visitor and would be entertaining him in my suite for an indefinite period of time, probably a few days. I asked that we be allowed unquestioned privacy and that food, water and wine be left outside the door twice a day. He should signal when the tray was delivered. I also requested that unless a dire emergency occurred, we were not to be disturbed.

His face remained determinedly passive, the mark of an exceptional servant. Nonetheless, I didn't want our conversation to end so impersonally.

"You can expect me to have a permanent smile on my face and be unbearably jovial from now on," I added.

"You know how much we all appreciate our position in this household," he replied. "We would be happy for your happiness and would bear the burden of your joy with a generous measure of joy ourselves."

"If the burden becomes too much, I know exactly what to do to make myself miserable again," I retorted.

He laughed heartily then assured me everything would be done to my specifications. "I will require absolute discretion," he promised. "But would you mind telling me, is your visitor the senator whom you and Alexios call Lucan?"

"It is indeed," I affirmed. "How did you know?"

"Your connection with him was evident the day he paid you a visit to welcome you here," he revealed. "It was clear your friendship went far beyond affection, and we hoped to see him again. But since he never returned, we assumed we were mistaken."

"It's a long story, one I will tell you some day over a full carafe of wine," I offered.

"I would be honored to hear you recount it," he declared, bowing slightly.

We both jumped a bit when a loud knock came from the door. "I'll get it," I said, knowing with every instinct it was Lucan.

"May the gods give you great pleasure and endless peace," the servant replied as he retreated to the kitchen, an evident if private smile on his face.

∞ ∞ ∞

I ran across the courtyard and peered through the filigreed portal to see who was standing outside. Just as Lucan was about to knock again, I unbolted the lock and swung the door wide open. He strode across the threshold, whisked me into his arms and twirled me around excitedly. Then without a word he put me down, closed and locked the gate, swept me into his arms again and carried me off to my suite.

I had left the door ajar. He shoved it aside with his foot, stepped into the room, closed the door with the same foot, went straight to the bed and laid me down in the middle of it.

He stood beside the bed for a moment, looking at me with eyes that were both tender and devouring. Then he reached down, untied the belt at my waist and opened my robe from top to bottom. I was naked underneath.

"I forgot how exquisite you are," he murmured after a quick intake of breath, "or maybe it would be more accurate to say I didn't allow myself to remember."

"Come here you great big, marvelous man," I said, reaching up to him, "and share my bed with me for the first of thousands of days and nights."

He sat down on the bed and leaned in to kiss me. His lips were delicious on mine, his tongue a delight. I wrapped my arms around his neck, and we let our lips communicate what we held back for so long. My entire body tingled in response. I wanted his hands all over me, his wicked tongue tantalizing me. But for the moment I was happy to settle for his kisses. They were glorious. Soon they became more languid and less urgent.

"I want to express my love in every way and take pleasure in your doing the same," he whispered. "Now we can celebrate the blessing of our love without restraint. This is the moment of our sacred union."

"My dearly beloved Lucan, I have hungered for you far too long," I replied, emotion spilling from my voice. "I want to experience our love with the certainty there will be no ensuing sadness, no interminable times apart, no conditions separating us. I can now receive you with a happy heart."

He began exploring my body with slow caresses and feather-light kisses. The heat of intimacy grew within me, melting into deep relaxation. And for the very first time I knew what lovers share when they are together without a care in the world.

His hand moved down to my belly, massaging it lovingly. I raised my hips in response to his touch. The quickening inside me was intensifying into erotic urgency. He gave me pleasure slowly then more insistently until I gave up trying to hold back my climax.

"It seems you haven't misplaced your capacity to lose yourself with my touch," he remarked, grinning. "Then again, you could probably lose yourself with just a kiss or two. Do you have any idea what a magnificently, phenomenally, irredeemably great lover you are?"

"All I did was lie back and let you do the work," I replied, deeply contented. "You are the outrageously great lover. I am simply the grateful recipient of your gentlemanly largess. Speaking of which, I detect substantial largess under the folds of your toga. It couldn't possibly be that the fabric is all bunched up there, could it?"

My hand grasped the bulge. Sure enough he was as hard as steel.

"I thought not," I said with satisfaction. "That endlessly draped garment of yours must be undraped immediately, or I will have to go hunting further myself."

Lucan kissed me on the nose, hopped out of bed and disrobed with dispatch. He stood before me, gorgeous and huge in just the right place.

"How wonderful that you are prepared to make me even happier than I was a few moments ago," I observed. "I am in danger of becoming the most permanently satisfied woman in the city, unless you want to count the wife of Marcus Leviticus, who I hear has taken so many lovers she will have to leave town to find a fresh supply."

"You will find all the supply you need right here," he laughed. "I am about to convince you of that once and for all. Well, most likely not just once."

Our bodies merged in exquisite oneness, bringing me to absolute surrender. I let go of everything that held me back before and made room for his love.

Tears erupted from my eyes. I wept tears of joy, relief and release; tears of oneness; tears of coming home to my love.

Lucan raised himself slightly, still on top of me, and kissed them away.

"I am forever doomed to making you cry," he murmured. "I would supply you with a corner of my toga, but that would require me to leave you. And I want to stay right where I am, inside you. So you will just have to make do with my kisses, and I will drink of your salty tears."

Lucan and I didn't leave my suite for five days. We read, took baths, napped, talked, massaged each other, laughed and romped playfully. But mostly we loved each other, ecstatically and thoroughly, redefining the boundaries of hedonism.

On the last morning, when we knew he must leave, Lucan reached for a small item he set aside soon after his arrival. It was the carved box he brought with him to the sea. My gifts to him were waiting as well.

"It was like a dagger to my heart when I opened the trunk you packed for me at Augustalis' villa and saw this box," Lucan revealed. "I was so cavalier about our time together, I neglected to give this gift to you. Then today I understood that was not the time for you to receive it. Now the moment has come."

He handed me the box. It was ancient, intricately carved with metaphysical symbols. It had traveled long distances, perhaps for eons, and finally found its way to me.

"I discovered this at an antiquarian shop," Lucan recalled. "Although it is neither exquisite nor extremely valuable, I knew it was yours." He paused. "I may be legally married to another, but I am joined in spirit with you. Please honor me, and our most sacred union, by wearing what is inside."

I opened the lid. The box contained a ring of gold and platinum woven together, engraved with hieroglyphs in an unknown language. I was holding the ring, studying it closely, when I had a feeling I had worn it before.

"Lucan," I whispered, almost inaudibly. "I believe this ring was mine in another lifetime."

"It was," he affirmed. "I gave it to you to commemorate our love and the sanctity of our oneness. Now I understand why I couldn't present it to you until now. We have been celebrating our eternal union these past few days. This ring honors the timelessness of our love."

He reached for the ring. Placing it on my finger, he vowed, "Graci, I love you now and everlastingly. I devote my life to our love and to you. This ring unites us with the strongest bond of all, which is our eternal love."

I pledged, "Lucan, I love you with the fire of the feminine. May our love bring us ecstasy and contentment in equal measure, and may we be ever mindful of how precious and steadfast our union has been, is, and will be."

We kissed with passion and compassion, sealing our infinite union.

"I found something for you as well before our trip to the sea," I recalled. "When I saw these two gifts, I knew they must be yours."

I walked over to a table by the window and picked up a leather pouch and a large wooden box. I handed the pouch to Lucan first. He reached inside and pulled out a gold chain.

Its links were long and straight, connected with eyelets, a tiny version of what surveyors use to measure distance.

Holding the chain in his hand, Lucan closed his eyes. "Incredibly, you found something for me from the same lifetime we shared when you wore the ring," he intuited. "This was mine, and it was most precious to me. It represents the role I played in bringing about sustainable peace after Rome invaded and conquered Britannia."

"Do you remember anything else?" I asked, anxious to learn more.

"I was the son of a king, and you and I were married," he said slowly. "Incongruously we befriended the officer who led the legions in the south then accompanied him when he returned to Rome. I became a diplomat and a businessman. We lived primarily in Rome, though we returned to Britannia many times."

"Vespasian was the officer!" I exclaimed. "Years ago when Augustalis selected an account of his life for me to read, his story seemed uncannily familiar to me. I have a feeling your second gift has something to do with Vespasian."

I handed Lucan the box. He opened the lid and gasped when he saw the gold goblet tucked inside. He lifted it, fingering its intertwined Celtic knots and admiring its craftsmanship. "This belonged to Alexios. We knew him in that lifetime."

"We were dear friends then as well," I affirmed, then paused to assure I was discerning new information clearly. "I think he was Vespasian."

Lucan's face expressed the shock of recognition. "Yes he was," he confirmed. "That explains so much, including his propensity to return to Britannia on trading missions."

"The three of us were together before, here in Rome as well as Britannia. Who knows what other lifetimes we've shared?" I mused. "Lucan, this is just a tiny fragment of a story that stretches beyond this incarnation. Everything links and relates. Our love is a reflection of what united us before, and no doubt it will bring us together again."

"Hopefully with less drama," Lucan remarked wryly. "I would be content living an ordinary life with you, where our only concern is how to make each other happier than we were the day before."

"That may indeed be possible," I conjectured. "But in the meantime we are accomplishing that quite admirably right now."

Lucan stood to go. We embraced with the deep gratitude of two lovers reunited. Rather than being our last embrace, this would be just one in an expanse of them defining our future together.

"I'll return soon," Lucan replied. "Until then I'll miss you every minute I am away."

I walked him through the courtyard and to the gate. I did so mostly to avoid being suddenly without him in the quarters we had shared. I also wanted to alert the staff that at long last we had emerged from my suite.

∞ ∞ ∞

Augustalis remained a dear friend after I left his service. Initially I saw little of him, most likely because he wanted to give me time to settle into my home and my redefined existence. Then one day he arrived unannounced, accompanied by servants laden with the most precious foods available in all of Rome.

"I sent Gaiana out to procure nothing but the best for you," he explained casually. "Not that I think you are spending time in the kitchen. At least, I hope not. It was more for you to enjoy without having to plan, purchase or prepare yourself. You can count on these deliveries at least once a month, although I can't promise I'll always ride along with them."

"Augustalis, it's so good to see you!" I exclaimed. "I've been on quite an adventure since I departed from your household. Do you have time to hear all about it?"

"I have an open calendar," he assured me.

"Good," I replied. "Then let me select a few things from this cornucopia of delicacies you brought. I will have them arranged impressively on trays, just for you of course, and we can adjourn to the sitting room. Or would you like to see the house first?"

"Since I've already toured the place, I suggest we start with a repast," he replied exuberantly. "When Alexios decided to make it your home, I gave it my stamp of approval. That was completely unnecessary. He managed on his own to select the perfect place for you."

"And for him, whenever he is in Rome," I reminded Augustalis.

"You look wonderful, by the way," he commented. "Without question, liberation is good for your soul."

"I have you and Alexios to thank for that," I replied.

"Not Lucan as well?" he asked.

"More indirectly," I agreed. "You and Alexios were the agents of my freedom. And the three of you together released me from any concerns regarding how I might survive on my own."

"You could have done so, though it wouldn't have been easy," Augustalis noted. "Each of us holds you in such high regard, there was no question about our doing everything possible to keep you from being cast out into the world, free but without resources. Are the servants working out for you?"

"They are indeed, and they even seem to be discreet," I commented lightly. "Although having been in service to a household myself, I have no doubt they talk about everything they see and hear. How are things going in Eirene's kitchen, by the way?"

"You are sorely missed," Augustalis told me. "I can't decide if it's more by those in the kitchen or the guests who attend our endless stream of social functions. Everyone is aware that banquets at my house aren't as spectacular as they once were because you are now a freedwoman. Word travels fast."

"Especially since I'm living in the neighborhood," I mused. "Did any of your guests object to your decision to release me on the grounds you were doing them an unconscionable disservice?"

"Yes, and on more than one occasion," Augustalis chuckled. "I simply told them they could take their gluttony elsewhere."

We talked amicably, enjoying the marvelous assortment of foods he brought.

"And how is Lucan?" Augustalis asked finally.

I told him about the visit from Euphemia and the time Lucan and I spent together immediately afterward. He listened intently.

"You two were given your freedom simultaneously," Augustalis observed. "Lucan was freed first by his father's death and then after your arrival here, by Euphemia. May I reveal something to you?"

"Of course," I replied.

"One of the reasons I was so anxious to grant your freedom when I received the letter from Alexios' grandfather was that I knew Lucan's father had just died," Augustalis explained. "Had he not, I might have delayed the decision. It would have been a terrible fate for you to be living in this house, a stone's throw from Lucan, with his father constantly looking over his shoulder. As for Euphemia, I didn't anticipate she would be so open-minded, though I'm not surprised. She was always a perceptive observer and an independent thinker, not unlike you."

"I too noticed our similarities," I admitted. "It's interesting that Lucan ended up with two women who are so alike but from such different circumstances."

"One of life's great mysteries, which most likely won't be explained until the afterlife, if in fact one exists," Augustalis commented.

"I am confident that one exists," I replied. "We'll have one fabulous celebration once we have all gathered there."

Then my tone changed. "Thank you, Augustalis, for all you have done to look out for me from the day I left Greece with you. I couldn't have asked for a more caring person to come into my life at that time, and it was all the doing of Alexios' grandfather."

"As well as Alexios," Augustalis added.

"Absolutely," I agreed.

"You just happened to stop by for a visit after Alexios was sent away," I recalled. "Then again, maybe you didn't just happen to be there at all."

"If you are implying I was conscious of a larger purpose for my arriving at that particular location uninvited, the answer is, I was not," Augustalis observed.

"You weren't conscious of anything in particular, but you may have been guided there by a higher power we can neither see nor understand with our intellect," I proposed. "I believe you stopped by specifically to save me from my mother and bring me to Rome so I could meet Lucan. After all, he and I were thrown together at your dinner party less than a week after my arrival."

"You weren't exactly thrown together," Augustalis laughed. "It was more that he insisted on meeting with you alone after he laid eyes on you."

"Still, you gave us an unmistakable opportunity to meet," I contended, "and despite all odds we are now free to be in each other's lives."

"The gods be praised," Augustalis declared.

"And you as well," I added. "Would you like to return again for a visit with Lucan and a chance to savor your favorite dishes?"

"Of course," Augustalis replied immediately. "I can always find the time to enjoy your company as well as whatever emerges from your kitchen. Besides, it will be a pleasure to see you and Lucan together as a couple with nothing standing in your way. I hoped to create that for you before his marriage, but it was not to be. Now that it has come to pass, I definitely want to be a witness to it!"

∞ ∞ ∞

I was determined to establish a routine of my own so I could live independently of Lucan's availability to visit me. Becoming bored and morose in between our interludes would serve no one, especially me.

I set out redesigning the garden, planting herbs and fragrant flowers to use in my cooking and aromatic oils. I refer to my cooking, although I was not directly engaged in preparing meals.

I was training the cook, which required considerable patience on my part. She was devoid of creativity. Had she been a man she would have been well suited for the Praetorian Guard, so adept was she at taking orders. But since discipline is preferable to laziness, I decided it was better to have someone dependable if a bit too literal than to be dealing with an artist in the kitchen who couldn't plan her way through a mid-day repast.

I took her to the market stalls where the most superb spices were sold. We ate exotic foods proffered by street vendors. Gradually she developed the sensibilities underlying the various marinades, vinaigrettes and sauces she was learning to prepare. I was pleased with her progress.

Along the way I began to write. It happened rather by accident, although I have come to believe there is no such thing as a random event. One day I was looking at scrolls for possible purchase from a bookseller who dealt in the works of rare Greek philosophers. He mentioned he had a new shipment of top quality vellum. Although it was exceedingly expensive – a rare splurge – when I saw the sheets I knew I must buy them all. I selected a bronze inkpot and pen, and he recommended the preferred ink for writing on vellum. I also bought a split-tipped reed pen in case it proved to be a more effective writing instrument than the bronze one. Everything would be delivered to my home the next day.

The library in my suite had a desk as comfortable as it was beautiful. It was a joy to look at, with ivory inlays featuring birds and flowers cascading in profusion, and it turned out also to be a most inspiring place to write.

When I sat down for the first time with a vellum page placed perfectly before me, the inkpot filled and my pen poised, I hadn't an inkling of what I was going to write. Almost immediately a story began to be told through me. It was about a time and place so fantastic, I had no way of relating to the context. Yet the characters were entirely real to me. I wrote into the evening, hearing a voice that flowed unobstructed through me like a bubbling steam. Although I wondered more than once if this exercise was not a waste of high quality vellum, I kept on writing.

This became a favorite pastime of mine. I spent more on writing materials than I did on anything else. Who needs another gold brooch when for the same price I could purchase enough vellum to last two or three moon cycles?

I wrote in the courtyard, where a special table and chair were situated in the shade. I wrote in my library surrounded by stories of all sorts. I even wrote in a nearby taberna, which had a quiet table surrounded by climbing roses that invariably encouraged narratives of love to tumble forth.

As I wrote a new Graci emerged. I became the protagonist, or perhaps she took over my being. Subtly and profoundly the vestiges of my former identify as a slave dropped away. I was a freedwoman, a storyteller and a female of substance defined as more than a home and a financial account, though I was grateful for both. I was an intelligent, independent, creative woman whose avocation was the written word.

I had always been fascinated with the drama and ideas in the writings of others. Philosophical treatises, histories, plays and cultural commentaries consistently intrigued me. I assumed they were an escape, a respite from the intractable reality of my enslavement. But in truth the volumes I read were food for my starved soul and my equally hungry intellect. They kept my spirit alive in a way nothing else could have.

I came by my love of writing naturally, as an offshoot of my love of reading. But it became more than that. Like my cooking, it served as a venue through which I could express myself, if not to the world, then to my own soul. In the process of writing I became acquainted with the freedwoman I so unexpectedly had become.

∞ ∞ ∞

Another factor in my emergence was my growing friendship with Euphemia. The fact that the same man was central to our lives served more as a foundation for our relationship than a wedge between us. With that said, our acquaintance also transcended Lucan. We sincerely liked and appreciated each other. And since neither jealousy nor defensiveness created a barrier between us, our closeness blossomed naturally.

Euphemia made the first gesture. She invited me for lunch and what she called a "private concert" to hear her play the stringed cithara. I experienced a moment of trepidation as I was about to present myself at the door of the home she and Lucan shared with their children. It would be exceedingly uncomfortable if I saw him. How would I feel being where he lived with another woman who just happened to be his wife?

Euphemia met me at the door and escorted me through the house herself. It was imposing, almost the size of Augustalis' estate. The furnishings were well chosen and thoughtfully arranged. Euphemia had the effortless good taste of one who grew up in beautifully appointed rooms. Still, there was nothing ostentatious about their home. It was a spacious dwelling occupied by a large, active, wealthy family.

"The children are at their lessons right now, and Lucan is attending endless debates in the Senate," she mentioned. "We have time to ourselves before disruptions begin in the late afternoon. Let's retire to my rooms and spend a few uneventful hours together."

Her suite was open and airy. Serene naturalistic frescoes complemented furnishings covered in rose, pale orange and muted gold silk. The floors featured complex mosaics of zodiac signs and symbols.

"I love this house mostly because of these rooms," Euphemia commented. "They have been used for a number of purposes, from the tutor's quarters to a guest suite. Finally I appropriated them for myself."

Lunch was arranged in a private courtyard off the suite's sitting room. It was lush with climbing plants, blossoming jasmine and a bubbling fountain. "I would spend all my time in this spot, it is so relaxing," I said appreciatively.

"I love to play the cithara out here," Euphemia revealed. "The only problem is that the birds gather whenever I do. They start singing along with me, and soon they are chirping so loudly they drown out my playing. I take it as a compliment that their chorus appreciates my accompaniment."

During lunch we chatted like old friends. Euphemia told me about each of her children and their idiosyncrasies. I was impressed with her combination of affection and objectivity. No one could accuse her of coddling them or being blind to their foibles. Nonetheless, she obviously thought the world of them, and I presumed they did of her as well.

"Lucan and I agree there will be no arranged marriages in our family," she said decisively. "Each of our children will have the opportunity to marry for love, which isn't as easy as it sounds. He tends to be overly protective, and I am too quick to see through our children's false assumptions. Both of us must try not to second-guess them, but I believe it can be done."

"It is gratifying to hear your stories about your children and their relationship with you," I told her. "Every child should be so blessed as to have a mother like you."

"It has nothing to do with how I was raised." she replied. "I had the most self-involved, narcissistic, emotionally unstable mother in the Empire."

"I would argue the same about my mother," I laughed. "The two of them might well be tied for first place. It took me years to release the protection around my heart that resulted from my mother's abuse."

"Lucan told me about your early years," Euphemia noted. "Any time you want to talk about them with me, I am available."

"There's not much to tell," I responded. "I was unwanted and left to die after I was born. In later years my mother became even more resentful of me, if that is possible."

"She resented your striking beauty," Euphemia commented.

"I wouldn't go that far," I demurred, "but I will say she couldn't bear to witness my budding development into womanhood. My mother was sexually promiscuous in the extreme, and when I got older she saw me as a competitor. It never occurred to her that the last thing I wanted were the favors of anonymous men. Her desperate need for love is what killed her."

"How terribly sad, for you and for her," Euphemia said with compassion.

"She is released from a lifetime she could barely tolerate, and I have transcended the ways her rejection and abandonment limited me," I observed. "We both experienced a resurrection of sorts."

"I appreciate your candor," Euphemia acknowledged. "You have an indomitable spirit, and I would like one of our daughters to benefit from it. Would you consider taking Placidia under your wing? She tends to remain in the shadow of her older sister's high spirits, and yet of the two she has more depth and potential power as a woman."

"I would gladly welcome Placidia into my life," I replied appreciatively. "Since I have no children of my own, I would love to have someone to mentor. I promise not to suffocate her with too much advice and attention."

"She will be quite taken with you," Euphemia predicted. "Perhaps I can make the connection before you leave today. I will introduce you as a new friend who recently moved into a house around the corner. You can take it from there."

"What do your children know of you and their father?" I asked, perhaps too boldly.

"The older ones are well aware of the implications of my own living quarters," Euphemia explained. "But when they see us together, we are happier than ever, so they don't think much more about it. They understand the consequences of arranged marriages and are grateful we focus on the positive in the context of our own."

"And Placidia?" I queried.

"She is only eight years old and unaware of what her older siblings have discerned," Euphemia explained. "You can expect her to be quite innocent, refreshingly so."

"You have done so much for me," I commented. "First came your consideration of Lucan in relation to me. Then I became the beneficiary of your willingness to invite me into your home, and now into your life. It is an honor I can repay with nothing but my commitment to reciprocate abundantly."

"The honor flows in both directions," Euphemia assured me. "I recognized at the outset that you were the kind of woman I could admire and appreciate enough to be my friend. I have no intention of checking up on Lucan through my acquaintance with you. Quite the opposite is true. I want us to be friends apart from Lucan's presence in our lives. Beyond that, it pleases me to see how genuinely at peace he is now. He has been a different man since the two of you came together. More than anything I want that for both of you."

"This may sound strange, but I will say it anyway. Despite the dubious intent behind your forced marriage, your families did a superb job of matching the two of you," I observed. "Your sensibilities are very much aligned."

"We both chose to make the best of an unfortunate fate," Euphemia explained. "If we opted to remain angry and vindictive, we would have become as similar as night and day. Thank goodness Lucan was mature and wise enough to propose a more amicable approach and lead the way for me. His love for you provided the insight for his actions. You see, Graci, when it comes to Lucan, all roads lead to you. And vice versa."

"I give thanks that you created your own path to my door then invited me through yours," I replied.

We went inside, where Euphemia played the cithara for an audience of one. Her sublime music transported me to the nether realms, where nothing but love and goodwill existed. Listening to her, I understood why it was believed the Muses and Apollo, the gods of music, gave cithara players their gift to mesmerize listeners.

I closed my eyes and floated on the wings of her genius. I remained in a meditative state, drifting along with the harmonious chords of the music. When Euphemia ceased playing, I returned to my body and opened my eyes.

"Euphemia, your melodies are exquisite," I said, still immersed in serenity. "They carried me to a place of peace. Thank you for sharing your gift with me."

"And with me," I heard Lucan say from somewhere behind me. He approached our circle of chairs and sat down halfway between us, casual and comfortable.

"I wasn't aware you arrived home," I said, stating the obvious.

"The debates today were particularly petty, so I decided to leave early," he explained. "When I got here I heard Euphemia's playing and was drawn into this room. There you two were, peaceful and unperturbed."

"The music brought you here," Euphemia observed. "I was hoping the three of us could spend time in each other's company today, but I knew it couldn't be planned in advance."

"Lucan, you have an extraordinary wife," I said appreciatively. "She gives you too much credit for her remarkable nature, but I am convinced her exceptional qualities were there all along."

"If anything is remarkable, it is that the three of us are likely to get along better than we do with almost anyone else," Euphemia retorted. "The gods are smiling down upon us, and we should endeavor to make the most of it."

"Graci, would you like to stay for dinner?" Lucan asked unexpectedly. "It is about time you met the rest of the family. And they need to get to know their new neighbor. I will arrange to have another place set for you at the table. Unless someone is late, we should be gathering in an hour or so. Meanwhile, I will be in my office."

"Thank you, Lucan," Euphemia replied. "I couldn't have extended that invitation without your agreement. I am glad you did."

"The gladness is all mine," Lucan assured her. "My life is now complete in ways I thought would perpetually elude me. I have you both to thank for my obvious contentment."

Dinner was a joy. I loved the children. I loved their family. I loved Lucan. I found another home.

PART THREE
YESHUA AND ALEXIOS

I was relieved when Lucan offered to walk me home after dinner. As far as I could tell, none of the children considered it to be anything other than the gesture of their unfailingly thoughtful father toward a new neighbor.

"What a great family you have!" I commented as we were leaving, in case anyone was still within earshot. "Each of your children is an absolute delight."

"Incredibly, they seem to be getting even better with age," he replied lightheartedly.

We kept our distance on the street, since it was likely he would be acquainted with many of the people we encountered. It took no time at all to reach my house. I knocked, the servant came to unlock the door, and I ushered Lucan in.

It was over a month since I had seen him. The last time we were together was after Euphemia freed him to be with me. I understood he faced numerous demands, but his absence was disconcerting nonetheless. I was unsure of my ability to experience such intense lovemaking followed by weeks of solitude.

I asked for wine to be brought to the receiving room, having decided it was preferable to continue our conversation there than to presume he escorted me home for the sole purpose of adjourning to my suite. I decided not to ask why he stayed away after our transcendent reunion.

"Euphemia suggested I develop a relationship with Placidia," I remarked. "She seems to be a lovely girl. It would be wonderful to get to know her better."

"She asked me if I thought the two of you would be a good match, and I told her putting you together was a great idea," Lucan affirmed.

"I'll invite Placidia to visit me here and nurture our acquaintance slowly over time," I suggested. "I don't want to overwhelm her with too much attention."

"Graci, I have some explaining to do," Lucan offered, shifting the conversation in a direction I welcomed. "I want to tell you what I've been doing and thinking since I last saw you."

"Please do," I encouraged, relieved.

"When I arrived home after being with you, it was as if I entered a world completely foreign to me," Lucan revealed. "While we were together, I became so immersed in our oneness, nothing else seemed real or relevant. Then suddenly I was a father once more and the Senate was squabbling again. I was adrift, unable to relate to the immediate aspects of my life. That surprised me, since for years they constituted my daily existence.

"I began to ponder what would enable me to move back and forth between two worlds, yours and my family's, frequently and seamlessly. The issue was not Euphemia, since we have her full support. Something else was at work.

"I thought it might be my need to keep up appearances with the children. But I knew if I could be with them as I have in the past, they would be fine. Besides, the older ones want me in their lives less these days. That wasn't the problem."

"What was it?" I couldn't help asking.

"Something more fundamental." Lucan continued. "I can't experience my time with you as an interlude amidst the demands of a life lived elsewhere. I don't want our relationship to be built on an ongoing sequence of visits. I want to be at home with you. But I also need to be at home with my family."

"How can you have both?" I questioned.

"The only alternative is to establish that fact overtly," he declared. "All five of my children will need to know I am spending a great deal of time here from now on, assuming that is acceptable to you. Would you be willing to have them here during the day or for meals, essentially whenever they choose? I want them to feel as at home here as they do in the residence their mother and I created for them."

"I would love that!" I exclaimed.

"Are you sure?" Lucan probed. "I'm asking you to give up a great deal of privacy by opening your house to my family, children and wife included. That represents a colossal change in your life."

"No more than the other changes I experienced lately," I reminded him.

"That's an understatement," Lucan averred. "It was clear to me today that Euphemia would be very much in favor of this arrangement. She respects you and enjoys your company, and she was delighted to see how well you got along with the children tonight. So what do you think?"

"The only thing that could make me happier than enjoying your presence here would be to have your family streaming in and out as well," I assured him. "You do me great honor to consider sharing your children with me. As for Euphemia, she and I are already well on our way to a close friendship."

"Are you certain you'd welcome my family?" Lucan cautioned. "Once we've introduced this change, there is no turning back."

"I am as certain of that as I am of our love," I declared.

"Wonderful!" Lucan exclaimed. "I'll sit down with my three oldest children and explain the situation to them honestly. They would figure it out eventually anyway if I regularly spent nights away from home. I can't credibly continue to claim I am attending to an emergency in the Senate. And besides, that's not the truth.

"It may take them a while to become accustomed to this arrangement, and no doubt they'll discuss it with their mother. When they find out she approves of it and is more content than ever, they'll come around.

"Eventually they might ask to stay here on occasion, when they are more comfortable with the fact that I'm spending many of my evenings and nights with you. Until the transition is more solidly in place, I'll be home with them in the late afternoon and during evening meals."

"Take your time," I advised. "This represents an enormous shift in your children's lives. Although you and Euphemia are aware of how the terms of your marriage affected your relationship, your children may be blind to it. I don't want them to see me as the other woman, even though to some extent that is inevitable. If we allow the unfolding to proceed differently for each of your children, everyone will benefit. I have infinite patience in this regard, since I never dared hope for anything so gratifying."

"I'll exert no pressure on any of the children to accept or adapt right away to this arrangement," Lucan promised. "Meanwhile, you can get to know Placidia if she is amenable to it."

"That's a good first step," I replied.

"I can't wait to celebrate the day when we are together more rather than less," Lucan commented. "I'd also like to move a few of my things into your rooms just to feel more at home here, assuming that is acceptable to you."

"You can move everything in here if you want," I declared. "I would revel in seeing your senatorial decrees strewn around, along with a toga or two draped over the back of the furniture."

"And not in a puddle on the floor beside the bed?" he asked playfully.

"That too, where it would remain as a daily reminder of the incalculable joy you bring to my life," I retorted.

"Even a temporary puddle would be preferable to none at all," Lucan suggested.

"Yes it would," I confirmed, the aching inside me becoming more acute.

"Then, my marvelous Graci, now that our plans are in place we should celebrate their impending realization," he whispered seductively.

I took his hand, and we walked to my suite. He closed and locked the door behind him then held me in his embrace. I let myself lean into him, as I so loved to do. We stood there silently and with gentle closeness.

We were sharing yet another first – the blessed knowing that our togetherness need no longer be a struggle, an interlude of oneness marked before and after by protracted periods of separation. There was no reason to rush, no desperate desire to squeeze every last drop of ecstasy from the moment. We could even spend the night in the same bed and not make love, though I doubted that would be another first on this particular evening.

Lucan kissed the top of my head. "Let's nestle, then make meandering love, then nestle some more," he murmured. He carried me to bed and laid me down tenderly.

Our lovemaking that evening was relaxed and intimate. An entirely new facet emerged as a result of our freedom to enjoy one another without restraint. The pillow-soft sweetness when we were silent, caressing each other and breathing in an identical rhythm, became a new touchstone.

"I may not have truly known you until this evening," I whispered as we cuddled. "I longed for you so mercilessly, the only way I could approach our private time was passionately. But you are more than an ecstatic lover. You hold me with such tranquility, I may never be able to separate myself from you."

"There's no need for that," Lucan assured me. "From now on even when we are apart, we won't be separate. The constraints we faced before no longer exist. This uncomplicated completeness is altogether different from what we shared before. It's as if we have been this way together for decades, not hours."

"Or lifetimes," I added.

"Or lifetimes," he affirmed.

We talked into the night as longtime couples do, discussing everything from the political convolutions he was facing in the Senate to my latest adventures as a writer. We considered different ways to include his children in our lives, and he revealed each one's perspectives and predilections with remarkable clarity.

As daybreak interrupted the darkness, Lucan began preparing to leave. "I should be home before the children are up and about," he told me. "I'll stop by later today to tell you how my conversations with the oldest ones went."

"Use your best fatherly instincts," I advised. "There's no need to rush. Everything will unfold beautifully in its own good time."

"Agreed, but I have a particular interest in returning to you and what I hope you come to think of as our bed, as soon as I reasonably can," Lucan declared. "I am more determined than patient, which may not be altogether unfortunate. Rest well, and I'll see you later."

He kissed me languidly, and I thought perhaps he might not be ready to leave quite yet. But he found a modicum of willpower and was out the door.

I spent the day considering how to rearrange the house to accommodate a brood of five, and perhaps their mother as well, for meals and informal gatherings. After evaluating different alternatives, I decided since the dining room could easily accommodate twelve, nothing else needed to be done. I would assure ample food was always on hand, and whoever wanted to sleep over could be offered a guest bed or a couch.

This improvisational approach to integrating Lucan's family into my life served us all well. It took less time than I anticipated for his two older sons to start coming around with him. Curiosity was their primary motivation initially. Their earliest visits were defined more by gallant defense of their mother than any desire to accept me into their lives. But I let them know how much I appreciated her and showed no signs of being desperate for their approval, mostly because I wasn't. After numerous tests of my resilience and intentions, they dropped their guard and began to settle into a routine I enjoyed immensely.

Both boys were exceedingly bright and equally inquisitive. They discovered they could converse candidly with their father and me about topics that wouldn't be discussed at home. It wasn't that the subjects were unacceptable. Rather, in a family with five children, opportunities for significant conversations with their father were rare.

They commented on how well read I was, "better than our tutors" as they noted. I discussed a wide range of topics, expressing my opinions without apology. They observed their father relishing such moments and hopefully concluded that the Graci they were getting to know wasn't a woman adopting pretense to impress them.

I made a few overtures to Placidia, but she hadn't yet agreed to visit me. Then it occurred to me that she might enjoy accompanying me when I went shopping for spices. She accepted my invitation immediately.

We had a marvelous day together, exploring areas of Rome she hadn't seen before, buying exotic bangles for her and tasting unusual foods. I was happy to discover she was intrepid in that regard. As we were nearing our neighborhood, I asked her if she would enjoy a cooking lesson at my house with the spices we purchased.

"Really?" she asked excitedly. "Could I do that?"

"You can experiment with me any time," I assured her.

"How about tomorrow?" she suggested.

"Tomorrow would be great, as long as your mother agrees to it," I confirmed.

Euphemia was walking through the courtyard of their home when we entered. "Mama, look what Graci bought me!" Placidia exclaimed, displaying her new jewelry. "And we picked out spices and ate strange but tasty food, and she invited me to come over to learn how to cook. Please, may I go to her house tomorrow?"

"Of course you may, my dear," Euphemia replied, smiling happily. "But you must promise to bring me a taste of whatever you create, so I can enjoy how delicious it is."

"I can do that," Placidia replied happily.

"And there's one more thing. Invite your father to dinner at Graci's so the three of you can share the meal you prepare," she suggested.

"Wonderful!" Placidia agreed.

That is how it all began. Placidia grew accustomed to the idea that her father dined with me even when she wasn't there. Lucan's two older sons sometimes invited themselves, since they preferred the cooking at my house. Most evenings two or three of Lucan's children had dinner with us. Euphemia was a frequent visitor as well. The family was coalescing around my home as a gathering spot, and I loved every moment of it.

Just as I hoped, Lucan's belongings became evident throughout my suite. I even bought a large desk for him to use in the library. We were as close to being a couple as we ever could be. I was content, profoundly so.

∞ ∞ ∞

I often revisit this time in our lives, when the joy was endless and the appreciation we all had for each other provided a backdrop for everything and everyone else.

Lucan's oldest son Hypatius was turning eighteen and wanted to study with a Greek scholar in Athens. He had his father's intelligence, but his sensibilities were more aligned with academic pursuits than with politics. Lucan, however, was hesitant.

"I can't comprehend why his continuing studies are so controversial to you," I told Lucan one evening after dinner. "Can you blame him for wanting to avoid politics? It is a thankless pursuit for a young man. Corruption and irresponsibility pervade the Senate, and other governmental offices are ruled by patronage. If I were in his position, I'd want to be a scholar for a while longer, too."

"But if he gets caught up in academics and my second son Carisius does what he desires, which is to accompany Alexios on his travels, who will follow in my footsteps?" Lucan interjected.

I couldn't believe what I was hearing. "Lucan, for the first time since I've known you I fear you are well on the way to becoming your father, and if not certainly your father's son," I objected. "Wouldn't you rather have all your children pursuing their passion than succumbing to the restrictions imposed by their patrician lineage? What does it matter if you are the last senator in the family line? You are committed to transforming the Senate anyway. Do your work, and let your sons choose theirs."

A broad smile came over Lucan's face. "In case you've been wondering lately how I feel about you, let me clarify one thing," he began. "You are more than my equal in all ways. You are awake where I am asleep, astute where I am obstinate and empathetic where I am insistent. But for you I would become a crotchety old curmudgeon.

"I depend on you to keep me in my place and remind me of what really matters in life. And what really matters is that I love you with ever more appreciation and understanding. Then, of course, there is the fact that you are the most exquisite lover a man could possibly wish for, one I can only hope to satisfy every now and again."

"Translated that means you agree with me about Hypatius' further studies in Greece?" I asked playfully.

"I agree with you. But more importantly, I love you for keeping me honest," Lucan replied.

We were sitting across from each other in the sitting room. He reached out for my hand, and I walked over to put it in his. Then he pulled me to him and brought me onto his lap. He placed his arms around me in one fluid motion and planted kisses on both of my cheeks.

"Here's one kiss for each of my older sons, and a peck on your nose for the youngest one," he offered. "As for my daughters, they wouldn't want me to settle for anything less than something within range of your lips."

We kissed and I snuggled into Lucan's embrace. I loved that lap of his, which always seemed so available to me. We remained together, silent for a long while until I noticed his breathing changed. He had fallen asleep.

I thanked our Creator for making it possible for us to spend this precious time together. Then I thought if for whatever reason it is cut short, we will have this moment and many others like it – enough of them already to stretch into infinity.

I curled up and drifted off to sleep myself.

∞ ∞ ∞

I continued to find time to write in the morning after Lucan left. It was a treat I never took for granted, since I spent mornings during three decades of my life working. Even when Lucan remained with me, I usually adjourned to the library and my pages of vellum.

One morning Lucan interrupted me with a kiss on the top of my head.

"What's happening with your intrepid heroine today?" he asked cheerfully. "I haven't had an update in a while. The last I heard she was trying to get her husband out of prison."

"She succeeded with some help," I reported. "Now she's working with him and a few others to reverse corruption throughout the land. It's turning out to be more difficult than pulling a few weeds and making room for flowers to grow."

"And her husband is integral to rooting out every trace of vileness?" Lucan asked.

"He is the consummate hero: steadfast, courageous, ethical, generous, spirited and madly in love with her," I affirmed.

"I will never measure up to all that," he groaned with simulated distress.

"You already have," I assured him. "You do so every day. Haven't you discerned yet that he is you?"

"And she?" Lucan queried.

"I couldn't presume to have all her admirable qualities," I replied lightheartedly, "except that like me she is a good cook. She makes delicious soup that contains mysterious healing qualities. The herbs and plants she grows communicate with her, revealing their unique properties so she can use them to best advantage. Actually, she is an alchemist as well as a cook. She heals the masses while she feeds them. The narrative is quite fantastic."

"And you believe you don't also do that, my dear little alchemist?" Lucan quipped.

"Not consciously," I admitted. "But that particular capacity may be latent within me. It drew you to me immediately after my arrival from Greece."

"What draws me to you is love," he observed, "although it was your wizardry with spices that got my attention before I ever laid eyes on you."

"I wonder if there isn't some sort of memory involved in my writing," I commented. "I often sense I am summoning up experiences that occurred before this lifetime. I feel as if I am documenting my past, not telling fictional stories, and you are central to them all."

"And a good thing that is, since I couldn't live up to the competition otherwise," Lucan remarked wryly. "Have you thought of getting your stories copied so you can sell them? That is all the rage with women who have the means to purchase manuscripts and the time to read them."

"I doubt my literary indulgences would resonate with anyone else," I objected.

"There's one way to find out," Lucan suggested. "Ask Euphemia to be your hypothetical audience and see what she recommends."

"I'll do that," I agreed, mostly to put Lucan's idea to rest. "I expect her to suggest, diplomatically of course, that the stories go no further."

"What happens next?" Euphemia asked me when we met a week after I turned over my vellum pages to her. "You must tell me! You left me at a critical moment, with no assurance the hero will be rescued!"

"First, what did you think of the story?" I asked. "Certainly it isn't something that would be widely read."

"It's fabulous!" she exclaimed. "I went to sleep last night thinking about the two protagonists. Graci, you must seriously consider selling copies of this narrative for a significant sum of money. Everyone in Rome will be talking about it. None of us has enough romance in our lives."

"You see it as a romance?" I asked, surprised.

"Of course," she confirmed. "It is a grand love story, with obstacles and convolutions thrown in to keep things interesting. But mostly it is about love – huge, all-encompassing, unequivocal, enticing love. What could be better than that?"

"Nothing is better than that," I agreed.

"I have an idea," she continued. "I'll invite a few friends to my house one evening so you can read assorted passages to them. We'll see how they respond. If they can't wait to peruse the tray of sweets before they leave, you can write in private and that will be that. But if they want to hear more, you may need to consider taking your writing public. If they request it, I'm willing to have my friends over a few more times so they can follow the lovers through to the conclusion. Besides, I want to know how the story ends."

I agreed to participate in Euphemia's gathering. I was intimidated by the prospect of sharing a private manuscript publicly, so I selected passages that provided an evocative glimpse into the characters and story line. Although I expected to see squirming after the first half hour, everyone was glued to their cushions. When I completed my reading, they asked, "When can we get together again?"

∞ ∞ ∞

Thus I became a novelist. I commissioned scribes to make copies of my stories by hand. They sold out as fast as they could be produced and were passed around

Rome, then Italy and the Empire. Alexios reported attending a banquet in Syria where the women couldn't stop talking about one of my novels. Apparently a copy made it that far.

I wrote in Greek as a convenience, since that was the language in which I had been taught to read and write. Doing so inadvertently gave my stories more credibility than they deserved. Greek was considered the more literate language, even for something as insignificant as a romance novel.

"You are becoming blatantly controversial in the Senate," Lucan noted one afternoon as we sipped pomegranate juice in the courtyard. "A number of my colleagues tell me you are setting an impossible standard for the men of Rome. Their wives expect them to behave heroically, not to mention being faithful in their marriage."

"And what's wrong with that?" I asked playfully. "This city could use a little heroism and fidelity. Sometimes I think we'd be better off if the barbarians invaded us. At least then the men of Rome would stop consulting with each other about the latest inanity and be induced to fight for something worthwhile. Your peers relegated heroism to the legions and now stand for very little."

"That's quite a damning statement, damning but true," Lucan said, showing no sign of having taken offense, thank goodness. "Do you include me in that group? Then again, I needn't ask. If you don't, you should."

"I have no doubt you want things to change," I replied. "Every now and then you speak out against the omnipotence of the Caesar and the appalling dishonesty that shrouds most dealings in Rome. But nothing much changes as a result. I can understand your reluctance to pursue what seems to be a lost cause. What is one voice in a cacophonous sea of cynicism and duplicity?"

"Every chorus consists of individual voices coming together in unison and harmony," Lucan observed. "It can't happen if the voices are intermittent, or if they are available only at the convenience of each participant."

"What exactly are you saying?" I asked, though I understood his point.

"I'm saying I may have lost my way," Lucan admitted. "I've grown comfortable and satisfied with my life. That represents great fortune, something I will never take for granted.

"But I've lost sight of my role in the Senate as a catalyst for improvement. I do more complaining than anything else, and I rarely suggest solutions that go beyond short-term, superficial modifications. We need more than that."

"Like what?" I pursued.

"We need a complete reapportionment of power, starting with the emperor and the Senate, and moving through every official position in the governmental structure," Lucan declared. "As long as the emperor is omnipotent and everyone else does his bidding, with the armed encouragement of the Praetorian Guard, nothing will change.

"You and I had many conversations about this when you were still serving in Augustalis' household. When my attempts to introduce reform were ineffective, I claimed my growing family was a distraction. But deep down I felt it was too big a challenge to take on. Now the opposite is true. I am so content, I avoid anything that might roil the placid waters of my life."

"You sound as if you are ready to stir things up," I observed.

"Over the years I've engaged in informal conversations with Marcus Aurelius about possible change," Lucan revealed. "Despite his authoritarian tendencies he is a reasonable, evenhanded ruler. He is willing to entertain a gradual realignment of power away from the emperor and toward representative bodies of the people.

"Before that can happen the Senate must be appreciably more responsible than it is now. Its members need to address significant issues and do more than talk volubly, which would be a shock to most of them. The emperor amassed the power that inheres in his role because over time the Senate abdicated its responsibilities. They relinquished their power out of indolence, narcissism and entitlement."

"Can a shift in power be accomplished without the violent overthrow of the emperor or a string of murders thinly disguised as suicides?" I asked anxiously.

"Yes, provided the emperor decrees such sweeping change," Lucan posited. "It must be accomplished during Marcus' reign. Beyond that, he would need to choose a successor committed to maintaining his vision. If his power hungry son Commodus were to succeed him, our efforts would be nullified."

"Do you plan to discuss this seriously with Marcus and others?" I inquired.

"There has never been a better opportunity to do so," Lucan noted. "And if we don't succeed, at least we'll have failed trying instead of accepting a corrupt situation perpetuated by our lethargy."

"Who says I write only fiction?" I quipped. "I do believe I have a true hero in my midst. How can I help you accomplish this objective of yours despite all odds?"

"May I use this house as a gathering place for others besides my family and our mutual friends?" Lucan requested.

"Yes of course," I agreed at once. "You can meet here whenever you want. If your strategizing becomes too raucous, I can always take refuge in my suite. Please establish this as your customary location. I'll make sure everyone is so well fed, they transform the apparently impossible into a purpose worth pursuing."

"Marcus has returned from endless campaigns in Germania," Lucan reported. "I'll try to schedule an audience with him in the next few weeks. Then based on how he responds to my inquiry, I can decide what to do next."

"Will you be in any danger?" I asked, suddenly apprehensive.

"First you remind me that my heroism leaves a great deal to be desired," Lucan commented good-naturedly, "then when I offer to step forward and pursue a significant agenda, you ask if I'll be putting myself in harm's way. You can't have it both ways, Graci. Heroism has inherent dangers.

"Complacency is rampant because people would rather avoid taking risks, especially ones that could cost them their lives or their fortunes. The history of the Empire is riddled with examples of power struggles that ended in death in one form or another. I won't assure you there are no risks involved. They lurk around every corner."

"I'm sorry I asked," I interjected.

"The alternative is unacceptable, as we both know," Lucan declared. "The concentration of supremacy in one person or position invites abuse, and exploitation is evident everywhere. I don't blame Marcus Aurelius for this. He stepped into a top-heavy power structure when he became emperor. He has made his share of arbitrary decisions, punishing Christians for example, which may lead one to believe he is as ruthless as all other Caesars since Vespasian and Titus. But he is an intellectual and a philosopher as well as a soldier. I plan to appeal to his more thoughtful side."

"How well do you know him?" I asked

"Quite well, actually," Lucan revealed. "We met during a debate about the importance of stoicism in Roman culture. I took the position that it had little impact compared to other factors such as slavery and the perpetual expansion of the Empire. He argued that much of the Roman way of life derives from the fundamentals of stoicism. We both debated our perspectives with more passion than we actually felt, as I discovered later, then we continued our conversation over wine at a nearby taberna. We have appreciated each other ever since, though we enjoy only infrequent meetings now that he is Caesar."

"Can he be trusted?" I questioned.

"I believe so," Lucan replied. "Marcus can be progressive and is definitely concerned about the future of Rome. Now is as good a time as any to see if he is willing to hand over a measure of the emperor's power for the good of all."

"I'll support your efforts in every way I can, even if my contribution involves nothing more than listening thoughtfully," I vowed. "This is an important mission, one worth the inherent risks.

"I say this from experience, not innocence. I say this as a former slave who understands the destructive force of powerlessness and the potential latent in liberation. You'll be doing what you can to enhance that potential for all. That is heroic."

"Save your accolades, and especially your triumphs, for when we know whether I am successful," Lucan cautioned. "I won't overstate my chances of making a difference. They're modest at best."

∞ ∞ ∞

As much as I desired regular updates from Lucan, I refrained from asking if he met with the emperor or discussed his ideas with other like-minded senators and influential politicians. I learned a long time ago that he would speak his mind when he was ready, usually when I least expected it.

Meanwhile I continued to write my novels. I cleared my mind of all thoughts and allowed the words to flow through me like water in an aqueduct. I wrote on the vellum pages exactly what I heard. The tales presented themselves fluently and effortlessly.

I unveiled each new volume before an audience of Euphemia's friends. Although I continued to fret that the stories would become tedious, the opposite was true. The women could hardly wait for me to announce it was time for another gathering. I enjoyed reading the stories aloud since I forgot much of the narrative as soon as the words arrived. It was like discovering the story anew along with my audience.

Years later I ran across counterfeit replicas of my volumes. The stories and characters were changed so arbitrarily, the tales barely held together. Despite the discontinuities and unimaginative prose, each well-worn manuscript had clearly been read many times over.

Besides my writing I continued to collect accounts told in the first person by those who were with Yeshua when he was alive. The most prominent booksellers in Rome knew of my interest in this topic and my willingness to spend whatever was necessary to acquire every available text. They kept an updated list of the volumes in my collection, assured that any acquisition they made on my behalf would result in a sale. Over time I developed one of the most comprehensive collections on this topic in the city.

I purchased these volumes not because I was intent on owning more of them than anyone else. Rather, I wanted the manuscripts on hand so I could read them again and again. They quickened something precious within me, an abiding faith in the benevolence of the Source of all existence.

I spoke to only a few about my deepening conviction. My beliefs were a private matter, one that transcended words and defied description. I could honor the sanctity of my faith most authentically if I lived according to Yeshua's wisdom, quietly and without fanfare.

Most who followed the teachings of Yeshua gathered quietly and unobtrusively. Sharing their beliefs in the context of a spiritual community was enough. They didn't attempt to convert others actively, but they did welcome all seekers.

Nonetheless the more radical believers created unrest for everyone else. They openly opposed the notion that the Caesar was a deity who would become a god upon death, and argued against the pagan practices that pervaded the Empire. Marcus Aurelius saw their claims as treasonous, warranting decisive action to silence them. He sent them to the mines as punishment.

Although I deemed this to be extreme, I didn't see a connection between the public denunciation of Christianity and my own abiding belief in Yeshua the prophet. Mine was an intimate matter involving my collection of books, which I read in private, and my prayers.

Lucan's children were growing up and leaving home. His oldest son Hypatius convinced an erudite Greek scholar to teach him everything he knew about philosophy and its underpinnings. He was immersed in his studies, and although he repeated in his letters that he missed his family and friends, it was obvious he was never more fulfilled. I credited Lucan for not insisting his son follow in his footsteps.

His second son Carisius was traveling with Alexios, learning about trade and commerce from one of the best. Not only was his mentor experienced and successful, he was also ethical and highly regarded throughout the Empire. I could see an informal legacy being created. Alexios had no children. And yet here was the perfect son for him, a young man passionate about his business who relished traveling with him.

Lucan was pleased that Alexios had this additional connection to the family. His biggest concern for his children was that they would lead meaningful, happy lives. The man was definitely mellowing with age.

His older daughter Janina fell in love with a wealthy patrician's son assigned to a legion in Germania. She swooned over his frequent love letters, none of which showed any signs of bloody battle. When she wasn't swooning, she worried about his safety. I couldn't devise any credible arguments why she should refrain from her incessant handwringing except to assert that his protection would be better assured by her confidence than her concerns.

She and Placidia were frequent visitors at my house, where we chatted about their preoccupations. Through them I became acquainted with the lifestyle of wealthy Roman girls. They saw me as more of a good-natured, supportive aunt than a surrogate mother, which pleased me to no end.

I engaged in their emotional peregrinations without feeling responsible to help them make acceptable choices. Perhaps because of my relative objectivity, they often found their own way to the decision I would have recommended. I cherished my relationship with them as much as the one I shared with their mother.

One afternoon we were sitting in the shade of the courtyard, a cool breeze alleviating oppressive summer heat. The two protagonists in my current novel provided an additional distraction. They were facing intractable uncertainty about every aspect of their lives but one, their love for each other. Regarding that there was no question.

"How did you and my father fall in love?" Placidia asked me matter-of-factly. The children had long ago accepted our relationship.

"It was my cooking," I replied lightly, "which proves how wise you have been, my dear, to learn my tricks with spices and herbs. Maybe you'll meet the love of your life the same way."

"But how did you meet?" she persisted. "Weren't you a slave working in the kitchen? I can just see my father now, barging in on the cooks and demanding to meet the person who created such delicious dishes. You would then step forward and say, 'I did, sir,' and it would be love at first sight."

"I take that back," I told Placidia. "Maybe your cooking won't draw your love to you after all. You are a novelist at heart, with a good sense of emotional suspense and a great ear for dialogue. No doubt when you meet your beloved, he'll be hooked before he even realizes he has taken the bait."

"Well, if the bait is your cooking, he'll know instantly that he has consumed a gift from the gods," she laughed. "What happened after my father tasted your food?"

"I arrived from Greece the week before, and it was the first time I cooked for one of Augustalis' banquets," I recounted. "His guests appreciated the unusual flavors in the food and assumed someone new was in the kitchen. They asked that I present myself to receive their compliments. I did so reluctantly, since my clothes were splattered with sauces and dusted with spices. That's when your father saw me. He asked to speak to me privately after the other guests left, and everything happened from there."

"Did you know you loved him when you saw him?" Placidia asked eagerly.

"I did, but a part of me also denied it," I clarified. "Allowing myself to love him under such impossible circumstances would certainly break my heart."

"Doesn't love matter more than anything?" she wondered. "That is what I always hear from mother and father, who never cease to tell us we are to marry for love alone. Heaven help me if I fall in love with a slave like dad did!"

Then she paused, embarrassed. "I hope I haven't offended you, Graci."

"You haven't," I assured her. "I wouldn't wish on anyone what we faced. It's unspeakably sad to love another and not be free to act on that love."

"But you both are free now," she said cheerfully. "I wonder if mother will meet someone she can love the way you and my father love each other."

"Maybe, though she is extremely happy with her own wing of the house, her music and her outrageously great children," I replied. "She may not need a man to love."

"Don't we all?" Placidia asked, more urgent than innocent.

"Not necessarily," I told her. "I would have been content had I never met your father. Granted I wouldn't have become acquainted with his family, a huge loss to be sure. But I take pleasure in many things, each of which could otherwise keep me occupied and fulfilled. The same is true for you.

"Nonetheless, women of your class are expected to marry. I hope you meet someone who loves you more than you ever thought you could be loved, even by your parents or siblings."

"Or by you," she added.

"Or by me," I agreed.

"Does love end when we die?" Placidia ventured.

"Not at all," I assured her. "If anything, it becomes the pure essence of who we are. When we die our spirit lives on in love. We come together with the spirits of those we love and experience one long, joyous celebration."

"Like a wedding that lasts forever?" Placidia conjectured.

"Like one endless love fest," I declared.

"Are you angry that you and dad can never marry?" Placidia posed the ultimate question.

"I feel only gratitude for what we do share, not anger over what we can't have," I explained. "Every day with your father, and with your mother and each of you, is a gift I never take for granted. I bless your mother for making it possible. My life is full, and my heart overflows with love. Marriage to your father couldn't bring any more joy than I feel now."

"But would you marry my father if you could" she asked, striking at the heart of the matter.

"It would make me extremely happy to do so," I admitted. "You led me adroitly to my fundamental truth, which is that the consummate acknowledgment of the love your father and I feel for each other would be marriage. But since for many reasons that isn't possible, I've chosen to be undeniably happy without it."

"So am I," Placidia added. "I hope my life keeps getting better and better, just like yours."

"It will, my dear," I affirmed. "I've prayed for it. Consider your happiness a given."

That evening after the girls went home, Lucan and I retired to our rooms. I recounted my exchange with Placidia earlier in the day. He listened with interest that was both fatherly and friendly.

"She sounds just like you," Lucan observed. "When Euphemia asked you to take Placidia under your wing, she knew exactly what she was doing. And now we have a budding Graci on our hands. My question is, can the world handle two of you?"

He came up behind me, wrapped his arms around me, bent down and nuzzled my neck.

"Two of us, maybe, but certainly no more," I chuckled. "It would be too difficult for the potent politicians, and the impotent ones as well, to address our constant queries and endless challenges of the status quo."

"As far as politicians go, I am grateful I haven't yet declined into the impotent category," Lucan retorted. "Of course, I have you to keep me perpetually interested."

He grew hard against me, and I turned around slowly to respond face-to-face. "My dearly beloved lover, you may be turning gray but your virility is not in question," I assured him. "If anything, you are an even better lover than you were before. Everything takes a bit longer, which I thoroughly enjoy. As for that hardness I feel against my belly, it arouses me as it always does. Ecstasy awaits thanks to a potent politician. I am once again about to become the most satisfied woman in all of Rome."

We made love with slow, comfortable caresses and casual movements born of years of intimacy. I lay in Lucan's arms afterwards, feeling his chest rise and fall with his breathing.

"The emperor agreed to collaborate informally with me and a few other senators to structure a phased-in realignment of power," Lucan confided. "This is a major development. Even so, the path ahead is anything but certain.

"Marcus expects to spend much of his time at the front in Germania, so his personal involvement will be minimal. I hope the group can meet with him at least once before he leaves, so everyone can experience for himself the Caesar's support."

"This is the breakthrough you wanted," I noted enthusiastically.

"We must keep our plans confidential and our meetings clandestine," Lucan noted. "I regret the need for secrecy, but too many in Rome made their fortunes and amassed their power under the current governmental structure. They'll resist change, violently if necessary, because it will doubtlessly cost them money or influence or both. That would diminish their prestige, which they can't tolerate.

"The shift in power from the emperor to governing bodies can occur only if the emperor himself decrees it. But that would only be the first step, not the final one.

"We must be in a position to implement sweeping change almost immediately. If concerted opposition keeps that from happening, the result would be disastrous. Marcus would likely be killed and Commodus would become Caesar, after which he would reverse our progress and make things even worse than they were before."

"So the risks don't end even after the emperor takes official action," I realized.

"Unfortunately, that is the case," Lucan replied. "But I intend to pursue this course nonetheless. I plan to gather a half dozen of the most enlightened and effective senators and, behind closed doors, develop a strategy we can follow after Marcus announces the realignment of power. Knowing the risks, would you still allow us to meet here?"

"I was given this house for many reasons, one of which is to support you however I can," I asserted. "Please let me do it."

"Thank you, my fearless Graci," Lucan replied, relieved. "I'll require that everyone keep the meetings secret. I'll also make sure Alexios agrees to this arrangement. I don't want you to be in danger, or him and his business to be implicated in any way."

"I doubt that would be an issue," I commented. "And if it were, he could lease another place to live until your work is done. I see no obstacles, unless the emperor refuses to consider your suggestions or no support is forthcoming in the Senate."

"Both are possible," Lucan admitted. "But for now we have a workable arrangement, pending Alexios' reply."

"The lover in my bed is about to make history by helping realign the balance of power in the greatest empire on Earth," I proclaimed. "Perhaps your father was correct in giving you an ultimatum. It was imperative for you to preserve your position in the Senate."

"Mind you, I may not succeed," he warned.

"Your worthiness as a senator is in your willingness to act with good intent on what is in the best interests of the people," I declared.

"That I am doing," Lucan affirmed, "at long last."

"Which is more than most men in your position can say," I noted, rolling over and kissing him appreciatively.

"Do I take that as an invitation to seal our agreement with another round of lovemaking?" Lucan teased.

"Only if you are up for it," I countered playfully.

Taking my hand and moving it down his belly to his groin, he was pleased to reply, "Had you any doubt about that?"

∞   ∞   ∞

Lucan managed to arrange an initial meeting between Marcus Aurelius and the senators before the emperor left for the front. They agreed upon the priorities the senators would address and a confidential means of correspondence. All parties were convinced the goal was worth pursuing in private initially.

I continued to write in the morning and entertain at least one of Lucan's three youngest children in the afternoon. Euphemia visited as well, sometimes arriving with one of the children and a basket of fresh produce from the market.

"You have more mouths to feed than I do these days," she said, handing me her parcel. "I intended to bring a contribution to your pantry at least once a week. But I get so distracted with my music, the time vanishes. Thank the goddesses you are watching out for the children. I have become an irredeemably irresponsible mother."

"Irredeemably talented," I clarified. "No one plays the cithara more sensitively than you do."

"My music teacher informed me the other day there is nothing more he can do to help me improve," Euphemia commented. "He is now suggesting I start teaching others, beginning with him. When I thought he was joking, he insisted he was serious. Can you believe it?"

"Yes I can," I affirmed. "Your music comes from another place. It's as if your heart is connected to the strings, and your fingers are communicating divine love through them."

"In that case, I won't apologize for neglecting either you or my children," Euphemia quipped.

"Everyone is doing great," I asserted. "Obviously you are too, which pleases me to no end. Our lives are expansive, thanks to a particular visit you made to my house shortly after I moved in."

"What I did was more self-serving than altruistic," Euphemia recalled, deflecting my appreciation. "In the process I gained a dear friend and won my husband's eternal loyalty. He and I haven't had an angry word since he stepped across your threshold later that day."

Euphemia provided an update on the two older boys, who were each pursuing their passions, different though they may be. Then she mentioned Lucan's senatorial activities.

"I heard Lucan's meetings are no longer secret," she revealed. "Apparently one of the senators in the group drank too much at a party and bragged about his personal involvement in a private pact with the emperor. The other guests plied him with more wine, paid homage to his ego and he proceeded to tell all. Of course, he overstated his role and its importance, but the damage was done. Everyone is talking about it. Three different friends recounted this to me, all of whom are concerned for you and Lucan."

"Why me?" I asked.

"Because he also revealed the location of the clandestine meetings, the rat," Euphemia explained.

"Does Lucan know this?" I asked. "He hasn't said a word to me about it."

"He does," Euphemia affirmed. "He has been fully apprised and has already taken action to reprimand the offending senator. That served only to put the oaf on the defensive and fuel a major fit of pique.

"Now Lucan is in the toughest of all spots. If he ousts the man from the group, which is what he deserves, the senator will no doubt disclose every detail of the process so far. And if he allows him to remain involved, their work will be in constant jeopardy."

"Lucan has a third option," I offered, "which is to cease the meetings under the pretext that once the confidentiality was compromised, it would be unwise to continue. Then after a reasonable period of time, the meetings could be resumed in secret, but without the untrustworthy senator. The biggest risk would be his vengeance if he learned that meetings were occurring again without him."

"I agree," Euphemia replied. "Tell me, have you always been such an astute strategist, not to mention an excellent observer of human vicissitudes?"

"I am exhibiting nothing but survival skills, honed at a young age," I observed.

"I forget what you endured because you transcended it so completely," Euphemia commented. "Only the positive remains. I know many women who lead lives of ease and abundance and yet are resentful and bitter. You, on the other hand, find love or the potential for it wherever you can. And when that isn't possible, you adopt a realistic view of the situation."

"That's a choice I made long ago, when I was a slave with no hope of ever being freed," I recalled. "Although I couldn't control my destiny directly, I was mindful of how I approached every day. I could either do so as a pitiful, powerless person or as someone determined to make the most of a situation not of my own making. I selected the latter, and it served me well."

"Rather like what Lucan and I did when we married," Euphemia added.

"Precisely," I agreed. "The three of us are similar that way, which is one reason we get along so well.

"I'll find out how Lucan intends to proceed or not with the meetings and share with you what I learn. If you have an opportunity to discuss this with him before I do, you can let me know. You and I are of one mind regarding this unfortunate situation."

"As we are about everything else," Euphemia noted. "If I didn't know better, I'd think we were sisters. Or perhaps mother and daughter, though I'm not sure which would be which."

At that moment Lucan arrived and saw us in deep conversation. "Been planning my future as a senator, I suppose," he observed cheerfully.

"As a matter of fact, we have," I replied without hesitation. "Are you ready to receive our most considered recommendation?"

"Absolutely," Lucan said encouragingly. "But I should inform you first that I have nearly made up my mind about what to do. Would you like to wager how closely matched our approaches might be?"

"Ten to one in favor of a match," Euphemia predicted.

Lucan didn't take the bet. Had he, she would have won a substantial sum.

Lucan informed the secret group there would be no more meetings because of an irreparable breach in confidentiality. Then he waited for the gossips to communicate this news throughout the salons of Rome.

His strategy worked. In the ensuing weeks many Romans, senators and otherwise, expressed their condolences to Lucan over the cessation of his efforts. They decried the fool of a senator who exhibited such poor judgment. Lucan learned about numerous other instances when the man was untrustworthy. He was an unfortunate choice from the beginning.

Lucan waited until other intrigues occupied the tongues of the most adroit and informed rumormongers. Then when enough time passed with nary a whisper about the group, perhaps they would resume their meetings with one less member. Unfortunately, with the emperor almost permanently ensconced in Germania, and his tendencies toward being a philosopher instead of a philanderer, scandal was scarce.

In the meantime we enjoyed the luxury of unobstructed days and nights. There was nothing unattended, nothing left to accomplish, nothing we were avoiding, nothing we needed to address or change. Our contentment was real, not a fleeting illusion. When I remember that time I return to serenity.

We were in the Garden of Eden just before the fall.

∞ ∞ ∞

Augustalis made a surprise visit soon after the scandal broke about the secret meetings.

"I have just one reaction to the latest news," he announced. "Now that you and Lucan are no longer endeavoring to save the republic, I am packing you off to my villa rustica. I visit it only rarely, probably out of guilt or remorse for sending you two there the first time.

"No one in my family wants to vacation at that villa anymore because according to them it's too boring. Imagine, the dullness of a life by the sea, with no shopping and massages and who knows what else. Actually, I do know what else. I'd rather not think about it. So, how about it? Will you and Lucan take some well deserved time off and agree to another tryst at my seaside cottage?"

"I'd love to go, Augustalis, but I can't speak for Lucan," I replied. "As for trysting, I doubt our efforts would measure up to the records we set on our first visit."

"You consistently restore my faith in the power of love, and no doubt you'd do so again," he retorted. "But please, don't feel any obligation to give me a full report of your indulgences or lack thereof. You can arrive whenever you want and stay as long as it suits you. If Lucan would like his children to come along, that's fine too. Alexios is welcome as well. You can make it a family outing, but I highly recommend preserving some time for yourselves."

"It would be good to get away," I assured him. "And it might benefit us both to return to the place that holds such ambivalent memories. We could put them to rest."

"Indeed you could," Augustalis agreed. "By the way, does Lucan seem overly disappointed that his plans for the republic went the way of one too many jugs of wine and a stupidly indiscreet blowhard?"

"He's disappointed, of course, but he's taking it all in stride," I reported. "He was working to achieve an important end, which was gratifying to him. That's certainly preferable to doing nothing and making excuses for inaction."

"I hope you aren't referring to me," Augustalis noted. "And if you are, I won't take offense. How could I, when you'd be correct?"

"The thought never crossed my mind!" I exclaimed. "You're a courageous and open-minded man, exemplary in fact. You achieve important ends every day of your life."

"Perhaps, but I could always do more besides throw endless banquets for my increasingly pompous and irrelevant acquaintances," he admitted.

"Why don't you come to the sea with Lucan and me?" I suggested. "If he is unavailable, you and I could venture there alone. We could create the very scandal Lucan is hoping will surface to distract everyone's attention from him."

"That sounds promising," Augustalis mused. "It's been ages since I did anything scandalous."

"Seriously, would you consider joining us, or me, for at least part of the time?" I urged. "It's your place after all, and being there would offer you a welcome vacation from your dinner parties. Besides, we see far too little of you these days."

"If Lucan goes, I may as well join you," he assented. "Alexios can stop by whenever he returns from his latest voyage."

Lucan agreed to the trip immediately, and we made plans to leave within the week. I sent word to Alexios to take a detour if he happened to be sailing by Monte Circeo, then prepared the household staff to handle all responsibilities in my absence.

Augustalis planned to arrive after we settled in. I begged him to come with us, but he declined, offering the not very credible excuse that he was too busy to leave so quickly.

"More importantly, I heard you two know how to make the most of a journey together in a carriage," he added, eyes dancing.

"Whoever told you that?" I exclaimed, pretending offense. "Obviously it was someone with an exceptionally active imagination."

"The imagination, my dear, was apparently most evident inside the carriage," he laughed. "As far as being active is concerned, you and Lucan take the prize."

"We are older now," I rejoined. "Please inform those driving the carriage that the most they can expect this time is a complaint or two about how ruts in the road are paining our arthritic joints!"

"Whatever occurs or doesn't, enjoy your journey. I'll meet you there a week after your arrival," Augustalis concluded.

We enjoyed our journey a great deal more than I expected. When Lucan first kissed me after we alighted in the carriage, I took it as a "glad we're on our way" peck. But he had something else in mind. I can't claim our acrobatics were as impressive as they were before. But we did have a splendid time indulging in every position we could still reasonably assume, assisted by inescapable bumps in the road. I was well satisfied when we arrived.

"We're off to a commendable start on this holiday of ours," Lucan observed exultantly as the carriage rounded the bend to the villa. "The fresh sea air may add even more stamina to my youthful vigor. Consider this fair warning in case you'd rather fill up the blank pages of vellum you brought or re-read the volumes about Yeshua you packed in the spare trunk."

"Nothing, my love, can distract me from your amorous attentions or intentions," I crooned. "You can anticipate a variety of unreasonable performance expectations on my part. Preserve your strength. You'll need it later."

I had forgotten how sublime a respite from Rome could be. It was a relief to be away from the incessant political intrigue. A few days after we arrived, I contemplated the possibility of retreating to the sea on a regular basis.

"Would you consider leaving Rome for the better part of the year, once all the children are out of the house?" I asked Lucan. "I'd love to do so. The petty machinations of small-minded patricians are so tiresome. Every time you take significant steps toward change, some fool pisses all over your progress."

"Spoken like a member of the Roman upper class," Lucan quipped. "Yes, let's consider something for our retirement. Maybe Augustalis would sell me this place since no one in his family uses it."

"That would be perfect," I agreed. "But he would never sell it to you. I'm sure he would insist on our enjoying it as if it were ours, to assuage his regret regarding our first visit here."

"That's ancient history," Lucan remarked.

"I agree," I replied. "None of us needs to drag that grief around any longer."

"I can see us now, two crotchety but never senile freethinkers to the end, spending our days taking long, slow walks by the sea and, if we're lucky, making long, slow love on occasion," Lucan mused.

"If we're lucky, that last part won't be merely on occasion!" I retorted.

"Tell me, Graci, do you believe in happy endings?" Lucan wondered. "Your books all have them."

"I believe everyone creates their own happiness and contributes to or detracts from that of others," I replied.

"How do you think this will end?" Lucan pursued. "Us, I mean?"

I had a terrible sense of foreboding and dismissed it as a residual memory of our previous visit. Still, it felt like a premonition, quite disconcerting. Lucan observed the concern that moved across my face.

"What have you seen?" he asked anxiously.

"Nothing in particular," I replied. "It was just a vague presentiment. Let's not talk of endings but focus instead on perpetual beginnings. After all, an ending is nothing more than a chance for a new beginning."

Apparently Lucan didn't want to alarm me more than I already was. He dropped the subject.

Augustalis arrived a few days later, accompanied by carts laden with enough provisions for a dozen guests.

"We can now include you in our established daily rituals," I told him. "A late morning repast beneath the portico, a languorous afternoon nap, sunset walks by the sea and a delightful evening meal followed by dessert wine and conversation."

"Sounds divine, except that I prefer to nap alone," he joked. "The simplicity could become addictive, in which case I'll fall from grace the minute I return to Rome and cease being host to half the city. Imagine days and weeks on end with no need to make small talk or endure the effrontery of those with more money than brains. I may never be the same."

"Feel free to release all obligations to be the host here," I suggested. "And if you experience a spell of small talk coming on, just give one of us a nudge with your walking stick. We'd be happy to oblige you with profound conversation. Cicero, perhaps, or Socrates?"

"Or that Yeshua you are so fond of," Augustalis added.

"I would gladly please you with stories of his life and teachings," I offered. "And I promise it would never degenerate into mindless chatter."

"You are incapable of mindless chatter," Augustalis observed.

"More's the pity," Lucan chuckled. "I can never succumb to intellectual sloth. Graci catches me every time."

With Augustalis there this would prove to be a most agreeable wrinkle in time.

∞ ∞ ∞

"Isn't it interesting how notions of family can shift with the phases we go through?" I asked one morning over fresh fruit and honeyed bread. "For instance, first Alexios was my family, then Augustalis, Gaiana and Eirene, then Lucan, Euphemia and their brood. Now it is the three of us, happily residing under the same roof. It feels like we've lived this way forever."

"I had that same sense a few days ago," Augustalis admitted. "I'm more content than I've been in a long time, possibly ever. It isn't merely a function of having escaped from Rome, although that contributed to my prevailing sense of peace. Rather, it's a feeling of having arrived home, of being with my true family, which is the two of you. It defies reason, but then in my old age I'm less dependent on reason. Most of the truly important things in life aren't reasonable."

"If I were to expire on the spot, which by the way I don't intend to do, I would feel complete," I added. "The loving companionship I feel with you both is extraordinary. It was strong and steadfast before, but this is different. It feels timeless, eternal."

I looked at Lucan and remarked, "You asked about happy endings. This would qualify as one."

"One of many more to come," he vowed, taking my hand in his and kissing it lightly. Then he took the ring he gave me and twirled it between his fingers.

"Augustalis, this ring has quite a history," Lucan began. "I came across it in an antique shop just before our first trip here, and I knew immediately it was meant for Graci. It was in an old worn box, the origin of which was unknown. I bought them both and brought them with me to the villa. Then in my arrogance and obliviousness, I delayed presenting my gift to Graci.

"When I was called back to Rome unexpectedly, I departed with nothing. She was left with the task of packing my belongings as well as hers. Graci, being thorough, included the box in my trunk. When I opened it later and saw the container inside, I was crestfallen. How could I have missed my chance to give the ring to her? I put the box back in the trunk, planning never to lay eyes on it again.

"Years later when Euphemia told me she wanted Graci and me to be free to act on our love, I retrieved the box before I left for Graci's house. That evening I presented the ring to her. Our sacred union was finally celebrated openly and completely. The timing turned out to be auspicious after all. Graci has worn the ring ever since."

"This is my wedding band. It joins us in love," I said solemnly.

"I noticed the ring long ago, but I hadn't heard how you got it," Augustalis remarked. "Lucan, I'm intrigued that what you originally assumed to be a terrible mistake turned out to be impeccable timing."

"Another happy ending," I said joyfully, "the perfect ring proffered at the perfect moment. It doesn't get any better than that."

∞ ∞ ∞

Augustalis had been with us almost a month when I saw two familiar figures walking up the lane leading to the sea.

"Alexios! Carisius!" I exclaimed. "Welcome, a thousand times over."

They looked up, smiled and waved. Lucan shouted from the edge of the portico. "Do you have baggage to be brought up?"

"We left everything on board until we determined what we need," Alexios explained. "We can attend to that later."

As they approached the villa, I couldn't believe the change in Carisius. He was taller and his shoulders had broadened considerably. He looked years older than he did when he left with Alexios. The combination of ocean sailing and business dealings suited him. He had come into his own.

"Jupiter be praised, Carisius, you have become a man of the world!" Lucan exclaimed. "If you weren't under the trusted tutelage of my dearest and oldest friend, I would be concerned you had somehow been led astray. What I see instead is someone who found what he loves to do and is thriving on it. Am I correct?"

"You are indeed," Carisius affirmed. "And speaking of that, you never looked better yourself."

"Don't you just love this mutual admiration?" Alexios teased. "It must be a family trait, although I don't recall it was handed down by your father to you, Lucan. Here's to the beginning of a whole new tradition in your lineage, the celebration of how well everyone is doing!"

"Alexios, you old goat," Lucan laughed, giving his friend a vigorous embrace. "Your years at sea haven't mellowed you one iota. So much for the calming pleasures of being on the water."

"Oh, they are calm all right," Alexios assured Lucan, "as long as one doesn't encounter any tempestuous storms. On our voyage here, we were nearly sacrificed to Poseidon. But our ship held together, our crewmembers lashed themselves on board, and we were saved. We lost nothing but our direction and our dinner. Carisius is as seasoned a sailor as you'll encounter anywhere. Whatever he experiences from now on won't even be noteworthy after our last episode."

"Do you still want to pursue the business of trade?" Lucan asked Carisius.

"I do, but with the provision that I do so only in association with Alexios," Carisius revealed. "Had he not been willing to go to the expense of having the best ships constructed for his fleet, we wouldn't be here to tell the tale."

"That might be the most important lesson you learn from me," Alexios commented.

"I learned a great deal more than that," Carisius continued. "One characteristic separates Alexios from most other traders. He sails with his ships. He participates when necessary with his crew. He isn't a landlocked merchant who never sets foot on board his fleet and saves a few sesterces for himself by building unsound vessels. I have found my mentor, whom I respect absolutely."

"Well said," Lucan replied. Then turning to Alexios, "Thank you for bringing my son back safely, and for returning to dry land so you and I can tease each other relentlessly."

"You've gone easy on me so far," Alexios retorted. "You must be out of practice. I'll give you until evening to warm up your bristles and barbs. Meanwhile, Carisius and I will get settled and have much needed baths. Don't come too close, Graci. You may be so shocked at how ripe we are, you'll send us packing back to the ship, your invitation having been summarily rescinded."

"I'll show you to your rooms and your baths," I offered, "holding my nose if necessary. We'll see you back here for sunset, followed by dinner and continuous demands to hear every detail of your adventures."

"So you can include them in your next novel?" Alexios asked playfully.

"Of course," I admitted. "I'll be taking notes. My forthcoming volume will have two heroes, but I promise you won't be vying for the same ladylove."

"I learned my lesson on that score," Alexios declared. "Having done that already, I suggest you craft my character as a simple man with gentlemanly charm and a predisposition to remain a vagabond bachelor."

After so long a voyage, the men's clothes were in desperate need of repair and laundering. Lucan and Augustalis loaned Alexios and Carisius clean under-tunics and togas, and by evening they were ready to join us.

I expected Carisius to spend as much time describing the exotic women he saw as he did recounting his business dealings with Alexios. Surprisingly, he never mentioned the former. Carisius was a young man in his prime. I knew from my years in Greece that port towns were full of women ready to relieve a man of his desires as well as his cash.

"In the interest of research for my next novel, I'm curious about something," I ventured. "Carisius, I can't imagine your dealings were so focused on commerce you paid no heed to intriguing women in foreign ports. Were they comely or no match for Rome's memorable maidens?"

Carisius looked embarrassed, which I misread for his having sampled their wares more than once. I decided to say no more.

"Actually, I did meet someone in Britannia," he admitted. "Alexios knows that country well and has trade agreements with their most successful merchants. We attended a dinner at the home of one of them, and there I met his daughter. She is phenomenal! I've fallen hopelessly in love with her."

"Here we go," I said gaily. "A love story in the making, and it isn't even fiction. Do tell all."

"She has the most pleasing blonde hair and blue eyes, and a voice that would make the gods weep," Carisius effused. "Mostly she is strong like you, Graci. She demanded to be educated against her mother's wishes. Her father relented and she learned Greek, the language in which she was tutored. Fortunately I know Greek as well, so we conversed easily. But since Alexios understood every word we said, our chaperone was also a wily eavesdropper."

"Being a substitute father, I felt an obligation to make sure you didn't declare your undying love until your second visit, at least," Alexios replied jovially. "I remained within earshot at all times."

"She wants to come to Greece for further studies, which would put her closer to Rome," Carisius continued. "But her father won't allow her to travel so far away, unmarried and unaccompanied."

"Which will it be, a marriage or a chaperone?" Lucan queried.

"A marriage, I hope," Carisius admitted, "but not until I'm successful enough to afford a wife and family. Alexios, how long do you think that will take?"

"How long do you think you can hold out?" he asked in response.

"Three more trips at most," Carisius replied.

"Then three trips it is," Alexios announced, "followed by a wedding on trip number four."

"Trip number three," Carisius corrected him, "a wedding on trip number three."

"He has already become a wicked negotiator," Alexios noted proudly.

"He learned from the best," Lucan declared, "which leads me to state the obvious. You'll be acting on my behalf in these impending marriage negotiations. And since you are handling the role so adroitly, I hereby name you honorary father to Carisius and father-in-law to his bride. But when the blond- haired blue-eyed children start scampering around, I may want to step in as grandfather."

My sense of family shifted once again, this time to include Alexios and Carisius. We were united in love and generous appreciation. Our homecoming was ongoing, the harvest of peace profuse.

∞ ∞ ∞

Lucan and I were gone almost two months when we received word that Marcus Aurelius, who was still at the front in Germania, had failing health. Although he was aging he had until then remained vital, the residual effect of years as a soldier and commander.

I assumed the news was an overreaction by the Caesar's advisers, who earned their keep with unwarranted drama and incessant fretting. But Lucan saw it differently.

"I should return to Rome to gather additional facts from trusted sources," he announced. "I can't do so from here, and I won't relax if I remain uninformed. You are welcome to go with me or stay here. I intend to return, but I have no guarantee when that will be."

"I'll accompany you," I decided. "Augustalis has been talking of returning to Rome anyway, and Alexios and Carisius left a few days ago. This is a good time to depart."

"I agree," Lucan replied. "But there's no rush. If you want to stay a few more days or even another week, that's fine with me."

"We should leave soon," I suggested. "We can't continue in the mode we enjoy here when our thoughts are elsewhere and our concerns are growing."

"Very well then," Lucan agreed. "I'll talk with Augustalis. Perhaps we can travel together."

Two days later we presented the staff with money and gifts in acknowledgement of their exemplary service and the three of us were on our way. Before we left Lucan received news that the emperor was declining rapidly and Commodus was already strategizing to take his place.

"If a son was ever the opposite of his father, it is Commodus," Lucan commented. "The father is a philosopher; the son is a warrior who never sees battle. The father is appalled at the corruption that has overtaken Rome; the son would use it for his own ends and make it worse without compunction. The father intends to reduce the power of the emperor; the son would amass more power and insist on maintaining his reified status. The father prefers to give the people the benefit of the doubt; the son would give them crumbs, the better to manipulate them. If Marcus dies soon, the work our secret committee began will be lost."

"It's too early to despair," I urged. "Wait until you know more about the emperor's health."

"The changes we sought would be in place by now if one of the senators involved hadn't been so egomaniacal and drunkenly indiscrete," Lucan remarked ruefully.

"Lucan, I've learned one thing in my long and eventful life," I began. My voice was so fierce, Augustalis awoke from his nap in the carriage. "None of us can change the past. Even the emperor, who purports to imminent godly status, can't do so. Refrain from mourning the outcome that has escaped you so far and focus instead on what can still be accomplished once you determine the circumstances you face."

"Thank you for shaking me out of my remorse," Lucan replied. "I am overreacting because of what I anticipate will be awaiting me in Rome. I promise not to be so pessimistic until there is reason for it. Hopefully pessimism can be avoided altogether."

"What do you think your daughters have been up to while we were gone?" I asked in an obvious attempt to introduce a lighter subject into the mix.

"If they're anything like their older brother, we'll discover Placidia is about to be married before her sister's hero is back from the battle lines," Lucan mused.

"Stranger things have happened, which I have either experienced myself or written about in my books," I commented. "Sometimes both."

"Speaking of your books, you didn't get much writing done, did you?" Lucan noted.

"No, but I did draft an entire story in my head," I revealed. "It involves a dashing young sea trader, the son of an equally dashing Roman politician, and his passion for a most unlikely Celtic goddess of a girl. These characters will be everyone's favorites."

"Once you are home and unpacked, I won't be able to pull you away from your latest cache of heroes," Lucan observed. "Your only request of me will be to have more vellum delivered."

"Don't forget the ink!" I laughed.

∞ ∞ ∞

It was surprisingly good to be back. Walking through the courtyard, I was grateful once again for the lovely setting Alexios chose for me so long ago. With time it reflected more of my taste, which was comfortable and informal. I created interludes throughout the house were I could relax, read, write, converse with visitors or pray. I made it my home and Lucan's as well.

Lucan left immediately to gather current information on the Caesar's health. I went to our suite and began to unpack.

As I was unloading my trunk of reading material, a volume on Yeshua fell from my hands. The scroll was open to the place where I stopped reading when we left to return to Rome. It was a manuscript written by Thomas, who recorded the exact words of Yeshua. I knew most of the text by heart, having read it so many times.

I looked at the next passage, which read, "Blessed are you when you are hated and persecuted. Wherever you have been persecuted they will find no place."

Hope, 120 AD

How interesting that when I returned to Rome, that particular message presented itself.

I laid the scroll on the desk and sat down to meditate. I cleared my head of thoughts and waited for the customary void to appear along with the luminescence of the nether realms. Presently I heard an inner voice that said, "My dearly beloved Graci, you have come to a crossroads in your life when you will be called upon to make a choice requiring great courage. Know that whatever you decide, you are loved. Know that whatever path you take, it will be the path of love. Know that your life is eternal, as is your love. Remember this, and you will discover within yourself a flame of passion that transcends all else. I hold you in the hands of grace. I walk with you as a true follower. I share with you the emanation of the Divine. May peace be your touchstone, may love be your talisman, may the everlasting light of your Creator bring you home to me."

Those words pulsed through my being. They were real to me, yet I hadn't perceived them with my ears. I vibrated with the purity and power of that message. My body felt as light as a feather.

And then I was gone. I don't know where I went or how long I was away, but when I returned to my body and opened my eyes, everything looked different. The room pulsed with a golden glow that originated from within rather than being reflected from without. I gazed in awe at my surroundings.

I returned to my desk, picked up a fresh sheet of vellum, inked my pen, and wrote the message that was given to me. I recalled it verbatim. I closed my eyes and returned to the state of bliss that overcame me earlier. Yeshua appeared before me.

"Those are my words," he said. "Please accept them along with the love with which they were given to you."

"I dedicate myself to you, in love," I vowed fervently. The words came from deep within me. My voice sounded like an echo. Then I was gone again.

Later when I came back to my body, I noticed that the scroll containing Thomas' account had fallen to the floor. I had placed it carefully to one side of the desk before I wrote what I heard in meditation. I barely moved a muscle in the interim. How strange!

The scroll lay open near the beginning of the manuscript. It said, "Blessed is the lion which becomes man when consumed by man; and cursed is the man whom the lion consumes, and the lion becomes man."

I thought about that passage many times before. The lion was like Rome with its corrupt humanity, amoral values and human bondage. When people allow themselves to be consumed by those values, they are cursed. But when fallen consciousness is consumed by enlightenment, the lion is blessed. Those who were accursed are reborn into their divinity.

So it is with each of us as we make our daily choices. Do we allow the lion to consume us, rendering us less than we are capable of being and becoming? Or do we face and consume the lion, and in doing so take a step closer to the Divine?

∞ ∞ ∞

The story that remains to be told is fraught with drama. That may be an essential ingredient in fiction, but it isn't particularly welcome in everyday life. Or at least, it isn't welcome in my life. I have experienced enough drama for ten lifetimes. I needn't amass an even greater storehouse of impressive events to justify my existence.

Nonetheless, there is more drama to come in this narrative. Most dramas conclude as farce or tragedy, happiness being at the mercy of both. This drama ends with neither. Rather, the outcome is a more serene state of being for Lucan and me, although we each achieved it through different means.

The villain in this story is the emperor Commodus. Every drama needs such a character, and he was cast perfectly for the part. His actions were despicable, motivated by the basest human objectives. One could assert that what he did was unforgivable. But I don't see it that way.

Instead, I see Commodus as the person playing the most difficult role of all, one with few if any redeeming qualities. He performed it to perfection. Thanks to him, I experienced the clarity and strength of my faith. And thanks to him, Lucan found the courage and commitment to embody his truth without compromise. Commodus gave us both a supreme bequest, packaged as appalling abuse and unrelenting betrayal.

But I am getting ahead of myself. Where we are currently in the story is at the beginning of the third act, when everything is possible and little is known. The latent potential in both Lucan and me is yet to be discovered.

The story line was simpler when I was a slave, Lucan was enslaved through different means, and our love was hopeless if not unrequited. But the tale digressed toward happiness. We are now lovers, openly and with the encouragement of Lucan's wife. His children have accepted my relationship with their father. We continue to enjoy the lively companionship of our friends, and Lucan is maturing as a responsible politician. I have become a writer as well as a steadfast believer in the authenticity of Yeshua and his teachings. We are living multifaceted lives, separately and together. I would have it no other way.

Little in life is obvious or straightforward. We face crises and convolutions in order to experience ourselves as the courageous or compromising people we are. What we learn about ourselves during those times can be affirming and enlightening, or it can strengthen our denial and hasten our degradation.

I am at peace with everything that happened in my life. I am at peace because somehow, somewhere, I discovered within myself the capacity to forgive. I am at peace because I now see everything that occurred – even, or perhaps especially, my experience of slavery – as the warp and woof in the intricate tapestry of my life. I am at peace because in the end there is nothing but love. And in the end I know nothing but love.

∞ ∞ ∞

Within a week after our return to Rome, Lucan verified the rapidly declining health of Marcus Aurelius. No one could estimate how much time remained to redistribute power from the emperor to representatives of the people, but it was reasonable to conclude the opportunity to do so was abbreviated.

Lucan met individually with the five trusted senators involved in his secret group. Each had a slightly different opinion about what should occur next. One wanted to introduce the subject before the Senate as soon as possible in order to build enough momentum to force the next emperor's hand if he resisted the changes.

Yet another believed any further action, even clandestine, was wasted effort since Commodus was sure to undo whatever progress was made. Lucan listened to all perspectives, each of which had some degree of credibility.

"Have you decided how to proceed?" I asked one morning after both of us awakened early.

"Not really," Lucan replied. "Many factors are relevant, not the least of which is whether we have a week or a month or a year. Since that can't be determined in advance, we must assume the worst and take action accordingly.

"It's futile and foolhardy to introduce the issue to the Senate at this point. Senators have neither the capacity nor the inclination to rally behind a shared purpose. They have opinions, which they communicate only in private. Ask a senator to take a stand publicly that might represent a degree of risk, and he'll demur like a eunuch. Few have the temerity to challenge the emperor, and those who do so accomplish their ends by getting others to take action. The Senate has been powerless and in disarray for too long."

"Is it worth continuing?" I wondered.

"I asked myself that question," Lucan revealed. "Each time I consider the facts, I come to the same conclusion. If I'm not willing to continue, I should retire from the Senate. I couldn't bear doing nothing and remaining a member of a castrated governing body after Marcus' death."

"Do what you believe is necessary and in the best interests of the people and the Empire, regardless of how effective you might be," I advised. "Whatever the outcome, you will have succeeded if you support the resurrection of a republic and do so with integrity."

"Do you really believe that even if I fail to change anything, I will succeed for different reasons?" Lucan asked.

"It matters not whether you accomplish a huge shift or nothing at all," I replied. "You will have challenged the self-destructive and not incidentally, self-serving, patterns of the Senate. That makes you a worthy senator."

"But what if it puts me at risk, not just financially but physically as well?" Lucan pursued. "Could you live with that?"

"If you deem the risks to be too great compared to your potential impact, it makes sense to cease your initiatives and retire from the Senate," I confirmed. "You have served long and well.

"Promise me you'll neither pursue this purpose because you want to please me nor turn your back on it because you want to protect me. You please me with all that you are, and you protect me with the generosity of your love. Your actions, or lack thereof, will have no bearing on either."

I said all of that, even though I was tempted to plead with Lucan to leave the Senate immediately. He was perpetually frustrated as a member of that moribund governing body, and he had given more than enough to it. Lucan was too good for them. But he was born into the position of senator. It wasn't mine to take away from him.

I couldn't make Lucan's decision for him, nor could I legitimately influence it. In the short term he might prefer hearing a strong opinion from me, which no doubt would affect his choice. But eventually that could become a wedge between us. So I remained neutral.

Hope, 120 AD

Lucan decided to continue meeting in different locations with the senators he trusted. When the complicated logistics became problematic, I offered to have the gatherings at my house again.

The urgency of the group's task intensified with updates emphasizing Marcus' worsening condition. Lucan sent the emperor progress reports but rarely received a response. That served only to validate the claims of his declining health, since previously he was a frequent and incisive correspondent.

Lucan remained focused and committed. He guided the other senators through difficult conversations regarding how far to go with proposed changes, when to push for more radical shifts and when to be more conciliatory. I was involved only to the extent that Lucan desired my counsel at the end of a long day or the beginning of a new one.

∞ ∞ ∞

I meditated daily in the privacy of my suite, during which the emanation of Yeshua was often palpably present. His visitations had a profound impact on me. I desired only to spend my time in solitude when Lucan was otherwise occupied.

Entering into a meditative state came naturally to me. I would sit comfortably, clear my mind and allow my spirit to soar to the realms of the Divine. I couldn't move my body even if I wanted to. Invariably when I returned I was filled with love. Whatever concerned me before was gone. Every aspect of my life, and the lives of those I loved, was unfolding in perfect order. I was sure of it.

I spoke to Lucan about these experiences. He listened intently, admitting he had little capacity to accomplish such surrender. I explained that it wasn't an accomplishment but an active letting go of the need to control and even the need to know.

"The closest I come to that is during my experiences with you," Lucan observed. "It happened first when I met you while we were sleeping and we merged. Of course, there is the other merging we do so well, which is both physical and spiritual. I experience a type of surrender then. Are your meditative experiences in any way orgasmic?"

"There is a moment when I lose myself loving you and seem to exist separate from my body," I replied. "That is similar but more transient. During my meditations my spirit leaves my body and exists fully on its own. It doesn't need my body at all."

"Does your body need your spirit?" Lucan queried.

"Yes it does," I confirmed. "I believe if my spirit were to abandon my body altogether, I couldn't sustain physical life. Even when I am far away during my meditations, my spirit remains connected with my body. It is the spark that arrives when life begins and leaves when it ends."

"Do you ever want to leave and not come back?" Lucan wondered.

"Never," I assured him. "How could I wish that when I have you to come back to?"

"But everything is so perfect in the realms you enter," he noted.

"That same perfection is available here as well," I stated emphatically. "The point of Yeshua's teaching is that every last one of us can access the blessing of divine grace while we are here, in these convoluted lifetimes of ours, if we choose to do so."

"My own purposes may be better served if I were to meditate instead of spending my days in meetings," Lucan mused.

"You are welcome to join me any time," I offered. "Just say the word, and you can accompany me on my journeys of peace and serenity."

"Which must necessarily be far, far away from Rome," Lucan sighed.

"Not so," I objected. "Such respites are available even in Rome. You need only bring them into your life."

Lucan never meditated with me. On occasion I told him of my experiences, but mostly I kept them to myself. They defied words anyway.

My writing adopted a different tone as well. When I completed the novel about the swashbuckling trader, his wise mentor and his beguiling ladylove, I had no more fiction left in me. Instead I wrote commentaries about the existence of the Divine in one's life and how to strengthen one's relationship with the spirit within. This writing intrigued me, though I had no illusions it would interest anyone else. I filled the vellum pages even faster than before.

At times I would take an entire afternoon to reread what I had written. Because I couldn't remember most of it, I felt as if I were perusing someone else's text. The ideas that landed on the page weren't mine. I studied my writings the same way I read the accounts and philosophies of others, and I often learned as much.

A spiritual journey is necessarily a solitary process. The terrain within is at once elusive and glorious. Moments of exaltation are followed by detours and complications, as if each new insight must be tested and then tested again before it can be integrated fully.

I released the ways I defined myself. I was no longer either a slave or freedwoman, alone or with a family, rejected by my mother or loved by Lucan. I just was, and in that simplicity I came to know my true self.

∞ ∞ ∞

Lucan and his senators reached an acceptable conclusion to their collaboration. After working night and day to commit their recommendations to writing, he handed them over to the group for one last review. Only a few alterations were proposed and agreed upon, after which Lucan prepared a final draft for the emperor.

"I'll deliver the document in person," he revealed to me. "I leave for Germania in the morning with two others. We must discuss our proposed plan with the emperor before, during and after he reads the text.

"This draft is a request for his commentary. We are prepared to make any revisions Marcus wants while we are there. Optimally we can gain his agreement on a final draft and obtain his signature on the resulting decree before we leave. Then whatever happens with him subsequently will be irrelevant. The deal will be done."

"Do you believe Marcus shares your sense of urgency and will be willing to approve your plan for restructuring so quickly?" I asked.

"We have kept him informed all along," Lucan reminded me. "Few of our proposals should be a surprise to him, provided our communications weren't intercepted and he has read and contemplated our suggestions. I can't be certain of that, since I heard so little from him of late."

"That's another reason to meet with him," I noted. "If he hasn't seen your messages, you can give him time to consider your recommendations."

"We're proposing a more rapid and aggressive shift of power from the emperor to the representatives of the people than we would suggest were Marcus' health not so fragile," Lucan explained. "My biggest concern is that he'll think we have gone too far and taken advantage of his goodwill toward us. If that appears to be the case, I will be candid with him about how his health constitutes a major consideration. He can't be blind to the messages flying back and forth about his weakened condition."

"I'll pray each day for you," I vowed, "that you return with a signed decree from the emperor along with his demand that it be implemented with all due haste. More importantly, I'll pray that you remain safe throughout your journey. I'm going to miss you."

"And I you," Lucan replied, his eyes growing sad.

"That look of melancholy reveals more than your anticipation of a temporary absence," I commented. "What is it?"

"I'm not sure," he admitted. "Something came over me this morning, a forewarning that I was about to seal our fates and knew nothing of the implications of my actions. I felt bereft of you, as if I lost you for good. I'll pray for your safety while I am gone. May the gods protect you."

After Lucan prepared everything for his trip, we sat up late contemplating our many blessings and celebrating our love with toast after toast from the best wine in our collection. I experienced a bittersweet sense of completion, as if we were about to embark on separate journeys taking us in different directions. I told myself that even if he was gone for two or three months, such time would be short compared to the years we had shared in this house.

Our lovemaking that night was a sacred act. It swept over me with wave after wave of blissful oneness. Lucan knew exactly how to honor me with his love, and I him. We were older and satiated more quickly. But our naps in between, holding each other tenderly, were serene. We spent every moment immersed in the love that united us.

A servant knocked on our door to announce the carriage was waiting for Lucan outside.

"I don't want to say goodbye to you with anyone else around," Lucan said.

He sat on the bed next to me, leaned down and kissed me gently. Then he took both of my hands in his, opened the palms and touched them with his lips. "Please hold me in the hands of your generosity and love. And when I return, be ready to hold me in all the other ways we both cherish so dearly. I love you Graci, with all that I am."

"Goodbye, my love," I said to him. "Serve your purpose and remain safe. And know that I love you, always and forever."

∞ ∞ ∞

I spent the next few weeks obsessively putting everything in the household in order. I created perfection as a means of coping with the elusiveness of the situation in Germania, where Lucan was engaged in a battle of diplomacy if not military might. I heard nothing from him about either his journey or his conversations with the emperor, assuming he arrived safely. I didn't expect regular updates, given the distance and his location near the front lines. Nonetheless, the silence was distressing.

Lucan was gone just over a month when I received the first communication from him. He sounded optimistic on the surface, but I could tell he was concerned. The emperor was frail. People constantly accosted him, hoping to receive favors before his ultimate demise. Lucan and his collaborators endured interminable delays and insolence from the Caesar's protectors before they were granted an audience.

When they met with Marcus at last, it was at the end of a long day. The emperor was fatigued and capable of little more than hearing an overview of their recommendations. They left a draft document with him and secured his commitment to review it within the week.

Marcus hadn't read a word of the proposal before their next meeting. Lucan summarized priorities, most of which Marcus supported. Lucan hoped that after one or two additional meetings, the emperor might be willing to sign the document into an official decree. Then they could return to Rome, announce the declaration before a meeting of the full Senate and determine a strategy for implementation.

To keep my mind off of Lucan's potential travails, I meditated regularly and read my collection of volumes about Yeshua's life. A new manuscript contained a description of him from none other than Pontius Pilate, in a letter he sent to Tiberius Caesar.

TO TIBERIUS CAESAR:

A young man appeared in Galilee preaching with humble unction, a new law in the Name of the God that had sent Him. At first I was apprehensive that His design was to stir up the people against the Romans, but my fears were soon dispelled. Yeshua of Nazareth spoke rather as a friend of the Romans than of the Jews. One day I observed in the midst of a group of people a young man who was leaning against a tree, calmly addressing the multitude. I was told it was Yeshua. This I could easily have suspected so great was the difference between Him and those who were listening to Him. His golden colored hair and beard gave to his appearance a celestial aspect. He appeared to be about thirty years of age. Never have I seen a sweeter or more serene countenance. What a contrast between Him and His bearers with their black beards and tawny complexions! Unwilling to interrupt Him by my presence, I continued my walk but signified to my secretary to join the group and listen. Later, my secretary reported that never had he seen in the works of all the philosophers anything that compared to the teachings of Yeshua. He told me that Yeshua was neither seditious nor rebellious, so we extended to Him our protection. He was at liberty to act, to speak, to assemble and to address the people. This unlimited freedom provoked the Jews – not the poor but the rich and powerful.

Later, I wrote to Yeshua requesting an interview with Him at the Praetorium. He came. When the Nazarene made His appearance I was having my morning walk and as I faced Him my feet seemed fastened with an iron hand to the marble pavement and I trembled in every limb as a guilty culprit, though he was calm. For some time I stood admiring this extraordinary Man. There was nothing in Him that was repelling, nor in His character, yet I felt awed in His presence. I told Him that there was a magnetic simplicity about Him and

His personality that elevated Him far above the philosophers and teachers of His day.

Now, Noble Sovereign, these are the facts concerning Yeshua of Nazareth and I have taken the time to write you in detail concerning these matters. I say that such a man who could convert water into wine, change death into life, disease into health; calm the stormy seas, is not guilty of any criminal offense and as others have said, we must agree — truly this is the Son of God.

> *Your most obedient servant,*
> *Pontius Pilate*

The man Pontius Pilate described was the same spirit who accompanied me to the realms of the Divine during my meditations. He calmed the stormy seas in my life when I returned, always filled with quiet joy and sweet peace.

Two more letters arrived from Lucan the next month. Progress was slow, and Marcus was listening to senators with opposing viewpoints. They were vocal, credible and effective rivals. Marcus hesitated. The momentum of Lucan's mission faded along with Marcus' vitality and commitment to support sweeping change.

Those letters were followed by a long and disconcerting silence. Worse, my connection with him vanished. In all the years after his marriage, when we neither saw nor communicated with each other, that connection remained intact. And now it was gone. I tried not to panic, but it was useless. I did anyway.

I considered filling my days with social activities, the better to endure this excruciating waiting period. But I was incapable of making casual conversation, even with Euphemia and Lucan's family.

I remained in relative solitude meditating, praying and trying to keep the faith.

∞ ∞ ∞

I was in my rooms one afternoon, reading a favorite Yeshua text, when I heard an insistent knock on my door.

"Graci, it is Euphemia," she entreated, rushing in flushed and flustered. "I just got word from a reliable source that Marcus is dead and has been succeeded by Commodus. Do you have any information from Lucan about what he accomplished before Marcus left this world?"

"No, I don't," I told her. "When did Marcus die?"

"Two and a half weeks ago," Euphemia revealed.

"That is when I began to sense a shift, and it wasn't positive," I recalled. "Do you know if Lucan is on his way back to Rome? And if so, how long would the journey take?"

"It depends on the weather, how many are in his party, and how soon he could appropriately depart after Commodus' succession," she explained. "Hopefully he will arrive soon. What shall we do in the interim?"

"We can do little for Lucan, so we'd best take care of ourselves – you playing the cithara and me reading and meditating," I observed.

"Let's do so together," Euphemia suggested. "Why don't you come to our house for a while? There's plenty of room for you now. After Lucan returns, you can resume the routine here that suits you both so well."

I accepted Euphemia's invitation with relief. She was correct. Remaining alone only escalated my concerns. Time with her would be good for me.

"Give me the rest of the day to put things in order and tell the servants where I will be staying," I requested. "I'll pack only a few clothes and books, since I can easily stop by here for anything I might need later. You can expect me at your home later this afternoon."

"That will give me time to have your rooms prepared and filled with fresh flowers," she confirmed.

There was little for me to arrange. The servants were reliable, and my life had simplified to such an extent they were able to accommodate my requests with ease and efficiency. Two of the servants helped carry my belongings to Euphemia's house. When I was settled into my rooms, I joined her for music before dinner.

"How can I express my appreciation for the many ways you stood by me over the years?" I asked her. "The heroines in my novels are nothing compared to you."

"We came together for a reason," she replied. "Initially that reason was Lucan. But our relationship expanded to encompass significantly more than our connection with him. And now it has no bounds at all."

"Boundless friendship," I said. "Women come by it easily. When I first arrived in Rome as a slave, two other female slaves stepped in early to befriend and guide me."

"Tell me, are you worried about Lucan?" she asked.

"Yes, I am," I admitted. "He risked alienating the emperor's staff, the military and the Senate when he decided to lead such a significant restructuring of power. It's one thing to do so with the knowledge and support of the emperor. It's something else to do so only to have a new emperor oppose such action."

"But we don't know for certain that Commodus would oppose it," Euphemia objected.

"We know enough to assume he wouldn't willingly hand over a scrap of power to the Senate, which is what Lucan was trying to accomplish," I explained. "At a minimum Lucan will be ridiculed and ostracized by the new emperor. That wouldn't faze him. I fear, however, that the repercussions could be far worse."

"You are safe here," Euphemia assured me. "When Lucan has returned and Commodus is paying more attention to his new playthings as emperor, female and otherwise, you'll have no more need for concern. He'll forget all about Lucan's negotiations with his father."

"I hope you are correct," I replied, unconvinced. "Unchallenged power is dangerous in the hands of one as ruthless as Commodus. He is capable of anything."

"I don't refute that, but I am hoping he has a short attention span and gets caught up in more interesting melodramas than a failed decree his father never got around to signing," Euphemia said dryly.

"Failed and therefore irrelevant," I noted. "I pray it is so."

"Whom do you pray to, might I ask?" Euphemia wondered.

"Yeshua," I replied. "I have developed a personal relationship with him."

"Did that result from your extensive reading?" she pursued.

"At first yes, then he started appearing in my meditations," I revealed. "I am more than superficially taken with Yeshua and his teachings. I am a believer."

"Do you attend Christian gatherings?" Euphemia asked.

"Mine is a more private experience," I explained. "I neither need nor want a community to support the central place Yeshua occupies in my life."

"You sound as if he were a person alive today, not a prophet born 180 years ago," Euphemia observed.

"I've always been fascinated by accounts of his life," I admitted. "But now I am doing less reading and more communing, if I can describe it that way."

"You most certainly can," Euphemia assured me. "I have no doubt he visits you. His spirit must be drawn not just to your devotion to him, but also to the way you live according to the precepts he preached."

"You see that?" I asked, surprised at her observation.

"I have for quite some time," Euphemia disclosed. "Perhaps you were a follower of his in an earlier lifetime. You may even have written one of those accounts in your extensive collection. Be that as it may, you embody the essential meaning of his messages. That is what counts."

"Thank you for the acknowledgement," I said softly. "I try to do so."

Suddenly a servant pounded on the door to Euphemia's suite.

"Euphemia, you are wanted immediately," he announced in alarm.

"Wait here," she whispered to me.

Something terrible was occurring. I could feel it. Maybe she was about to receive bad news about Lucan. After all, it would be brought to his wife first.

When Euphemia returned to the room, her face was white with fear. I had never seen her so shaken.

"Soldiers of the Praetorian Guard are outside," she said quickly. "They have come to arrest you. I told them you weren't here, but apparently one of your servants revealed where you were staying. If you don't present yourself, they will search the house. They insist you can't escape, since guards are posted at every entrance. What shall we do?"

"Did they tell you my offense?" I asked, panic-stricken.

"You are under arrest for being a Christian," Euphemia revealed. "The order was received directly from the emperor."

"This is his way of punishing Lucan, or intimidating him into dropping his plans for change," I cried. "Commodus will take his recourse out on me rather than attacking Lucan directly. He can arrest me and send a clear message to Lucan without damaging his reputation. It's an astute move on his part, and a preemptive one as well. He made sure it happened before Lucan arrived back in Rome."

"You could try to escape, or hide somewhere in the house," Euphemia proposed. "I know a number of places the children used to hide. They'd never find you."

"And then we would be under house arrest," I concluded. "If I escaped later, I would be hunted and arrested if I am lucky or killed if I am not."

"If we can delay your arrest, Lucan might return in time to demand the Guard cease their harassment," Euphemia suggested.

"Only the emperor can do that," I noted. "It won't happen."

"What shall we do?" Euphemia asked desperately. "I'll protect you if I can."

"That won't be necessary," I stated firmly. "I'll turn myself over to the Guard. There is no other choice. We must pray that Lucan can use his influence to have me freed when he returns to Rome."

"I'll go with you then," Euphemia offered.

"Thank you but no," I replied. "You can do more from here. Now let's leave so I can allow myself to be arrested."

"I need to know where they are taking you," Euphemia insisted.

"Hopefully they are at liberty to say," I commented. "Thank you, Euphemia, for looking out for me once again. You are my sister in more ways than one. I love you."

"I love you, too," she choked out, tears flooding her eyes. "They can't be doing this to you!"

"But they are," I replied, "and we are powerless to resist without jeopardizing our own lives and the lives of our loved ones. This is the only alternative. Please let Lucan know what has happened as soon as he is back in Rome. I'm confident the situation can be resolved once Commodus knows he has threatened Lucan sufficiently to force him to back down."

"But will Lucan back down?" Euphemia questioned.

"He may as well do so," I replied realistically. "He has no influence now. At least Lucan can tell himself he did what he could when success was within reach."

Euphemia walked with me to the courtyard. I was bound in chains and taken away. The guards gave her no information about my destination. As the gate closed behind me, I heard a wail leave her throat that was both angry and mournful.

∞ ∞ ∞

I was locked in a horrifying prison where people who committed a real or perceived crime against the state were incarcerated. Marcus Aurelius hadn't been kind to the Christians. Many were arrested and kept there along with an assortment of malcontents.

What a perfect solution for Commodus to have contrived! This early in his regime, he could declare he was merely following his father's example by rounding up one more heretical Christian with the audacity to believe in a god disassociated from the emperor. Was that not unquestionably treasonous?

The cell into which I was thrown was beyond wretched. Two dozen people occupied a miniscule space with no amenities and absolute lack of privacy. Even those who arrived with the best of Christian intentions eventually devolved into something baser. My cellmates left me alone, as I obviously preferred.

Decades as a slave prepared me somewhat for my imprisonment. Rather than resisting it, I found a spot of my own and considered my new circumstances. My options were limited at best and nonexistent at worst. I needed to review everything that transpired and pray for guidance, discernment and patience.

Three days after my arrival Euphemia appeared with a basket of food and more importantly, some news. An armed guard stood next to her as we talked. The basket had been searched to assure she wasn't smuggling in anything that might enable my escape.

"How did you find me?" I asked.

"I went to Augustalis immediately after your arrest and urged him to use his influence to discover where you were taken," she explained. "Of course he was willing to do everything possible to help you, and he continues to do so.

"I received a note from him this morning asking that I pay him a visit. When I arrived in his office, I could tell the news wasn't good. He started by revealing where you were being held, but he knew more than that.

"Commodus' current plan is to hold 150 days of games in the Colosseum to commemorate the reign of his father. Nothing could be more perverse and cynical, given that Marcus despised such exhibitions. He saw them as the epitome of human depravity, which they are.

"The killing of Christians will be one of the main spectacles. You are to be among those sacrificed. We have no information about the timing. It could be tomorrow or months from now. We must proceed with even greater haste to have you freed."

"How is that possible?" I asked, feeling powerless and desperate.

"Augustalis is demanding your release, using every shred of his considerable influence," Euphemia assured me. "Lucan can do the same when he is back. This week Augustalis will call upon the Senate to attest to your innocence. He is meeting privately with the senators who are his closest friends to obtain their commitment to provide outspoken support for your cause.

"As you know, Augustalis can be compelling and persuasive. He told me if all else fails, he plans to resort to guilt. He'll insist they owe you this after devouring so many of your delectable banquets over the years. He is hopeful that with enough pressure the senators will call for your immediate release."

"Leave it to Augustalis to call for a quid pro quo such as that," I observed.

"You have strong support in extremely high places," she reminded me. "Beyond that, I won't stop until you are unchained, nor will Lucan once he returns to Rome.

"Now eat this food, which everyone in my kitchen lovingly prepared for you. I hope you especially enjoy the cakes. Placidia made them exactly as you taught her."

"Thank you, my dearly beloved Euphemia," I said, tears spilling from my eyes. "Your love and courage mean the world to me. That and this food will sustain me, though I intend to share the latter with everyone here."

"In that case, I'll bring a bigger basket filled to the brim next time, along with even more money for bribing the guards," Euphemia replied, trying unsuccessfully to appear lighthearted. "Hold steadfast to your faith, Graci, and remain confident you'll be home soon."

She handed me the food through the iron bars. When the basket was empty, she squeezed my hands, smiled reassuringly and took her leave.

A few days later Euphemia returned with an enormous trunk of provisions.

"You must have given the guards a month's wages to get that through the door," I quipped when I saw what she brought.

"More than that, but it was for a good cause," she replied. "They waived inspection of the contents, which would have taken forever. The guard will look over everything before I hand it through to you."

"Be sure to tell Placidia everyone loved her cakes," I commented. "Are there more?"

"She spent all day yesterday making them," Euphemia revealed. "It calms her nerves to do this for you, and she is grateful others can enjoy them as well. That isn't to say any of us are glad you have company here. We all wish the cell were empty."

"If I get out of here, I'll spend the remainder of my days campaigning against the arbitrary arrest of Christians," I vowed. "We are a nonviolent spiritual community that poses no threat to anyone. We bear no grudge against the Caesar, and we never argue for his overthrow. No one in this cell committed a treasonous act, yet we are treated as people who plot the overthrow of the emperor as well as the Empire."

"You say 'we' as if you are an active participant in the Christian community," Euphemia observed. "And yet you are not. Is it advisable to associate yourself so closely with them? Please don't speak this way to anyone other than me."

"It matters not whether I practice my Christian beliefs alone or in the company of others," I insisted. "I am a follower of Yeshua, just as they are. If that makes me a Christian, which I believe it does, so be it."

"But you never called yourself a Christian until now," Euphemia noted correctly. "Why do so at this point, when it places you in even greater jeopardy?"

"I thought a great deal about this, Euphemia," I replied. "Please listen carefully and don't object. I am unwilling to denounce Yeshua and his teachings if it is required to gain my freedom. That is too great a price to pay for a longer life. I would be haunted by the constant awareness that I was too weak to stand by the most powerful truth of my existence."

"I know I am not to object," Euphemia qualified, "but let me ask you this. Isn't love the one most powerful truth? Could you not love, can I not love, in the absence of Yeshua's tradition?"

"Yes, but I can't reframe my life in a way that allows me to denounce his messages of love on the one hand and give and receive the gift of love on the other," I explained. "Doing so would kill me."

"So you would be killed otherwise," Euphemia concluded.

"I would. I must, if denunciation is the price to be exacted for my freedom," I confirmed. "Let's hope Augustalis and Lucan can use their influence to force my release with no recanting on my part."

"Lucan is on his way, but I have no information about his anticipated arrival," Euphemia revealed. "I hope it is soon. I want to see you walk out of here with no chains on your wrists and your beliefs intact."

"Thank you, Euphemia," I whispered gratefully. "Please take care of yourself and keep a fire lit under Augustalis."

"He needs no help in that regard," she assured me. "I have never seen him so focused or mobilized to accomplish a desired end. Then again he did many extraordinary things for you, and later for you and Lucan. That particular fire isn't unfamiliar to him."

"No it isn't," I agreed. "Please give my love and best regards to him and everyone in your family."

"I will," she whispered. "I'll be back in a few days' time."

She had been passing the food through the iron grating as we talked, and the trunk was now empty. My fellow cellmates could barely contain themselves.

"Time for a feast!" I exclaimed as Euphemia walked away. It was the easiest way to hide my terrible sadness.

∞ ∞ ∞

A persistent nightmare haunted my sleep. I was in the Colosseum along with the others imprisoned with me. We were chained to stakes. There was no means of escape. The bloodthirsty crowd was cheering. They couldn't wait to see us mauled by whatever starving wild animals were about to be unleashed upon us.

Hope, 120 AD

Doors in the center of the arena opened, and voracious lions appeared from underground cages. One huge male lion charged toward me. Everything shifted into slow motion.

My spirit rose above my body and communicated with the lion's spirit. "Please, be quick," I urged. He lunged for my heart. Just before his fangs pierced my chest, when my death was imminent, I was totally at peace. More than that, I was ecstatic.

The dream portended what was likely to occur despite attempts to force my release. I would endure ghastly experiences leading up to the moment when my spirit left my body upon my death. Then I would be received into serene stillness and divine light. That was of immeasurable comfort to me.

I recalled having read the passage from the writings of Thomas that presented itself the first time Yeshua came to me in meditation. "Blessed is the lion which becomes man when consumed by man; and cursed is the man whom the lion consumes, and the lion becomes man."

I hadn't taken the meaning of the text literally. Perhaps I was mistaken.

∞ ∞ ∞

My next visitor almost a week later was Lucan. I was so relieved he was alive and well, I almost forgot a prison cell separated us. I stuck my hands through the bars to touch him.

"I have the approval of the Praetorian commander to conduct a private meeting with you," he said formally, every bit the senator. "A guard will be placed outside the door. We have fifteen minutes."

The guard opened the gate and nodded for me to walk through it. I did so, with as much calm as I could exhibit given my quaking heart. Lucan escorted me silently to the assigned room. We entered and he closed the door behind him.

I ran to his arms, forgetting the fact it had been two weeks since I had enjoyed a bath or a change of clothes. He held me close. His chest heaved as he sobbed sorrowfully. I willed myself to retain my composure so he could regain his.

"What have I done to you?" he cried out, and the sobbing began anew.

"You've done nothing to me," I replied quietly. "This is the work of our new emperor, to teach you a lesson."

"It isn't that simple," Lucan replied. "I wish it were. There's much to tell you about what occurred in Germania, and no time to do so. Commodus discovered our plans and went into a rage with his father. He declared him senile and incapable of making any lasting decrees. Then he told a senator, no one in my group of course, that if Marcus persisted he would take more drastic measures to assure no decree was signed before his father's death.

"I thought those drastic measures would involve our expulsion. Then suddenly the emperor was dead. It may have been precipitated by the extreme agitation Commodus caused him, or it could have been patricide. However it happened, the realignment of power was no longer an option or an issue.

"I prepared to leave as soon as I honorably could, but Commodus prevented my departure. He made it clear I wouldn't be allowed to begin my journey for three weeks.

"Just before I left, Commodus summoned me for a private audience. He revealed to me that you were imprisoned as punishment for my deeds. I told him if he arrested anyone, it should be me. He sneered and said, 'I could never do that. You are too well loved and respected. It wouldn't serve me to turn you into a martyr. But your Christian whore is a different story. No one will protest when she is thrown to the lions. She will die and you will live. Every remaining day of your miserable life you will be reminded you can never again challenge the emperor.'"

"There is no recourse," I replied. "Even though Augustalis has been working day and night to obtain my release, nothing has succeeded."

"The emperor ordered that you are not to be discharged under any circumstances," Lucan informed me. "I met with Augustalis before I came here. Every effort he made on your behalf was rebuked by Commodus."

"I'll be thrown to the lions, then," I concluded.

"How can you give up so easily?" Lucan challenged.

"I'm not resigned, just realistic," I replied. "No one can defy the emperor. To believe otherwise is insanity, since the emperor is omnipotent. He may as well be a god, considering the unquestioned power the people have conferred upon him. There is nothing I or anyone else can do."

"But you can save yourself," Lucan urged. "If you declare you aren't a Christian and don't believe in the veracity of Yeshua's teachings, we can make a public case of your arrest. Commodus may hesitate. Public outcries make him vulnerable. I beg of you to do this."

"I cannot, Lucan," I said with conviction. "I am willing to denounce anything but the two truths in my life: my profound belief in the teachings of Yeshua and my undying love for you. Denying either one would slay my spirit. You ask the impossible of me."

"You would choose instead to die and leave me to spend the remainder of my life alone and grieving?" Lucan asked incredulously. "How is this possible?"

"I'll consider what you suggest in the context of my own convictions," I replied. "I contemplated more than once the expedient alternative of denying my Christianity. Each time I reached the same conclusion: I cannot do so. However, now you are here and my determination is wavering."

"I like to think I can still sweep you off your feet," Lucan replied, attempting a smile. "Come here. Let me hold you in the time we have left."

I leaned into him. The smell of him moved me to tears. I didn't know how I could let him go.

A loud rap came from the door. "Emerge now!" the soldier ordered.

"I walked away from you once," Lucan whispered, pained and struggling. "I can't let it happen again. I won't lose you a second time. Have faith in me as well as in Yeshua. Let us both serve and support you. I'll be back for you. I promise. I love you."

We kissed and he led me to the door. He opened it and waited for me to walk through it into a world of prison guards and religious persecution. I tried to look at him reassuringly, but all that came from me were more tears. He forced himself to leave as I was escorted to the cell.

The next morning Euphemia appeared with more provisions. She seemed unusually cheerful, given the circumstances.

"Thank the gods Lucan has returned," she exclaimed, clearly relieved. "Everything will work out for you now. You must believe that, Graci."

The imminence of my being sacrificed to the lions flashed into my mind. Interestingly, it served only to strengthen my conviction not to recant my belief in the prophet Yeshua.

"You just fled somewhere in your mind, and it wasn't the Elysian Fields," Euphemia observed. "Tell yourself this, Graci. You have been freed once. It can happen again. Hold that in your heart as inevitable and not a vague possibility."

"One way or the other, I'll be freed," I declared.

"You and I will grow old and recalcitrant together," she insisted. "Rome needs at least two elderly women who refuse to take no for an answer. We must start now by refusing to take no as an answer from the emperor himself."

I relented. Why perpetuate a vision of being consumed by a lion when I could instead imagine myself creaking around the city with a fellow octogenarian as unwilling as I to suffer fools?

"When I am released, I'll throw the biggest party Rome has seen since the conquest of Gaul," I promised her. "It will be such a grand celebration, we may have to commandeer Augustalis' estate to hold all the guests. I'll spend an entire week cooking my best creations to assure everyone in attendance is adequately indulged."

"You'll have your party, but I won't allow you within one hundred yards of the kitchen!" Euphemia chuckled. "Now, I must go. Enjoy sharing this food. I love you."

"I love you too," I replied. "Bless you."

The next day a guard appeared, singled me out and told me I would no longer be allowed to wear the clothing I had on when I arrived. He took me to a small room, pushed me inside and locked the door. A tunic made of rough cloth was lying on the floor. "Put it on," he barked gruffly through the door, "and leave your belongings and garments behind."

I undressed, took off my jewelry and donned the shift. It scratched my skin like a blanket of thistles. My body would be one big welt in a few days' time.

Lucan's ring was still on my finger. I couldn't bring myself to take it off. But if the guard saw it he would forcibly remove it. I'd rather have it end up in the lion's stomach than be sold for a few sesterces by some miserable prison guard.

I found a seam along one side of the shift that was wider than the others and determined the ring would fit inside. I could remove a few threads from the fabric and use them to refasten it. I took the ring off my finger, placed it in my mouth between my back teeth and my cheek and called out to the guard that I was ready. He uttered not a word to me on the way back to my cell, and I remained silent. The ring was safe. As soon as I could do so unobtrusively I fastened the ring securely inside the seam of the tunic.

The requirement that I wear the clothing of a prisoner was evidence that a decision had been made to have me killed. After accepting the inevitability of my execution, I spent my days recalling my favorite passages contained in Yeshua's teachings. They were a comfort to me. I also recounted the extraordinary life I led, full of more blessings than difficulties. It was an adventure spilling over with love.

Another week went by. I had no visitors and received no word of either an imminent trip to the Colosseum or the opposite. I surrendered to the benevolence of the Divine at an even deeper level. My prayer was a simple one. "Thy will be done. Thy will be done."

∞ ∞ ∞

I was sitting alone in a corner of the cell, infused with that very prayer, when a guard pointed to me.

"Hey, you!" he yelled. "Come here!" I stood up and walked over to him. "You have visitors. Follow me."

I stepped outside the cell and looked down the passageway, where Lucan, Augustalis and Euphemia were waiting. A magenta tunic and gold cloak were draped over her forearm. I walked up to them, unsure of what to expect. As I drew closer, I could see all three of them were beaming.

"You have been freed," Lucan said exultantly, picking me up and swinging me around, a most unusual gesture for a senator to be making in front of the Praetorian Guards. "The emperor signed your release. You are no longer under arrest."

"Come my dear," Euphemia said softly. "Change into these clothes and we'll take you out of here once and for all."

"One moment first," I said, digging into the seam of my shift and retrieving the ring. Handing it to Lucan, I said, "They made me give up everything, but I refused to let them have this ring. I found a secure hiding place for it. I never thought it would see the light of day again. Now that it has, would you please put it back on my finger?"

"With all of my heart and all of my love, yes," Lucan replied, slipping the ring slowly in place.

"A truly sacred union just occurred with witnesses, and in a prison no less," Augustalis announced. "A celebration is definitely in order. Put on these clothes, Graci, so we can remove ourselves from this unfortunate place."

The guard was watching the proceedings, itching to take action against us. His fingers kept clenching the hilt of his sword, but he restrained himself. I changed clothes in a nearby room, reemerged and we left. As we stepped outside into the sunshine, the iron prison door slammed and locked behind us.

"There is no more beautiful sound in the world than that one after you have just been allowed outside," Augustalis observed.

"And no more menacing one when you are on the other side of it," I recalled. "Now tell me exactly what happened and omit not a single detail."

"First you are going to the baths," Euphemia announced. "You are due for a long soak followed by the ministrations of the best masseuse in Rome. After that we will retire to my house for dinner and an evening of conversation. On the way you can learn what led up to this moment."

Augustalis' litter was waiting. We stepped inside. I was anxious to hear how they accomplished the impossible.

Lucan began, "We launched a three-pronged strategy to influence the emperor. Influence is the most potent of weapons, especially with Commodus.

"Augustalis built support for your release long before I arrived from Germania. He obtained the agreement in principle of over a third of the Senate to go on public record demanding your release. I won't fault his methods, although I will note they were more closely tied to the senators' stomachs than to their sense of justice."

"No one can accuse me of not utilizing every persuasive tactic at my disposal," Augustalis noted sardonically.

"Thanks to those powers of persuasion the stage was set for the most influential senators to protest your arrest and implied execution," Lucan continued. "When I finally arrived in Rome, Euphemia and I went directly to see Augustalis. We agreed he would call a meeting at his home so every senator committed to the cause could sign a petition on your behalf. I then prepared the second incentive for Commodus to release you, a formal statement confirming that as long as he is emperor I would engage in no attempt to restructure the allocation of power between him and the Senate."

"Are you at peace with that commitment?" I asked.

"Absolutely," Lucan assured me. "Commodus would swiftly and effectively thwart any further efforts on my part anyway. Last but certainly not least, Euphemia met with Commodus' favorite concubine, with whom she became acquainted at a clothing shop they both frequent. Euphemia knew her to be a Christian. She informed her of your situation and entreated upon her to intervene with Commodus."

"Commodus is consorting with a Christian?" I asked in disbelief.

"He is," Lucan confirmed. "Your belief in Yeshua was nothing but a lever he could use against me. He wouldn't hesitate to send you to the lions to thwart my attempts at change. Commodus does whatever is required to achieve his ends.

"Simultaneously we made our move. Augustalis presented to Commodus a petition with more than 250 signatures. I followed with a written statement committing to stay out of his way. Then Euphemia arrived with his concubine, who pleaded with him to have mercy on you.

"I have no delusions that the first two actions carried significant weight. But knowing they occurred, Commodus was won over by his concubine's convincing pleas. She happened to have with her a decree for your release, which we prepared in advance. She handed it to Commodus and he signed it."

"Brilliant!" I cried. "When the three of you combine forces, anything is possible. I owe you my life."

The litter stopped its forward motion and Euphemia peered through the curtain. "Time for your bath and massage," she said. "The rest of us will proceed to my place. We'll send the litter back for you."

"I'll return with it," Lucan insisted. "I don't want to miss a single opportunity to be with my dearly beloved Graci."

∞ ∞ ∞

Immersing myself in a deep pool of fragrant water, I cleansed more than the surface grime from my body. I floated, eyes closed, imagining that the hatred and manipulation, greed and corruption that sent me to prison were released permanently from my life. My existence from then on would be enveloped in peace.

Then I saw the many Christians whose fate would be different from mine. They would be sacrificed in every despicable way. I surrounded them with my love and committed to help usher them to the realms of the

Divine immediately after their spirits left their bodies upon death. I saw my own spirit floating above them in the Colosseum, arms wide, ready to receive them when the time came to take them home.

Yeshua appeared, as he had done so often before. "You forgot one thing: forgiveness," he whispered to me. "Forgive those who punished and persecuted you. Forgive the prison guards and duplicitous senators. Forgive Commodus. Forgive slaveholders and those who sell precious human beings into perpetual bondage. Forgive every last corrupt individual. Without forgiveness we cannot transform such actions into their opposite."

And so I forgave just as Yeshua advocated. At first I was so attached to my anger I could only utter the words, "I forgive, I forgive, I forgive."

But after a while a nascent capacity to forgive emerged within me. Eventually, perhaps for the first time, I experienced genuine forgiveness. I cleansed and released, then cleansed and released some more.

I prayed to Yeshua in thanksgiving and love. Tears fell into the pool as I sobbed and prayed. I was being purified. In the end every last facet of my being was reborn.

It wasn't lost on me that my rebirth was at the hands of Commodus. He was desperately in need of love. I prayed for his transcendence, however it might occur.

I emerged from the baths and prepared for my massage, during which I slept like an innocent child.

∞ ∞ ∞

After a quietly celebratory evening with Augustalis, Euphemia and Lucan, I grew tired and suggested it was time for Lucan and me to depart. I expressed my love and gratitude to my two dearest friends one more time, and we started home.

"You realize we both were given our lives back," Lucan commented as we walked. "I was altered by this experience, maybe not as much as you. But still, I am a different person. I want nothing but a simple life of loving you and indulging our children and grandchildren whenever possible."

"I'll cherish every moment of that simplicity, along with a healthy dose of gardening, meditating and spice gathering," I replied contentedly.

Just outside the gate to our home, we paused. Lucan pulled me to him and held me in a decisive embrace. Then we kissed slowly and with sweet intimacy.

"Let's continue this inside," he murmured.

"I can't wait," I whispered back.

As we entered the courtyard, Alexios came bounding out of his wing of the house. "I just got here," he announced. "After a six-month absence it's great to be back in Rome. Tell me, did anything exciting occur while I was gone? Probably not. You two lead such settled lives."

I looked at Lucan. Neither of us wanted to recount quite yet what we had been through.

"Nothing much," Lucan said casually. "We are both quite tired tonight and need to retire to our rooms. In the morning we can exchange stories of our mutual adventures or lack thereof."

"Very well, then. Sweet dreams," Alexios called to us as we headed down the hall.

Hope, 120 AD

ACKNOWLEDGEMENTS

For the past half century I have been blessed to be part of a constantly emerging, joyfully celebratory sisterhood. Each of these dear friends exhibits the divine feminine in all of her unhesitating acceptance, generous support and unconditional love. They are, in alphabetical order:

Susan Blake

Delinda Chapman

Linda Davidson

Choong Gaian

Davida Hartman

Sally Hudson

Trudie London

Sharon Mehdi

Regina Meredith

Pix Morgan

Sandra Tripp

Justine Turner

Wendy Weir

Hope, 120 AD

Explore additional books by Gates McKibbin at
www.lovehopegive.com

Epic Steps: *Rekindling Democracy, Unity and Peace*

One, Beyond Time
Love, 24 AD
Hope, 120 AD
Give, 1671 AD

The Light in the Living Room: *Dad's Messages from the Other Side*

Lovelines: *Notes from Spirit on Loving and Being Loved*

A Course in Courage: *Disarming the Darkness with Strength of Heart*

A Handbook on Hope: *Fusing Optimism and Action*

The Life of the Soul: *The Path of Spirit in Your Lifetimes*

Available Wisdom: *Insights from Beyond the Third Dimension*

Forging Faith: *Direct Experience of the Divine*

Printed in Great Britain
by Amazon